Prima Facie
Adam Stanley Thriller – Book 4

Netta Newbound

Junction Publishing
NZ

Copyright © 2016 by Author Name.

All rights reserved. No part of this publication may be reproduced, distributed or transmitted in any form or by any means, including photocopying, recording, or other electronic or mechanical methods, without the prior written permission of the publisher, except in the case of brief quotations embodied in critical reviews and certain other noncommercial uses permitted by copyright law. For permission requests, write to the publisher, addressed "Attention: Permissions Coordinator," at the address below.

Netta Newbound/Junction Publishing
Waihi
NZ
www.nettanewbound.com

Publisher's Note: This is a work of fiction. Names, characters, places, and incidents are a product of the author's imagination. Locales and public names are sometimes used for atmospheric purposes. Any resemblance to actual people, living or dead, or to businesses, companies, events, institutions, or locales is completely coincidental.

Ordering Information:
Quantity sales. Special discounts are available on quantity purchases by corporations, associations, and others. For details, contact the "Special Sales Department" at the address above.

Prima Facie/ Netta Newbound. -- 1st ed.
ISBN   978-1534930285

To my beautiful sister Sarah.

Prologue

The wooden window frame splinters as I twist the crowbar, making a gap wide enough for me to reach inside and unfasten the latch.

I glance around in the cold, crisp darkness and wait, hardly breathing. Most of the neighbours would've hit the sack hours ago, so I don't think anybody will get up to investigate the sound.

I stuff the crowbar into the rucksack at my feet, and shove it through the open window into the kitchen-dinette beyond. Dragging a chair from the wooden outdoor table set, I place it beside the wall, jump onto it and climb in through the window.

The apartment is silent and in total darkness as I knew it would be. I move quickly wasting no time. I flick on the light above the cooker and begin.

Methodically I go through each room, ransacking every drawer and cupboard, upending anything that isn't fastened down.

In the bedroom, I gag as I smear my message across the wall above the bed. I stand back to admire my handiwork.

Racing to the bathroom, I avoid my reflection in the mirror above the sink as I scrub my hands.

Back downstairs, I grab a five-inch knife from the knife block and head for the front door. A framed photograph I'd missed earlier taunts me. Using the butt of the knife, I smash the frame to smithereens, and with the blade I eliminate the smiling face.

With the rucksack on my back, I open the front door. The brightly lit corridor makes me wince and shield my eyes. I reach up and jab out the closest bulb with the knife. Now this end of the corridor is in partial darkness. I take a couple of steps towards the door opposite.

Michael is security-conscious and given the late hour will be extra vigilant. I knock and turn my back knowing he will look out through the peephole he loves so much and see the open door opposite. The dirty old bastard won't hesitate.

As I suspect, within moments, the door is thrown open.

"Sal?" he says, stepping forwards.

I turn to face him.

He's startled at first and takes a step back then smiles, relieved. "Oh, it's you. You had me worried for a second."

As I lift the knife, I spot the delicious terror in his eyes. But the reactions of this feeble old man are much too slow for me and the blade punctures his chest. I relish in that first blow. I smile at his confusion. I triumph as the realisation dawns on his face.

I push the old man inside and he falls backwards crashing into an old-fashioned cabinet, sending shards of glass in all directions.

I enter and close the door behind us.

Chapter 1

Adam's phone rang for the second time in as many minutes which wouldn't normally be an issue. However, the phone was deep in the pocket of the jeans currently in a pile around his ankles.

"Somebody's popular." The doctor chuckled as he gently examined Adam's testicles.

"Sorry, Doc. I'm on call." He fixed his eyes on the doctor's balding head. "Can you feel it?"

"I can feel a swelling, not surprising considering the trauma you suffered." He stood upright and snapped off his gloves. "You can get dressed again now." He stepped to the side of the room to wash his hands.

Adam pulled his boxers and jeans up and sat in the chair opposite the doctor who was now focused on the computer screen, his fingers moving at lightning speed across the keyboard.

"I need to ask a few questions, Adam."

"Okay."

"Did you experience any aches or discomfort in your testicles prior to the kick?"

"No. Nothing."

"That's a good sign. How about your sex life? Any problems there?"

"No. My wife is due to give birth in a few weeks, so obviously we don't...you know...too often."

The doctor smiled and nodded. "Of course. But when you have had intercourse recently, you didn't experience any problems?"

"No. None."

"Masturbation?"

The phone began ringing again. Adam reached for it and hit the mute button, trying to disguise his embarrassment. "I'm sorry?"

"Believe me, Adam, these questions are just as difficult for me to ask." He cleared his throat. "So, any problems masturbating?"

"No. I've had no problems in that department until last week when I took a size nine to the knackers. Since then, one of my balls has been swollen and bloody painful."

The doctor smiled again and nodded. "I'm going to give you some painkillers for the discomfort, but make an appointment to come back next week, and if it's no better I'll arrange for a scan."

"Okay, thanks, Doc."

Adam took the prescription straight to the pharmacist and checked his phone while he waited. Three missed calls from Frances. He called her back.

"Hey, Frances. Sorry, but you caught me with my pants down, literally. What's up?"

"I'm not even gonna ask you what you're up to—I don't want to know." She huffed. "There's been a homicide. Number fourteen Caspian Villas. I'm on my way over there now."

"Okay. I'll meet you there." He hung up and strode from the pharmacy, his painkillers forgotten.

*

He tooted his horn at Frances' car which was in front of him at the traffic lights, and then followed her to the crime scene.

They climbed out of their cars beside a row of eight redeveloped town houses. "So, fill me in." He braced himself as a blast of icy November wind bit through the fabric of his jacket.

He knew each townhouse had been converted into two lavish apartments from his flat hunting episode when he arrived from Manchester last year.

"We received a call from Sally Kemp. She came home this morning to find her apartment trashed, and when she knocked on the neighbour's door she found him dead. Stabbed."

"You think he may have disturbed the intruder?"

"Possibly. Here we are."

They ducked underneath the police tape that cordoned off the second-to-last house in the row. Before entering the crime scene, they paused to don bootees and gloves.

The shared hallway was long and narrow with two doorways at the end on either side. To the left, a body lay scrunched directly inside the door. The injuries made it impossible for him to work out the age of the victim.

"Anything?" He crouched down beside Felix, the medical examiner.

"Meet Michael Curtis, a retired sixty-eight-year-old naval officer. He's been dead around five hours. Multiple knife wounds. The blade snapped off in his skull."

Adam winced and touched the spot on his own head, just above the ear, where he'd been stabbed a few months ago. He stood upright and moved for Frances to take a look.

In the hallway he noticed the lightbulb above the doors had been smashed leaving jagged glass and the bayonet fitting still in place.

Frances stepped into the hallway, and he pointed his pen towards the light fitting and glass fragments on the carpet below.

She nodded.

The door to the right was wide open, and as Adam stepped over the threshold he gasped. The corridor had two doors off it, one closed, and the place had been ransacked. But the worst part was the awful smell. "What the hell?" he said, covering his nose and mouth with his forearm.

"Faeces." A uniformed officer appeared at the top of the stairs. "Come on up."

Adam blew out of his mouth and shook his head in disgust before he walked up the narrow staircase.

Frances followed close behind.

Off the small landing were a bathroom and two bedrooms. The officer led them into the master bedroom. It held a large, ornate, wooden double bed and matching furniture. Faeces smeared above the bed, across the cream and gold wallpaper, spelled out *DIE YOU BITCH*.

"Charming. Where's the owner? What's her name, Frances?"

"Sally Kemp," she said through the fabric of her shirt that she'd used to cover her mouth and nose.

"Sally Kemp. Where is she?" He turned back to the officer.

"She's next door at number sixteen. Clearly distraught at finding her dead neighbour. She says she knows who's responsible though."

"She does?"

"She reckons her ex, Miles Muldoon, did it."

*

Next door, a middle-aged woman with long, mousey, recently-styled curls and a small yapping dog shoved under one arm, led them through to her lounge. The woman's hair amazed Adam as they walked behind her. It moved like a solid piece of cardboard. She must have emptied a whole can of hairspray on it.

Sally Kemp, an incredibly attractive redhead who appeared to be in her late twenties, was rather more composed than Adam had expected.

She glanced up as they entered and darted a questioning glance to the mumsy-looking female officer sitting beside her.

The officer nodded and patted the younger woman's hand.

"Hi, Ms Kemp. I'm DI Adam Stanley and this is DS Holly Frances." They showed their badges.

"Take a seat, detectives." She motioned towards the black velour sofa opposite, an exact match to the one she and the officer were sitting on.

Adam took the lead as usual. "We need to ask you a few questions."

She nodded.

"Can you tell me exactly what happened and where you were last night?"

"Yes, of course. I've been staying at my father's house for the past few days. He's sick. The late stages of cancer."

"I'm sorry to hear that," he said.

She nodded. "You must know him, my dad. Charlie Kemp?"

Frances gasped.

Confused, Adam lifted his chin in question.

"He used to be Chief Constable up until a few years ago," Frances said.

"Yes, that's right. I've taken some time off work in order to help care for him. Well, among other reasons."

Adam's interest piqued, but he didn't interrupt.

"I only came back this morning to water the plants and pick up a change of clothes, and I walked into that." She pointed her manicured finger towards the adjoining wall. "Heaven knows when it happened."

Frances nodded. "How awful. What did you do?"

Sally took a deep, controlled breath. "I did what I always do in a crisis. I ran to see Michael. He never misses anything. But as I knocked, the door swung inwards and that's when I found him." She dropped her head, dabbing at the corners of her eyes with a screwed-up tissue. "I'm sorry," she whispered.

The officer put her hand on the woman's arm.

"That's okay. You've had a terrible shock," Adam said.

"I know who did this." She threw the tissue down, and her eyes flashed angrily.

"Okay." Adam nodded. "Maybe you can explain who you *think* may be responsible and *why*?"

"Miles Muldoon, my ex. He hated Michael and even accused us of having an affair! I mean, no disrespect to Michael, but he's old enough to be my granddad."

"What made Miles think there was more going on?"

"He's sick. I'm close to Michael, *was* close to Michael. I found him interesting and thoughtful. We just got on. Why does everybody immediately think a male-female relationship has to be sexual?"

Adam shrugged, tapping his pen on his chin. "But Miles didn't believe you?"

"Depending on what mood he was in. He knew the truth, but it still didn't stop him from throwing it in my face any time we had an argument. He hated him. Always called him a dirty old man and said he lusted after me."

"What did Michael say?"

"He didn't know. I didn't let on, and Miles would never accuse him to his face. He's not the type to air his dirty laundry in public. If you ask anybody, they'll tell you Miles is a true gent. Michael knew we were having problems, but I never discussed any of them with him."

"How long were the two of you an item?" Frances asked.

"Almost three years."

"And you think he's capable of doing something like this?" Adam frowned. "We're talking cold-blooded murder."

"I know. And yes, I do. I've seen how angry he can get."

"Is that why you split up with him?" Frances asked.

"No." She shook her head. "I was too scared to break up with him. He had a ferocious temper."

"Then how?" Frances shrugged.

"He left me for another woman. Someone we work with. Miles is our boss at Pinevale Publishing."

"Hang on a minute." Adam sat on the edge of the sofa and winced inwardly as the pain in his testicles almost brought tears to his eyes. He altered his position slightly and the pain decreased. "This doesn't make sense. If he left you, why would he come back and do something like this?"

"Because I warned Lana, the other woman. I told her to be careful because he was abusive. I didn't think she believed me at first. But then I got a call from Miles screaming that I'd pay—that we'd all pay."

"When was this?" Adam said.

"Last night."

"We're going to need to take your phone, if that's ok?"

A deep furrow appeared between her eyebrows. "How long for? My whole life is on that phone."

"I'll get our technician onto it right away and will have it back to you as soon as possible."

She took her phone from the black leather bag at her feet and handed it to the officer.

"Thanks." Adam got to his feet. "Now, we're going to need a formal statement from you at some stage. And can you give us Mr Muldoon's address?"

"He doesn't have one. He was staying at the hotel just past the roundabout on The Old Road. I can't remember the name of it."

"The Sentinel?" Frances suggested.

"Yeah, that's the one. He moved out of here last week after telling me about him and Lana." A fresh bout of tears began to flow.

Adam nodded to Frances and turned to leave.

Chapter 2

After dropping Frances' car off at the station, they headed to the offices of Pinevale Publishing.

Their destination was the first floor of a plush office block. He knew Frances disliked lifts, but there was no way he'd manage the stairs in his current state. He called the lift and Frances got in beside him, gritting her teeth for the entire five-second journey.

"We're looking for Miles Muldoon." Adam showed his badge to the wide-eyed young receptionist who had thick, black, drawn-on eyebrows.

She shook her glossy blonde hair dramatically. "I'm sorry. Miles didn't turn up to work today."

"And do you have any idea where he might be?"

"No. I don't, I'm afraid. It's unlike him not to call if he's going to be away."

"I see. Can I speak to his boss?"

"Julia Rothwell is away at a conference and won't be back until Monday."

Adam sighed. "How about Lana?" He paused, realising he didn't get her last name. He glanced at Frances who shook her head.

"Lana Davis? Yes, certainly, sir. Just take a seat."

They didn't sit down. Instead, they stayed at the reception desk while she made the call.

She twirled in her seat as though trying to put some distance between them. "Lana, there are a couple of detectives asking for you." She turned back to Adam as she hung up. "She'll be right with you. Please, take a seat."

Adam had no intention of sitting on a hard plastic chair with the current state of his private parts, so he walked to the window and looked down at the car park.

The sun poked through the clouds briefly, illuminating the cold grey day.

"What are you thinking?" Frances sidled up to him and perched on the windowsill.

"Can't put my finger on why, but I'm not convinced."

"Me neither."

Adam noticed his partner wasn't as well-groomed as usual. In fact, she looked like shit. Her normally tidy dark brown hair looked as though it could do with a good brush, and she had what appeared to be yesterday's make-up around her eyes. She didn't wear make-up to work. Heaven forbid the team may think she was girly. She'd fought hard to be accepted as one of the blokes.

"You okay?" He nodded at her.

"What? Me? I'm fine. Tired, that's all."

"Pull the other one. Something's wrong. What's happened?"

A small, timid-looking young woman suddenly appeared in the doorway. "Hi, I'm Lana Davis. Do you want to follow me?"

As soon as the woman spoke, she was gone again, back through the swinging door.

"This conversation isn't over," he hissed at Frances.

***

I stand behind a van in the car park looking up at the office block.

The detective appears at the window, the tall one with the funny walk. That bitch, Lana, will like him. He's her type—male. She'll be fawning all over him, fluttering her eyelashes, trying to captivate him with her naive and dewy-eyed charm.

The female detective appears, putting her back to the window. Then they both disappear.

I can imagine what Lana is telling them. Feeling sorry for herself—the fragile victim. Yeah, right. She's another one who's going to pay.

Chapter 3

Adam and Frances took off after the remarkably fast-walking woman dressed in a pale blue knitted skirt and matching jacket. The affected way she placed her feet caused an exaggerated wiggle, reminding Adam of Jessica Rabbit. He nudged Frances and nodded at the woman, grinning like an adolescent.

Frances nudged him back and shook her head, disapproval written all over her face.

What? He mimed, goggling his eyes and shrugging his shoulders.

She shoved him again in the ribs.

He groaned, changing it to a cough as Lana turned to see what the sound was.

"Excuse me," he said, clearing his throat.

"This way, please." She ushered them into a sparsely furnished office devoid of all personal items.

Adam suspected it wasn't *her* office but a neutral place used for interviews and private meetings.

They all took a seat, Adam carefully lowering himself into the least painful position.

Frances eyeballed him again.

Lana cocked her head in question. "What can I do for you, detectives?"

"I'm DI Adam Stanley and this is my colleague, DS Holly Frances."

She nodded, not making a sound.

"We're investigating a murder and would like to ask you a few questions," he said.

"Murder?" She appeared genuinely shocked.

Adam nodded. "Why else did you think we were here, Miss Davis?"

"What do you mean?" She fiddled with a locket at her throat.

"Well, you greeted us and brought us through here as though you'd been expecting us."

She shrugged, shaking her head. "Who's been murdered?"

"An elderly gentleman. Sally Kemp's neighbour."

She gasped.

"Can you tell us about your involvement with Miles Muldoon?"

"He's my boss."

"Any other connection?"

She shrugged. "We had a thing, but I ended it yesterday."

"Do you mind me asking why?"

"What does this have to do with the murder, detective?"

"It may have a great deal to do with the murder which is why I'm the one asking the questions."

She bit her lip, clearly annoyed.

"Well?" He pressed.

"His ex, Sally, told me a few stories about him."

"I see. Were you seeing Mr Muldoon while he was still having a relationship with Ms Kemp?"

Her cheeks and ears flushed. "We began seeing each other a few weeks ago. He told me their relationship was all but finished though."

"Oh, that old chestnut," Frances muttered.

"I'm sorry?"

"Never mind. Not important." Frances gave a fake smile.

"Do you know the current whereabouts of Mr Muldoon?" Adam continued.

"No. He was angry with me for believing Sally. In fact..." she slid her jacket off and raised the sleeve of her blouse, "...look at this."

Deep bruises covered her wrist and forearm. Adam knew without a doubt they were finger marks.

"That looks nasty. Did Mr Muldoon do that to you?"

"Yes. He would've probably done much worse, but my dad came home in the nick of time."

"You live with your dad?" Frances asked.

Lana nodded.

"Then what happened?" He couldn't tolerate the ache in his groin for a second longer. "I'm sorry, do you mind if I stand?" He eased himself to his feet wishing he'd waited for the painkillers.

"My dad punched him. That's what I thought you were here about. I waited all evening for something to come of it. Then, when Miles didn't show up to work this morning..." She began to cry.

"Don't worry about it, love. It seems your dad may have saved you from a beating." Frances put her hand on the younger woman's arm.

"I'm still in shock. I thought he loved me. He was always so lovely and gentle."

"They always are, love," Frances said.

Adam placed his card on the desk. "If you hear from him, anything at all, call me."

She snatched the card up with shaking fingers. "Do you think Miles killed that old man?"

"Put it this way. He's very high on the list of suspects, but it's still early days. In the meantime, if you notice anything remotely suspicious, just call—night or day."

"Do you think he might come back for me and my dad?"

"It's doubtful. My guess is he'd have done it last night if he intended to do anything at all. But still, it's advisable to be prepared." Adam shook her hand before limping off up the corridor.

Once they were in the lift, Frances looked at him, her eyebrows drawn tightly together. "What the heck's wrong with you? You don't look a bit well."

"I need to do a detour to the pharmacy next to the medical centre."

"What for?"

"Don't laugh."

"Would I?" she smirked.

"See? You're at it already."

"Honestly, boss. Look at me. I'm being serious. What's wrong?" She forced her face straight.

The lift door opened and they walked out of the foyer to the car park.

"That kick I took to the knackers last week is still killing me. My right bollock has swelled up the size of a bowling ball."

She sniggered and then straightened her face again when he looked at her. "Sorry."

"It's not funny. If you received an injury in the line of duty I'd sympathise. Just because it's my goolies, suddenly I'm the laughing stock of the fucking station," he hissed, glancing around to make sure nobody could hear him.

"You should get Amanda to bathe them for you." She sniggered again.

"Honestly. I'm working with a bunch of children. And not one word of this to Calvin."

She made a zipping motion to her lips.

"Why don't I believe you?" He shook his head.

They reached his grey Mondeo. "You can drive. I can't seem to position myself correctly. And it's even worse since the doctor fiddled about down there."

She belted out a laugh this time. "Sorry, boss. Truly, I am. Is that what you were doing when I called?"

He shook his head and raised his eyes to the heavens. "Just get in and drive, will you."

At the pharmacy, he picked up his painkillers.

Heading back to the car, he popped a couple of pills into his mouth and gagged as he swallowed them down dry.

"Where to next, boss?" Frances started the engine as he got back in the car.

"We need to call Calvin and tell him where we're up to."

"Already done. I called him while you were getting your pills."

"Did he have any news for us?"

Calvin Wade, their admin assistant, kept them all in order and single-handedly kept the department running smoothly.

"Not really. He sent me this." She showed him a photograph on her phone of a man, average build, in his early to mid-thirties, with close-cropped black hair and designer stubble.

"Is that our man?"

She nodded. "Miles Muldoon."

"Any form?"

"Just two minor offences. Urinating in a public place and drunk and disorderly. Both offences happened on the same night, nine years ago, when he was just twenty-three years old. The only other thing is a former girlfriend, Catherine Bailey, accused him of domestic abuse but dropped the charges the next day."

"We may need to have a chat with Ms Bailey. Anything else?"

"Calvin told me there's a team out conducting house to house enquiries to see if anybody saw or heard anything, but up to now, it's a big, fat zero."

"Then I think we should pay a visit to the hotel and see if we can locate our Mr Muldoon."

Chapter 4

As they drove, Adam noticed the throbbing ache in his groin subsiding. He turned to face Frances.

"So, come on. Tell me what's wrong with you this morning?"

"Nothing, boss. I just got up on the wrong side of the bed. You know how it is sometimes?"

"Yes, for Calvin or Les or Ginger Dave, even myself on occasion, but never with you. Come on. I told you about *my* delicate situation, didn't I?"

She grinned at the mere mention of his poor old gonads.

"I can't tell you. I'll have to show you and I promise I will, but not now. We have a murder to solve."

He didn't want to leave it at that, but he'd worked alongside Frances for months now, and she'd said nothing about her private life in all that time. The rest of the station thought she was a lesbian. She never corrected them, but he knew she was married to a man called Steve.

Adam had spoken to Steve on the phone a couple of times. Nobody had met him in person. Frances even attended his and Amanda's wedding alone.

He figured so long as she turned up every day and worked her backside off, what business was it of his? However, the past few weeks she'd taken the odd day off here and there, and she seemed preoccupied and distracted.

She pulled up outside the reception area of The Sentinel. A sign above the parking space threatened anyone parking there would be towed away. Frances shrugged when he pointed it out.

"You little rebel, you." He got out of the car slowly.

"Have the pills not started working yet?"

"Yes, I think my body's got used to moving like this," he laughed, trying to straighten himself up.

"Harden up, man!"

He slowly shook his head, half smiling. "It's easy for you to say—you were born with a pair of massive balls without the added complication of testicles."

"Aw, you saying I'm ballsy, boss?"

"You know you are. Stop fishing for compliments and get me across this car park with my street cred intact."

"What street cred?"

He made as though to cuff her around the earhole and she grinned.

After the first few steps, the pain subsided and he managed to walk relatively normal again.

"What did the doctor say?" Frances asked as they approached the huge glass automatic doors.

"That it's probably bruising. But I may have to go for a scan, just in case."

"That'll teach you. Next time you see a group of fellow officers struggling with a thug, leave them to it."

"Don't you bloody worry, I will."

The foyer of the hotel was deserted.

Adam slapped the flat of his hand against the counter.

"I won't be a minute," a female voice called from somewhere out the back.

Adam raised his eyebrows and scanned the room. "Strange name and branding, don't you think?"

Frances shrugged. "Not really thought about it, to be honest."

"Well, look at that sign. It shows a kind of medieval sentinel, hence the name of the hotel, The Sentinel. In this case, it's indicating a knight in shining armour, that kind of thing."

Frances nodded. "Ye-es."

"If I saw that on the internet, I'd be expecting historic and atmospheric accommodation with high ceilings and traditional architecture. If I arrived to find this sparsely furnished, uber-modern monstrosity, I'd be more than a little pissed."

She shrugged. "Looks alright to me."

He sucked his teeth. "I don't know. Grown-up conversation is wasted on you."

"I can't think of anything more boring than talking about architecture. Is that what you and Amanda talk about? She's an architect, isn't she?"

"No. She's an interior designer, not that she does much of it anymore. But yes, she is interested in architecture."

A delicate Asian woman appeared in the doorway. "I'm so sorry to keep you. We are experiencing a problem with the hotel security system, and they kept me on hold for ages." Her perfect English was better than most English people he knew.

Adam smiled, digging his ID out of his pocket. "We're looking for Miles Muldoon. We've been told he's staying here."

"Yes, that's correct. Hang on two ticks and I'll call him." She checked on the computer before picking up the phone.

He heard the ringing tone from where he stood.

The woman replaced the receiver. "I'm sorry, he doesn't appear to be answering. Would you like to leave a message?"

"I would prefer to check his room. We urgently need to speak to him regarding a serious matter."

She appeared flustered. "I'm here alone at the moment. Is there any chance you could come back later?"

"We don't need you to come with us. If you give us a key, we can go ourselves."

She shook her head. "No. I must be present. Hang on." She stepped back into the room behind reception and made a phone call. She came back and busied herself programming a swipe card. "Somebody is coming to cover me in a few minutes." She gestured they take a seat.

Moments later, another Asian woman appeared and they spoke between themselves for a few seconds. The first woman came from behind the counter and led them to the lift and up to the fourth floor.

The corridor they stepped into seemed dark and gloomy with no windows and only dimly-lit wall lamps to light the way. She stopped at number forty-six and tapped lightly on the door.

When nobody answered, she swiped the card and the door clicked open.

As expected, the room was empty. Adam found an Adidas holdall in the wardrobe and several items of clothing hanging up. On the dressing table lay a pile of loose change, a watch, and a mobile phone.

"Look at this," the woman said, pointing to a swipe card that had been left in the slot to power the electrics. "Why would he go without his card? He can't get back in without it."

On the bedside table were a bunch of car keys. "Do you know what car he drives?"

"We usually obtain all that information when they check in. It should be on the computer," she said.

"Okay. That's all we can do for now. When he comes back, he'll have no choice but to approach reception before he can access the room. If you would be good enough to inform us when he does, I'd appreciate it. And it's probably best you don't mention our visit. He's a very dangerous man."

Her eyes widened and Adam knew she would call as soon as he showed his face. The last thing she'd want is trouble in her hotel. If it turned out Miles was innocent, then no harm done.

Down in reception, she found Miles' car details. A blue Audi Quattro A4 and his number plate details.

Adam gave her his card.

They headed outside and he took his car keys off Frances. "I'll drive," he said.

"Feeling better?"

"Much. Thanks."

"So what do you make of that? All his personal belongings still in his room," she said.

Adam shook his head as they climbed into the Mondeo. "Seems a bit odd, but it's not the only thing that doesn't seem right about this whole scenario. Keep your eyes peeled for a blue Audi." He drove through the hotel car park, trawling up and down each aisle.

"There it is," Frances said, breathlessly.

He pulled into a space beside the Audi and checked the number plate. It was indeed the right one.

They got out and peered through the windows. The pristine leather interior gleamed. There wasn't a thing out of place. It could have been parked in a showroom.

"So now what?" Frances asked.

"We can't do any more right now. We might have to apply for a warrant to search the car and phone, but at this stage Miles is still just a suspect, and we don't have any right to go through his stuff."

"Shit. I'd love to know where he is."

"Let's head back to the station and see if anything else has come to light. Do you fancy a sandwich?"

She nodded. "Yeah, I'm starved."

He picked up two chicken and avocado sandwiches on granary bread on the way to the station.

As they walked in, he nodded to Tom Sullivan on the main desk.

Smirking, Tom winked at him.

"What the heck's tickled his fancy?" Adam said to Frances under his breath.

"I haven't the foggiest."

They climbed the single flight of stairs to their offices and, as they entered, everyone stood up and began singing and clapping.

Ging gang goolie, goolie, goolie, goolie, watcha
Ging gang goo. Ging gang goo
Ging gang goolie, goolie, goolie, goolie, watcha
Ging gang goo. Ging gang goo
Hayla, oh hayla Shayla, oh hayla Shayla, Shayla, oh-ho
Hayla, oh hayla Shayla, oh hayla, Shayla, Shayla, ho.

Then, they all doubled up laughing raucously.

Adam shook his head and stared at Frances, who was also laughing.

Covering her mouth with her hand, she said, "I'm sorry, boss. I only told Calvin."

"Right, you've had your fun. Get back to work, you horrible lot." He walked into his office and shut the door.

The noise stopped suddenly and he smiled to himself. They'd all be worrying that he was annoyed now. The last laugh definitely belonged to him.

Chapter 5

Adam waited a few minutes before calling Calvin into his office.

The door opened and Calvin waved a white paper tissue ahead of himself. He bobbed his head in and smiled sheepishly. "Is it safe to come in?"

Adam rolled his eyes at the slightly effeminate young black man and smiled. "Get in here, you fool. Anything you need to tell me?"

"It was all my doing, I'm sorry. We didn't mean to upset you."

"About the case, Calvin," Adam groaned.

"Oh, yes, boss. Of course." He came further into the room. "We've had no joy with the neighbours. Nobody saw or heard a thing. A few of them know Miles Muldoon and couldn't speak more highly of him."

"Anything else?"

"We don't have Muldoon's DNA on file, but his girlfriend found a hairbrush of his and we're currently waiting for the report to find out if it matches the faecal sample found at the scene."

Adam nodded. "We need that ASAP. If it does belong to our man then we can ramp up the search."

"I spoke to Jemima, at the lab and she's on it. Probably won't be back until tomorrow though. I'll bring you a printout of Muldoon's phone history and all we know about the bloke."

"Thanks, Calvin. And a cup of coffee wouldn't go amiss."

"Yes, boss."

Adam ate the sandwich while picking through the notes on his desk. One was from Amanda.

He returned her call and she answered breathlessly.

"Hi, babe. You okay?" he asked.

"I'm fine."

"You should have called my mobile. I've not been in the office all morning."

"I don't like to disturb you when you're working—you could be in the middle of cracking a case and the phone rings."

"Well, tough. I don't want to come back from an interview and find I've missed the birth of my son."

"Of course I'd call you then, and who says we're having a boy?"

"Me and Jakey need another boy to balance everything out."

She giggled. "Whatever. Anyway, I wondered how you got on at the doctors."

"He gave me some painkillers and at least I'm able to walk properly again. Calvin and Frances think it's hilarious, but they're worried I'm annoyed with them, so I'll wind them up a while longer."

Calvin appeared in the doorway with a cup of coffee and a pile of papers.

Adam indicated he place it on the desk and gave him the thumbs up.

"Meanie."

"Hey, you. You're supposed to be on my side."

She laughed. "I am! But don't be too hard on them. Is that all the doctor did? Give you painkillers?"

"He examined me, and made another appointment for next week. He said if it's no better he'll arrange a scan. No doubt the swelling will have gone by then."

"Let's hope. Oh, and can you spare me an hour or so tomorrow lunchtime? I want to test drive that SUV I've had my eye on. Once the baby arrives, we won't fit everyone in the car."

"Yeah, that should be fine. Just remind me in the morning. I've got a lot going on at the moment."

"Okay, I'll let you go. Love you."

"Love you too. See you later."

He hung up and read through the information Calvin had compiled on Miles Muldoon. He was thirty-two-years-old, born in Maidenhead, in Berkshire. His parents emigrated to Australia when he was four-years-old. He came back, aged twenty, and got a job in London with BP Global as a trading and business intern, leaving his parents and three younger sisters in Perth.

He stayed in that job for twelve months before getting in through the back door of a large publishing company as admin assistant. He managed to step up the ladder quite quickly from assistant editor, to sub editor, and became a section editor within four years.

At twenty-six, he moved to Pinevale Publishing as Editor, specialising in fiction, non-fiction and memoirs.

Adam dropped his pen and rubbed his face with both hands. It didn't make sense. Something made this guy go off his rocker and jeopardise such an impressive career he'd clearly worked his socks off for.

He switched on his PC and brought up the company website. In the *Meet the Team* tab, there was Julia Rothwell, the commissioning editor and company director. The photograph of Julia showed a woman in her thirties, but there was no telling how long ago the image was taken.

Below her were two acquisitions editors, Miles and a woman in her sixties called Muriel Grey.

Sally Kemp was listed in the next column of copy editors, along with two other women, Nigella Monks and Carol Griffiths.

Lana Davis didn't get a mention.

Turning back to the paperwork, the phone history showed Muldoon's last call was to Sally Kemp at 8.15 pm Tuesday night, and lasted three minutes. This confirmed Sally's version of events, and Adam couldn't help but think if not for her dad's cancer, things could have turned out much worse for her last night.

Adam hadn't heard of her dad. He'd been Chief Constable long before Adam moved down from Manchester. He punched the name into the search engine, Sir Charles David Kemp, and a whole host of information was instantly available. It seemed he had been in the position for thirteen years and in the force for over forty. He was even knighted by the queen in 2008 for services to policing. He retired four years ago aged sixty-one.

Adam sighed. All that and now the poor man is dying of cancer at sixty-five.

He got up and headed into the main office.

Frances glanced up from her desk and smiled at him.

"Calvin, did anybody check the airports to see if Muldoon left the country? He may have scarpered back to Australia, which would explain leaving his car and phone at the hotel."

"Good point. I'm onto it, boss."

"Any luck in finding a next-of-kin for Michael Curtis?"

"Nothing yet. His parents and sister are dead. Apparently there's a niece somewhere but no luck yet." Calvin turned back to his computer screen.

Frances hung up the phone and jumped to her feet. "We've had confirmation of Muldoon's fingerprints all over the place, which isn't surprising considering he lived there up until last week. However, the crowbar used to break in the dining room window is also covered in his prints."

"Bingo. Let's get a warrant to search the hotel room and his car."

Chapter 6

The hotel room and phone gave them nothing at all, although several overseas numbers were found which would save Calvin a lot of time in his search for Muldoon's parents.

Adam didn't hold out much hope for the car after their earlier inspection, but he went with Frances to check it out.

Frances unlocked the top-of-the-range Audi with the key fob as they approached it. Adam opened the driver's door while Frances walked around to the passenger side. As he slid into the seat, the throbbing in his privates started up again, and he quickly pushed the chair back a few inches.

"Is it bad again?" Frances asked, sliding in beside him.

Unsure if she was taking the piss again, he didn't reply giving her a dirty look instead.

The owner's manual and service history books were the only items in the glove box. Two CDs, Adele and Ed Sheeran, were in the centre console and apart from the local Audi dealer's business card in the sun visor, the vehicle was clean.

"Get on the phone to Jimmy. We need his team down here to sweep for blood. There's bound to be some if he used this after the murder."

"Will do, boss." Frances got out and checked the boot.

He swung his legs out and held his breath as the throbbing ache returned with a vengeance.

"Oh, my God!" Frances said.

"What is it?" He raced to her side, his pain forgotten.

A single plastic bag sat in the totally clean boot.

Frances positioned it for him to peer inside at the blood-soaked grey clothing.

He whistled as he pulled his phone out of his pocket and dialled the station. "Calvin, it appears we've found the clothing the killer used. We need to upscale the search right away. It seems Miles Muldoon is definitely our man."

*

Adam was exhausted by the time he arrived home. He wanted a beer, his dinner, a bath and bed in that order. As he turned the key in the lock, he realised it wasn't going to happen.

Emma, Amanda's five-year-old daughter, stood in the hallway, screaming at the top of her lungs. Her usually pretty little face had turned bright red.

"Hey, hey, hey! What's going on?" he said.

"I don't like sausages and Mummy said I've got to eat them or go to bed," she sobbed.

"Come here." He held his arms out and she ran to him, and wrapped her arms and legs around him as he picked her up.

Amanda appeared in the kitchen doorway. "She's got a mood on her. This is the third temper tantrum since coming home from school. She even hit Jacob with a book earlier."

He tried to look at Emma's face, but she'd buried it in his neck. "Is that true, Em?"

She gave her head several quick shakes.

"Emma?" he said, sternly.

"Well, Jacob put his dirty fingers on my book and I told him to stop but he wouldn't."

"So, was it kind to hit him with it?" He bent to kiss his wife and stroked her rapidly growing baby bump.

"No," she whined.

"Where is Jacob now?"

"Eating his dinner." She pointed to the kitchen-dining room.

"How about we go in to see him, and you can apologise?"

"He didn't say sorry to me for touching my book."

"But he's only three. He doesn't understand. You're his big sister and should be caring for him, not hitting him with books."

She made a *humph* sound and shook her head again. She looked at him and his heart broke at the sight of her huge tear-filled eyes.

"Are you sorry for hurting your little brother?"

She nodded.

"How about we go and tell him. And maybe you could eat some of your dinner to make Mummy happy too. Okay, squirt?"

She nodded again.

Once Emma was all smiles, happily munching on sausages with Jacob, he left them to it.

Amanda had her back to them at the kitchen sink, and he could tell by her whole demeanour she was unhappy. He put his hands on her hips and slowly turned her to face him.

"Thanks, love," she said, putting her arms around him and holding him close—or as close as she could with a massive bump in the way.

He kissed her on the head. "Are you alright, Mand? You're looking a bit down in the mouth."

"I've just had one of those days. How about you?"

"I'll tell you right after you fill me in about yours." He lifted her chin up and looked into her eyes.

"You saw Emma. She's been like that since coming home from school. On top of that, Mary decided to go off with one of her mates without letting me know, so, as you can imagine, I was beside myself. Thankfully, the girl's mum thought to give me a call, or else I'd have been calling your lot out. She's due home soon, and I'll be having a serious chat with her."

"That's not like Mary. She knows you'll worry, especially with everything..."

Mary was Amanda's niece. That was the official explanation anyway. In truth, she was Amanda's daughter who'd been given up at birth. Andrew, Amanda's fugitive brother, had kidnapped the child from her adopted waste-of-space, druggy parents.

Amanda pulled away as she always did if she thought he might mention her brother. She checked in the oven. "Chicken casserole for dinner?"

"Sounds lovely, but I would have made do with sausages. You don't need to make two meals every day, you know. No wonder you're tired out."

"You need a proper meal after the hours you work, and that little madam..." she pointed at Emma, "...would throw it back at me if I tried to feed her casserole."

"Right, you." He twirled her around on the spot and faced her to the door. "You go and put your feet up. I'm in charge now."

"No, but I..."

He placed a finger on her lips. "No arguments. Get yourself on the sofa. I can dish up the dinner and afterwards, I'll sort out their bath, and bedtime stories."

"I couldn't possibly let you do that." She reached for the oven gloves.

He got to them first and pointed at the door. "Go!"

"Go, Mummy," Emma said.

"Go!" Jacob copied her, laughing.

"See? You've been told." He raised his eyebrows and cocked his head towards the door.

As she walked away, he flicked her bottom with the oven gloves. She caught them and threw them back at him. "Watch it, you." She smiled.

So much for a quiet night, he thought. He popped a couple of painkillers in his mouth and swallowed them down with a glass of water, then filled the kettle.

"How's it going in there?" he asked. "Have you finished your sausages yet?"

The room was large, the kitchen area was separated with a breakfast bar and the dining area held a dining set as well as a small sofa. Kids' toys were piled all around the room.

"Ye-es," they said, giggling.

"Who wants yoghurt?"

"Me, me, me," they chanted.

He set about cleaning tomato sauce from Jacob's hands, face and every surface in arms' reach of him. "Flipping heck, Jacob, how did you manage to get it everywhere?"

"Everywhere," Jacob said, holding his hands up to him for inspection.

Adam laughed and ruffled the boy's fine blond hair.

He got two pots of strawberry yoghurt from the fridge and two spoons. "Come on, you two. Eat up and then its bath time."

He made Amanda a cup of her favourite herbal tea and carried it through to the lounge.

She was curled up on the sofa, sleeping soundly.

He smiled as he placed the cup beside her on the coffee table and stroked a finger along her face. He went back to the kitchen, closing the door behind him.

An hour later, the kids had been bathed, changed, and read to. They insisted on giving their mum a kiss before going to bed.

He popped his head into the lounge and Amanda opened her eyes.

"Oh, hello," she said. "Is everything alright?"

"Wonderful. Kids are all ready for bed. Can I send them in to say goodnight?"

"Of course." She struggled into a sitting position.

"Come on, you two, quick kiss, then bed. Mummy's worn out."

The giggling children ran in and pounced on Amanda who kissed and tickled them.

"Okay, you little tinkers. Say goodnight to Mummy."

Chapter 7

I wait in the back alley until all the lights go out. Then I reach over the gate and unfasten the bolt.

A dog in the house next door begins barking continually. Quickly closing the gate, I press myself up against the brick wall of the tiny back yard.

"Shut up, you bloody nuisance," the dog's owner yells.

I creep to the kitchen window that I'd forced open earlier when the house was empty. Pulling it, I'm relieved when it opens.

A deep rumbling growl comes from next door followed by the dog scratching and whining to be let out.

Needing to move fast, I jump up and pull myself through the open window, step onto the kitchen sink and down onto the tiled floor.

The kitchen seems different in the dark. Bigger and more cluttered somehow. I wait for my eyes to adjust before I head for the door.

My movements are slow and careful. One wrong move and the whole thing will go tits up.

My feet tap lightly on the wooden floorboards, and I pause in relief as I reach the carpeted stairs.

Keeping my feet close to the edge, I climb one step at a time, reach the top and take a moment to assess the lay of the land.

Both bedroom doors are closed, but the bathroom door is open allowing a glow from the streetlight to illuminate my way.

I almost jump out of my skin as I step onto the landing and the floorboards creek. My pulse quickens and I wait to see if anybody has heard.

Two more silent steps and I'm standing outside the first bedroom door.

Fingers on the handle, I relish the thrill of adrenalin coursing through my veins.

I turn the handle and gentle snores reach my ears as I push the door slowly inwards. The sickly scent she always wears assaults my nostrils causing my stomach to clench.

A moment of weakness almost has me tearing out of the place. But the thought of her lying there, sleeping soundly when my life had turned seven shades of shit, spurs me on.

I close the door and stand above the bed, yet her snores never falter or lose momentum. How fortunate for her when I've not managed a wink of sleep in days.

The room is softly lit by the salt lamp she always recommends to anybody who will listen. And for once, I agree as I'm soothed by the pale pink glow.

My fingers slide easily around the handle of the hunting knife in my pocket. I shudder and take a deep breath in anticipation of her reaction.

Goosebumps cover my entire body causing delicious ripples of pleasure, and I smile savouring the moment.

My breath escapes in short pants reminding me of that moment just before an intense orgasm—that point of no return, and I almost cry out in sheer ecstasy.

When I grab her face, it surprises even me.

Her eyes open, slowly at first. Then, with a sharp intake of breath against my gloved hand, the terror reaches her eyes and she begins to squirm.

I wish I could stretch this part out, but the presence of her dad across the landing gives me no choice.

The knife cuts through her flesh with ease.

She blinks. Once. Twice. Three times and I feel her body sag.

A crimson stain spreads around her leaving a beautiful pattern in its wake.

I watch trying to take in every last detail, needing to etch it to my memory so I can recall it at will.

I would like to take photographs, but I'm not that stupid. Physical evidence is a no-no.

I lose all track of time. Her once beautiful face first turning grey, then purple and waxy and her lips now have a strange white tinge.

I force myself to my feet and wipe the knife and my gloved hands on the bottom of the pale blue bedspread.

With one final glance back at the body, I step out onto the landing.

I still have work to do.

***

Adam rolled over as Amanda climbed into bed. "What time is it?" he asked.

"Shhh. Go back to sleep."

"Shit, it's still the middle of the night. Are you feeling alright?"

"I'm fine. Just bloody uncomfortable," she said.

He pulled her head down onto his chest. "Do you want me to sing to you?"

She chuckled. "No, thanks. Can you even sing?"

"Yes, I can sing. Cheeky bugger."

"Well, I've never heard you."

"You have. I'm always singing in the car," he said.

"Oh, is that what you call it?"

It was his turn to laugh. "Get to sleep, woman. I've got a lot on tomorrow."

"Stop talking to me, and I will."

He shook his head and rolled his eyes.

He listened as her steady breathing turned to gentle snores when she fell asleep. But, wide awake himself, he glanced at the clock again—4.08am.

He eased out from underneath Amanda placing her head gently on the pillow. He went for a pee before heading down the stairs.

Amanda worried him. So used to keeping her problems inside, she often struggled to confide in him if something bothered her.

He knew she was concerned about Mary. Who wouldn't be? The poor girl had been through a lot in the past year beginning with the death of her mum to acute multiple sclerosis. That in itself was too much for a girl to cope with who, at that stage, hadn't even reached her teens. The disappearance of her dad, resulted in her being left with Amanda, the aunt she'd only just met. As if finding out about his arrest and the murder charges weren't enough, he escaped and returned to kidnap her.

Not in his right mind by then, Andrew locked Mary in a small closet for hours while he went out to plan the next stage of their escape. However, he had an accident and was killed outright.

They found Mary just in time.

So, if the girl had been playing up a bit, he couldn't blame her.

He checked his phone, almost 5.30am. There'd be no point going back to bed. He needed to be up in an hour anyway. He made himself a strong coffee and curled up on the sofa to ponder the case.

Muldoon was clearly angry at Sally Kemp for destroying his relationship with Lana. But mad enough to kill her old neighbour in cold blood? Something didn't ring true. There had to be some other reason. He'd ransacked her apartment, left his fingerprints on the crowbar, probably his DNA all over the wall. So, to kill a man, knowing he would be in the frame from the get go, he must have been pretty pissed off at something. But what?

The most likely explanation was Michael caught him trashing the apartment, but there didn't seem to be any signs of a scuffle. In fact, it appeared that Michael had fallen backwards after opening his front door and was butchered on the spot.

And where the hell could Muldoon be without his car and phone? Since withdrawing five hundred quid on Tuesday, his bank balance was also left untouched.

He turned as the door opened, and Amanda padded in holding a full coffee pot.

"Want a top-up?" she said, sitting beside him.

He held out his empty cup and smiled as she poured. "What are you doing up so early?" he asked.

"Couldn't sleep without you."

"I'm sorry, Mand. I've got a lot going on at work."

She snuggled in to him. "Anything I can help you with?"

"Not really. It's early days for the case I'm working on, but the problem isn't who the culprit is this time. It's why, and where the hell is he?"

"You already know who killed that old man?"

"Prima facie, as they say in court."

"Prima what?"

"Facie. It means we have enough evidence to prove he did it."

"Does it matter why? Who knows why anybody does anything?"

He rubbed his chin, nodding. "But you know me. I like things as tidy as possible."

"Once you find him, I'm sure he'll tell you why, especially if you can prove he did it."

He kissed the tip of her nose and sat forward. "You're right, as usual. Thanks, Mand. I'll get a quick shower and shoot off. It won't do me any harm to get in early for a change."

Chapter 8

He found Calvin already ensconced behind his computer when he walked in the office.

"Oh, my. Did you piss the bed or something?" Adam asked.

"Ha, ha. No, actually. I'm behind with paperwork and thought I'd catch up before the troops arrive."

"Good thinking. Anything you need me to do?"

"Denise Foley rang. She wants to know if you've got anywhere with her husband's murder."

Adam exhaled noisily. "We've got nothing to report. She's not being entirely truthful with me, and, until she does, we'll get no further."

William Foley, a two-bit drug dealer, was attacked in the park at a supposed drug meet. His wife Denise knew who he'd arranged to meet but refused to tell, so Adam's hands were tied.

"Can you call her, boss?"

"Leave it with me." He sighed.

He closed himself in his office, and, after replying to several emails, he called Denise for his weekly ear chewing.

As he hung up, Frances knocked on his door.

"Can I have a word, boss?"

He gestured with a nod she take a seat. "Are you alright, Holly?" He rarely used her Christian name at work as she tried to maintain a kick-ass persona, but Adam could tell she was far from alright—far from kick-ass for that matter.

Tears filled her eyes and she didn't even try to hide them.

He made to stand up to comfort her somehow. But she held a hand out to stop him.

"No. Please. This is hard enough as it is."

"What is? What's happened?"

"I told you yesterday I needed to show you. Are you free for half an hour?"

"Of course." He grabbed his jacket from the back of his chair. "Come on. Let's go."

She got to her feet and dabbed at her eyes, then smiled.

They were almost blown across the car park to his car. "When will this bloody wind die down?" he complained, as he slammed the door.

"Soon, I hope."

He pulled out of the car park. "Where to?"

"My house."

He nodded, not knowing what the hell to expect from this much-awaited visit to her home.

They parked up on the street outside her house, and she placed a hand on his arm.

"Before we go in, I want to tell you something."

He swallowed hard.

"I need to explain why I've kept this from you for so long."

He shook his head. "What? I don't understand."

"I needed my work life to be a complete contrast to my home life. I wanted to be accepted and judged on my own merit as a good detective."

"You're a great detective," he said, totally confused.

"Thank you." She smiled, but her lips were turned down in the corners. "I want you to meet my husband, Steve."

"Okay."

"Just be yourself, and if you have any questions save them until we're back in the car."

"Frances, you're worrying me now. Can't you tell me what I'm to expect in there?"

She closed her eyes and breathed deeply. "It will all make sense soon."

She led the way down the path and in through the front door of the plain semi.

A terrible stench he didn't recognise hit his nostrils as he crossed the threshold.

"Excuse the smell. It happens twice a day," she whispered.

A woman appeared at the top of the stairs, her arms filled with sheets.

"Oh, it's you, Holly, love. I was just changing the beds." She threw the sheets down in a heap and made a tidying motion with her hands over her permed mousey-brown hair and down her pink T-shirt and blue tracksuit bottoms.

"Val, this is Adam, my boss."

Smiling, the woman rushed down the stairs holding her hand out to him. "How nice to finally put a face to the name."

He shook her hand. "Pleased to meet you too, Mrs...?" He glanced at Frances for help.

"Call me Val, lovey." She patted his arm. "Come on through. Are you staying for a cuppa?"

"I'm not sure." Once again, Adam glanced at Frances to make the decision.

"No, I don't think so, Val. We've not got much time."

"Then I won't keep you. It was lovely to meet you at long last, Adam."

"And you, Val."

"Come on." Frances paused at the first door on the right. "Ready?"

He nodded and braced himself as she turned the handle.

The stink was worse *inside* the room, and his eyes began to smart.

"Hi, love. I finally managed to drag Adam in to meet you," she said, as she entered. "I'll open a window, shall I?"

"Yeah, it stinks in here."

Adam glanced in the direction of the slow drawl.

A man, who appeared to be in his mid-thirties, was sitting up in bed. He was clean-shaven and his hair was the same mousy shade as the woman in the hall. He presumed they were mother and son.

"Hi, Adam," Steve said, with a twisted smile.

"Steve, how nice to meet you." Adam held his hand out towards Steve, but Steve didn't move.

Frances, suddenly back behind him, shook her head and shoved in between them. She lifted Steve's hand into hers.

"So, to what do we owe the pleasure?" Steve asked, his eyes still on Adam.

"We were passing, and I've been meaning to introduce you both for ages," Frances said.

Steve smiled at his wife. "Are you investigating an exciting murder?"

She gave him a stern look. "We're not allowed to discuss my work, as you're well aware."

"Spoilsport." His mouth opened in a soundless laugh.

Frances wiped his mouth with a tissue before bending to kiss him. "We can't stop, honey, but I didn't want to pass the street without popping in."

Steve nodded. "Don't worry. I know how important your job is."

Adam smiled, totally at a loss for words. He'd had no clue what Frances had to deal with and felt terrible for piling all the extra work on her over the past few months.

They said their goodbyes and she shouted to Val they were leaving. Val came to the door and waved them off.

"Well?" Frances said as they got in the car.

"I feel like a lousy shit." He shook his head. "Why didn't you tell me?"

"Don't. Don't pity me, Adam. I'm serious."

"But I could've helped. All this time, instead of piling more and more on you, I could have helped."

"I didn't want your help. I wanted to be treated equally. I still do."

"What's wrong with Steve?"

"He had a car accident six years ago, three months after our wedding."

"Fuck! And they could do nothing for him?"

She shook her head. "He broke his neck. He was lucky he didn't die. Not that he agrees. He wishes he'd died instantly."

"I can understand that. He won't want to be a burden to you."

"You sound just like him. He's not a burden to me. He's the love of my life." Silent tears rolled down her face.

"I know, but he probably feels like he's a burden. Look at him. A young man in the prime of his life, and he's stuck in his bed."

"He wasn't always stuck in bed. He used to come into the lounge and into the garden. But lately, he's been too sick."

"When I spoke to him on the phone, I had no idea."

"You wouldn't have. He sounded normal. But now his pressure sores are infected with MRSA."

"MRSA? The hospital bug?"

"Yes, although his wasn't contracted from the hospital."

"Isn't it highly contagious?"

She smiled and nodded. "It is, but Steve's sores are cleaned and redressed twice a day. That awful smell is his rotting flesh. They can't treat him. He'll die soon."

"Why not? I mean, there must be something they can do."

She shook her head, sadly. "No. None of the antibiotics will touch it. He's on morphine for the pain. I won't go into too much detail, but there's nothing they can do."

"So how long? Weeks, months?"

"Could be days. Weeks at the most."

Adam felt as though he'd been slammed into a brick wall. He couldn't think straight. "How the hell have you kept this to yourself for so long?" he eventually said.

"It was easier at first. After the accident, I came in to work too numb to discuss it and found focusing on my work helped. But the past year or so, working with you and Calvin, I felt as though I was betraying you somehow, and wanted to tell you so badly. But there was never a right time. That's how it is with lies or omissions. The longer the gap, the harder it is to come clean."

"I'll take you back to the station to pick up your car, and then take as long as you like. I'll cover you."

"I don't intend to go home and wait for him to die. He has his mum and the care staff coming and going all day. We have a murder to investigate. Call me selfish, but it's the only way I can cope."

"Shit, Frances. You're far from selfish. But don't you want to spend time with him now, while you can? You might regret it if you don't."

"I hate the daytime. All the doctors and nurses parading through, treat him like he's just a number. I get angry with them which is why he's not going into hospital. He will die at home, and when the time comes that I'm needed there, I'll take time off."

"If you need me to do anything..."

"I'll ask. Now, if you don't mind, can we get back to work?"

"One last question. What about Cal and the team?"

"Can you tell them for me?"

Chapter 9

Adam felt gutted for what Frances had been dealing with—was still dealing with. He admired her strength and devotion to her job, and couldn't help but feel she was making a huge mistake by not being at her husband's side. Shit! The mere thought of losing Amanda made him want to run home and hold her tight.

His first wife had been killed by a hit-and-run driver. She died instantly, and he didn't get the chance to say goodbye. But if he had, nothing would have convinced him to leave her side.

They made the trip back to the station in silence. He had no choice but to carry on as normal, and, like she said, they had a murder to investigate.

He put a hand on Frances' shoulder and gave her a reassuring smile before they reached the office.

She nodded and gripped his fingers as she opened the door and entered.

"Ah, there you are," Cal said. "I was about to call you. Lana Davis didn't turn up for work this morning."

Adam screwed his face up. "Why is that a matter for us?"

"Well, she isn't answering her phone and she's never had a sick day since she's been working there. Shall I get uniform to check the house out?"

Adam glanced at Frances, his eyebrows raised in question.

She nodded.

"No, it's okay, Cal. We'll check it out."

Within minutes, they pulled up outside a row of terraced houses a few streets from the station.

When their knocks went unanswered, Adam peered through the lace-covered front window into the tidy lounge.

"Can I help you, mate?"

The deep voice startled Adam, and he turned to find a burly man wearing a beanie and khaki-coloured jumper with holes in the sleeves, standing behind him. The man held a large, vicious looking Rottweiler by the collar.

"I'm looking for Lana Davis." Adam flashed his ID. "Do you know where she is?"

"Not today. Why? What's she done?"

"She's not *done* anything. We just need to locate her."

The dog growled at Adam, and the man pulled it's choker-chain tighter. "I've not seen her since yesterday."

"And you are?"

"Bruce. Bruce Campbell. I live next door."

"Have you seen or heard anything unusual from your neighbours?"

"No." He shook his head. "Although Lana's car is still here, which is unusual." He shoved the dog inside his house and pulled the door shut.

Adam glanced up and down the street. "Which one's her car?"

"The red Fiesta over the road."

Adam and Frances walked across the road to the car. The back seat and the foot-well were full of junk, crisp packets, takeaway burger boxes and all sorts of other stuff.

"You know what an untidy car says about the owner, don't you?" Frances said, under her breath.

"My guess is scruffy bitch."

"Well, in this case, yeah, I agree with you."

"Anything untoward, detective?" Bruce shouted from his doorstep.

"Nope. I don't think so." Adam walked back towards the house.

Frances tried the car doors before following.

"Shall I call the house phone? See if she answers?" Bruce pulled his phone out of his pocket.

"You can do." Adam nodded. "You don't happen to have a key, do you?"

Bruce held a finger up as the phone began ringing.

Adam could hear it from inside the house.

"No answer," he said, ending the call. "Hey, Dean's car's parked over there too."

"Who's Dean?" Frances joined them on the pavement.

"Lana's dad."

"I'll check around the back of the house," Adam said.

"Here you are, mate. Come on through. Much faster than going all the way around." He shut the dog in the first room on the left.

They followed him down the hallway and through the dining room into the kitchen. The houses went further back than Adam expected.

Lana's back gate swung open.

"Strange. That's always locked." Bruce followed close behind.

"And that?" Adam pointed to the kitchen window.

Bruce gasped. "No way would they go out and leave the house unlocked."

Adam hammered on the back door.

"Call for back-up, Frances. I'm going in."

He took a step backwards and kicked the door, groaning as the impact caused his testicles to throb.

The door didn't budge.

"You could climb through the window, you know?" Frances said, shaking her head.

"Here you go, mate. Let me have a turn." Bruce slammed his shoulder into the door several times before it shot open and banged into the wall behind it.

"Wait here," Adam told them both, before stepping inside. "Hello? Anybody home?"

A familiar stench reached his nostrils. *Oh no*, he thought. He made his way through the house. Frances appeared behind him as he reached the stairs.

"Is that what I think it is?" she asked, pinching her nose.

He shrugged. "I hope not."

They reached the first closed door, and Adam braced himself taking a deep breath.

Lana lay on the bed, her head almost severed from her neck.

Frances cried out and staggered back from the room, leaning against the wall in shock.

"Frances. Go downstairs."

"I told you already. Don't mollycoddle me." She straightened up in defiance.

A similar scene awaited them in the room opposite—a middle-aged man with his throat cut. Adam doubted he'd even woken before the attack as the bedding was all in place.

On the wall above the bed, scrawled in shit, just like before, were the words YOU DESERVED IT.

Adam accompanied Frances downstairs and out the front door, taking several deep, nostril-cleansing breaths.

Bruce appeared on his front doorstep again. "What's happened? Did you find them?"

Adam nodded. "I'm sorry."

Bruce made as if to run inside.

Adam barred his way. "I can't allow you to do that, sir. I'm afraid it's a crime scene now."

Within minutes, the street swarmed with crime scene examiners.

After handing over responsibility of the scene, he found Frances leaning against his car.

"Come on, you. I'm taking you for a coffee."

"I told you, boss. Don't mo—"

He pressed his finger to her lips. "Don't mollycoddle you. Yeah, yeah, I get the message. But not everything's about you. Maybe I need a bit of mollycoddling. It's not every day you're faced with a scene like that."

"You're a homicide detective. It's what you do."

He shrugged. "Never-the-less, this shit gets to you sometimes, doesn't it?"

*

Adam's phone rang as he walked to the table. He hurriedly placed the tray on the table and fumbled in his pocket as it stopped ringing. He rolled his eyes. "For God's..."

Frances' phone rang.

"Cal," they both said in unison.

She handed him her phone.

"Yes, Cal?"

"Hey, boss. The faeces results are back."

"And."

"Definitely a match to Miles Muldoon."

"Well, you can add Lana Davis and her dad, Dean Davis, to the list of his victims."

"They're dead?"

"Both had their throats slashed while sleeping. The killer left his calling card smeared on the wall with another message."

"Yuck."

"Tell me about it. We're just grabbing a coffee and we'll be back. Can you find next-of-kin for the victims and also book a press release? We're going to need the public's assistance with this one. Someone knows where Miles Muldoon is hiding out."

"Gotcha, boss."

"And contact Pinevale Publishing. They might even have Lana's next of kin on file."

"Will do."

"Oh, and one other thing, Cal." Adam looked over his shoulder to make sure Frances was out of earshot. "I need to speak to you and the team later. Can you arrange for them to be available?"

Frances, absently making shapes in the froth on her latte with a teaspoon, looked up when he returned to the table.

"It was a match on the..." he glanced around and lowered his voice, "...faeces."

She nodded. "I'm not surprised."

"We will need to speak to Sally Kemp and warn her Muldoon means business."

"Do you want to go now?"

"Drink your coffee first." He popped two pills into his mouth and sipped his.

"We also need to find Muldoon's closest friends. He must have some."

"Sally should be able to help with that too. They were together for a while."

He nodded. "Yeah. Let's hope so."

Chapter 10

Sally Kemp opened the front door of the detached stone cottage, on the outskirts of Pinevale, before Adam and Frances had the chance to knock.

"I'm sorry. I've been waiting for the nurse to come and sit with dad, and then I planned to come in, I promise."

"Sorry?" Adam shrugged, confused.

"To make my statement. That is why you're here, isn't it?" She shook her head and her long red curls swished.

"Actually, no, that isn't why we're here. Do you mind if we come in?"

She stepped back and allowed them to enter the spacious and tastefully decorated entrance hall.

"I don't have much time. Dad's regular nurse called in sick this morning and I'm waiting for a replacement." She padded barefoot on the thick cream-coloured carpet through to the lounge.

They followed and Adam admired the beautiful room adorned with exquisite artwork and quality antiques.

"Take a seat." Sally motioned to the two chunky, cream leather sofas.

He and Frances sat side by side.

"So, why are you here? Did you catch Miles? The news last night said you were trying to find him, so he must be the one who killed poor Michael."

"I'm afraid not. But we did receive confirmation that Mr Muldoon's DNA is a match for the faeces found at your apartment."

"So you came all the way over here to tell me that?"

With a nod of his head, Adam gestured for Frances to take over. She was more sensitive than him.

Frances cleared her throat. "I'm sorry, Sally. But it looks as though the killer has struck again."

"I don't understand." Her eyebrows screwed tight together.

"There's no easy way to tell you this, but Lana Davis and her father, Dean, were found dead this morning."

Sally gasped and clawed at the fine fabric at her throat as though suddenly claustrophobic.

Frances moved across the room and sat beside the other woman.

Sally crumpled into her arms and began to sob. Adam marvelled over how different it was having that woman's touch at times like these.

After a few moments, Sally wiped her face and tried to pull herself together. However, she still held Frances' hand tightly in hers.

"I had my issues with Lana, but she was just a gullible child really, you know?"

Frances nodded.

"I couldn't blame her for falling for Miles' patter. I did the same myself once upon a time." She closed her eyes and struggled to fight back the tears. "I must go and check on Daddy. I won't be a sec."

She scurried from the room. Adam couldn't help notice the delicate beige fabric of her calf-length trousers looked like something most women would wear on a night out, not for dossing around the house in.

"Poor woman must be petrified," Frances said.

"I'll ask Cal to arrange for someone to keep an eye on the house for a few days. I can't help but think we should've arranged the same for Lana yesterday."

"We didn't know he would be back. It's not your fault, boss."

Adam shrugged. "Makes you think though, doesn't it? Lana asked if we thought he might come back for them. If we'd said yes, they may not have even stayed at home last night."

"Well, I certainly didn't think he would be back."

"As detectives, we should be one step ahead of the game. There was a chance he'd come back. He killed Michael for much less than what Lana and her dad had done."

"Hindsight is a marvellous thing, boss."

He nodded. "Yeah, you're right. But I'm not making the same mistake with Sally and her dad."

"Fair enough."

Sally returned a short while later. "Sorry. Daddy could tell I was upset and made me explain everything."

"Well, he doesn't need to worry. We'll make sure someone is watching the house before dark."

Sally slouched in relief. "Thank God for that. I was wondering how I'd cope. Daddy can't be moved, he's too sick."

"Sally, can you give us a list of all Miles' friends and acquaintances?" Frances asked.

"He doesn't have many outside of the office. He used to be close to a guy called Joey when I first met him. He was the brother of his ex, and they didn't stay in touch once he moved in with me."

"Who was his ex? Do you know?"

"Yes. She made my life hell for months. Her name's Natasha Barker. She's the Department Manager in the Bed Superstore in Pinevale—or she was last I heard."

"And her brother used to be Miles' closest friend?" Adam said.

"Well, he was back then."

"Anything else you can tell us? Somewhere you think he might go? Someone he may turn to for help?" Adam ran a hand through his close-cropped hair.

"No. He would just work, work, work. Drove me mad, to be honest. He said we didn't need anybody else, we had each other. Then, once he made me shun all my friends, he up and left."

Adam got to his feet. "We'll let you get back to your father. If you think of anything else, no matter how small, call us. The sooner we get the nasty piece of work off the streets the better."

Adam called Cal as they walked back to the car.

"Cal, I need you to arrange for an officer to watch over Sally Kemp's father's house. The address is Waverley Lodge, Sutton Lane, Upper Pinevale."

"The DCI won't like it, boss. He's always going on about the budget, yada, yada, yada, but I'll see what I can do."

"See they are aware he used to be Chief of Police and now he's dying of cancer. It's the least we can do to keep them safe."

"Leave it with me, boss."

Chapter 11

Natasha Barker, a slightly overweight, thirty-something brunette, still worked at the Bed Superstore, but she was now the Store Manager.

A member of staff pointed her out, and, as they approached, they witnessed her tearing strips off a geeky-looking man in his twenties who appeared to be wearing his father's suit.

"If a customer keeps looking in your direction, you pounce. They're not going to hand over hundreds of hard-earned pounds if you can't be arsed checking what they're looking for."

"But the last person told me to back off. They treated me like a stalker."

"There's a world of difference between a stalker and a good salesperson, you idiot. Now get out there and bloody sell something."

She did a double take as she realised Adam and Frances were standing behind them. "Can I help you?" she snapped.

"Natasha Barker?" Adam raised his eyebrows. He'd already decided he didn't like this woman.

"Yes. What can I do for you?"

"DI Stanley and DS Frances." They held up their badges. "Can you spare us a minute while we ask you a few questions?"

Deep furrows appeared between her eyes. "What about?"

"May we?" Adam gestured to her office door.

As she stomped into the office, Adam wondered how the heels on her court shoes didn't disintegrate under the sheer pressure.

Piles of vacuum-packed pillows filled the small room, and Natasha climbed over them to get to her chair on the other side of the desk. "Excuse the mess. We had a double delivery by mistake, and we've got nowhere else for them to go."

"Don't worry about it," Adam said, glad of the chance to stand. The drawing ache in his scrotum was returning. He gestured that Frances take the only other seat.

"We believe you're acquainted with Miles Muldoon."

Natasha inhaled quickly and coughed. "A long time ago, maybe."

"*How* long ago?"

"Two years. Give or take."

"Two? Sally Kemp said she's been seeing him for almost three years." Adam scratched his head.

Natasha shrugged, a smile playing at the corners of her mouth.

"Are you saying you were still seeing him after he moved in with Sally?"

She shrugged one shoulder flippantly. "Not a crime, is it? What the hell's this about? I need to get back to work."

"We have reason to believe Miles has brutally murdered three people."

She gasped and jumped to her feet, her hands covering her mouth.

"And I seriously suggest if you have any idea where he is, you inform us immediately."

"I haven't a clue. Like I told you, I've not seen him for months."

Adam placed his elbow on the doorjamb and leaned against it, exhaling loudly. "You actually said your last contact with him was two years ago. Which is it?"

"When he left, I was heartbroken. We'd practically lived together for six months, until Miss Prissy Knickers set her sights on him, and he was putty in her hands."

"He left you for Sally?" Frances' voice was gentle.

Adam backed off and let her fly with it.

"Yes, but not for long. He kept coming back telling me he'd made a mistake by leaving me."

"And you'd sleep with him?"

"You've got to understand how much I loved the man."

Frances nodded. "I do understand. Go on, what else happened?"

"This continued for a few weeks on and off. He said he loved me and I stopped taking my pill. I thought if I got pregnant he would leave her once and for all."

"But it didn't work?"

She shook her head, her face twisted in disgust. "He found out and just stopped coming. Wouldn't accept my calls or anything. So, one night, after a few too many glasses of wine, I sent his bimbo a message on Facebook. I told her everything."

"And what happened?"

"The bitch got me banned off Facebook. And I never saw Miles again until he arrived on my doorstep around six months ago."

"What did he want after all that time?"

Natasha raised her eyebrows. "What do they always want?"

Frances' eyes widened. "Sex?"

"Got it in one. A booty call. I told him to sling his hook. I'd been engaged to Stu for a couple of months by then, and Miles was livid when he found out. I don't think he's used to being turned down."

"So what did he do?"

"Said some horrible stuff, upended the coffee table and left. He didn't contact me again."

"He wasn't violent towards you?"

"Not then."

"But he had been in the past?"

"A few times. Nothing too bad. I mean, he didn't hospitalise me or anything. Just the odd slap here and there. Oh, and he bit me once, that's all."

"That's all?" Adam snapped, startling her. "A man lays his hands on you and even bites you and you say, *that's all.*"

"Well, I meant it wasn't a serious assault." She flushed deep red from the neck up.

Adam barked out a laugh and raised his eyes to the ceiling, incredulous.

"Any assault is serious, Natasha," Frances said, eyeballing Adam to shut him up. "So, that was six months ago?"

Sufficiently put in her place, Natasha squirmed. "Near enough."

Frances smiled. "And your brother, Joey. Sally said they used to be friends. Are they still in touch?"

"No. Not since the Facebook episode. They used to be good friends too, but Joey couldn't stand Sally. He said she was a controlling bitch."

Adam pursed his lips, making a loud sucking sound.

Frances bristled slightly, but ignored him. "Where can we find Joey?"

"He's touring South America with his new wife. Won't be back for another month or so."

"Do you know Catherine Bailey?" Adam abruptly changed the subject.

"Erm, yes. She used to go out with Miles before I met him. I don't know where she lives now, though.

You could try the gym on the High Street. She used to be an aerobics instructor there."

"Let me guess. He was still seeing her when he met you?"

"They were living in the same house, but they hadn't been intimate for months."

"Really?" Adam grinned. "You know, he told Sally the exact same thing about you."

"The lying bastard." She shook her head in obvious disgust. "I'm such an idiot."

"Don't worry about it, Natasha. He sounds like a pro." Frances got to her feet. "Maybe you should lie low for a while. Can you stay with friends or family for a few days, at least until he's caught? It seems he's targeting anybody who rebuffed him, and you may well be on that list."

"Okay. Thanks for the warning, but I'd like to see him try."

***

Amanda looked at her watch for what felt like the hundredth time—2.15pm. "Where the bloody hell are you, Adam?"

She got up off the stylish plastic chair and waved at the smarmy car salesman.

"Are you all set?" he asked, rubbing his hands together.

She shrugged. "I guess so. My husband must've been held up."

"We can reschedule if you like?"

Amanda sighed. "No. It's okay. If he's not here then he can't object if I buy a car he doesn't like."

"If that's the case, I have a nifty, blue sports car that would look fantastic with you in the driver's seat."

She laughed. "I couldn't fit four kids and my detective inspector husband in a nifty blue sports car."

He coughed, straightening his tie. "Fair point. I'll just grab the keys for you."

Chapter 12

When they got back to the car, Adam noticed he'd missed a call from Cal. He dialled the station.

"Hi, boss, a couple of things. I traced Lana's mother and two sisters. They live in Devon. A local officer is going around there to inform her and arrange for someone to identify the bodies."

"That's a relief. We've got one more stop to see if we can find Catherine Bailey before we head back. I'll fill you in on everything then. What was the other thing?"

"I managed to arrange for the PPU to keep watch over Sally for a couple of nights. If you want any more than that, you'll have to square it with the DCI yourself. He gives me the wild shites."

Adam laughed. "That'll do for now. Speak later." He hung up and turned back to Frances who seemed miles away again. "You hungry?"

She shook her head, sadly.

"Tough. You're having something to eat whether you like it or not. How's fish and chips sound?"

"Fattening."

"Good brain food is what it is."

Frances shook her head as he pulled the car out into the street.

A few minutes later, he marched her into the local greasy spoon and ordered two fish meals with a large pot of tea.

"I've told you. I really don't want you treating me differently."

Adam popped a pill in his mouth and swallowed it with a glass of water. "Wind your neck in. I'm hungry, that's all."

"You don't fool me. This is the second cafe we've been in today."

"It's all in your head."

"Alright then. When, before today, were we last in a cafe?"

He shrugged. "I dunno."

Their food arrived, and Adam busied himself pouring the tea. She was right, of course. He did feel different towards her.

"I'm sorry." He gave her a cockeyed smile. "I can't help it. I'm worried about you."

"Do you understand why I didn't tell you before now?"

"I think you should go home. Steve needs you by his side."

"You don't know anything about it." She looked totally exhausted.

"I know enough. He's your husband. You're his wife. You love each other. Right?"

She nodded, turned away and began dabbing at her eyes.

"He must be so scared, Holly."

She took a deep breath and closed her eyes tightly, her lips quivering.

Adam reached for her hand. "And you need to spend as much time with him as you can. Believe me. You will never get this time back."

She gripped his fingers and sobbed.

"Now come on. All this sentimentality's given me an appetite."

Frances smiled and wiped her eyes on a napkin.

"I'll take some time off once we find Muldoon. Deal?"

He shrugged. "We'll see. Now eat up."

*

"Do you feel guilty coming in here after scoffing all those calories?" Adam said, holding the door to the gym open.

"*You* should. You ate half of mine."

"I'm a growing boy." He laughed.

"Good afternoon," the bronzed, muscle-bound woman said from the front desk.

"Does Catherine Bailey still work here?" Adam asked.

"She sure does. Who shall I say wants her?" The woman picked up the phone.

"Detective Inspector Stanley."

The woman's already high eyebrows rose a little higher. She picked up the phone. "Cathy, you're wanted in reception. A detective."

The woman who appeared a few seconds later was nothing like any of Muldoon's other girlfriends, which was strange. Most people tend to stick to a certain type but clearly not Muldoon. Catherine Bailey was short and dumpy-looking, considering she was a fitness instructor. She had fine, silky blonde tresses that had no body or shape whatsoever, and her nose could've been moulded out of Plasticine by a two-year-old.

"Can I help you," she said, in a breathless voice.

"Catherine Bailey?" Adam showed her his badge.

She nodded, her gaze travelling between him and Frances.

"Is there somewhere private we can talk?"

"Is it Amy?"

"Amy?"

"Has something happened to my daughter?"

"No. Nothing like that."

She visibly relaxed. "Oh, thank God for that. Follow me."

They walked through a large open area filled with weightlifting equipment. A handful of people were dotted around the gym, in various states of undress.

The mirrored glass partition at the back turned out to be the outer wall of the office.

"You must see all sorts of sights from in here." Adam chuckled.

"You're not kidding." She smiled, perching on the desk. "So, what can I do for you?"

"We believe you know Miles Muldoon?"

Her face dropped into a scowl. "What about him?"

"How long were you an item for?"

"Too long. What's this about?"

"We're investigating several murders and Muldoon is our prime suspect."

"Miles?" She frowned.

Adam nodded.

"A murderer?"

He nodded again.

"That's insane." She shook her head. "Miles wouldn't hurt anyone."

"I believe you made assault claims against him?"

"I was going to, but I changed my mind. It was more a misunderstanding."

"A misunderstanding?" Adam shook his head in confusion. "How do you misunderstand something like that? You were either assaulted or you weren't."

"I wasn't. We had a fight and I slapped him. I just didn't expect him to slap me back."

"Did you find him to be the jealous type?" Frances asked, her voice a little gentler.

"I guess, but isn't everyone?"

"I don't think so." Frances frowned. "But even so, there's a difference between a few flatteringly jealous remarks and an all-encompassing, destructive kind of jealousy."

"I guess. Then I would say Miles' jealousy started off mild, making me feel loved and special. But by the end of our relationship, he could be downright nasty. Which makes me laugh, considering he was the one who went on to have an affair."

"Dirty thinkers are dirty doers, according to my dad," Frances said.

Catherine's face lit up as she laughed. "That's a good one. I might have to tweet it."

"Be my guest."

Adam cut in. "About Amy…"

"My Amy? What about her?"

"How old is she?"

"Three. She's just started nursery. That's why I panicked when you arrived."

"Is Muldoon her father?"

"What?" Her eyes shot poison darts at Adam. "No, he's bloody not."

"He left you three and a half years ago. That would have made you three months pregnant. Did you make the decision to keep it from him?"

"What is this?" She turned back to Frances. "I don't need to answer him, do I?"

Frances winced and cocked one shoulder. "Not if you don't want to, but it looks as though Miles is targeting anyone who has, in his opinion, double-crossed him. If there's anything you're keeping from us, you may be putting yourself and your daughter at risk."

"If I tell you in confidence, will you promise to keep it to yourself?"

Adam nodded. "Until such a time that I can't." He knew he was being abrupt, but he couldn't help it. His testicles were throbbing and he'd left his pills at the station.

"What the fuck's that supposed to mean?" Her lips curled.

"He means..." Frances eyeballed Adam. "...that we will keep it to ourselves unless a situation occurs where it's no longer safe to do so."

"I still don't understand."

"Well, say Muldoon decides to pay you a visit and we need to intervene and get you safety, then any secrets you tell us may need to be shared with the rest of our team."

"You think it could come to that?" Tears spilled from her eyes.

"I would like to say no, but to be honest, we haven't a clue what's going on in his head at the moment," Frances explained. "That's why we need as much information as we can get."

A massive muscle-man squared himself up in front of the office and began swinging dumbbells. Clearly he couldn't see them in the office as he posed at his reflection, all but blowing himself a kiss.

Catherine shoved past Adam and Frances and hammered on the window with the palm of her hand.

Startled, the weightlifter dropped the dumbbells and scowled. The way his nostrils flared resembled an angry bull. Adam was pleased when he sauntered to the other side of the room.

"Okay. You're right. Amy is Miles' daughter. I never told him, but he wouldn't be interested if I had. He made it perfectly clear he never wanted kids."

Frances frowned. "Pinevale isn't a big place. I'm surprised he didn't hear about her from a mutual friend before now."

"I didn't intend to keep it from him, initially, but Miles wasn't interested enough in me or my life once he'd scarpered. After all this time, I doubt he'll find out. Amy and I don't need him or anyone else in our lives right now."

"Hopefully, before too long, he'll be locked up for the foreseeable." Adam forced a gentler tone to his voice. "In the meantime, is there anywhere you can stay? Just in case."

Wringing her hands, Catherine nodded. "I could stay at our Karl's. Miles was always scared of my brothers."

"Where does Karl live?"

"Opposite the high school. I can't think of the number but it's the one with the awful green caravan in the front garden."

He nodded. "I know the one."

Chapter 13

Amanda still hadn't heard from Adam by the time she collected the kids from school. She knew he wouldn't have stood her up if it wasn't important, but it didn't stop her feeling a little rejected.

She smiled, shaking her head. It must be the hormones, causing her to be so touchy and emotional.

The school run comprised of three stops. The daycare for Jacob, primary for Emma, and she had to wait on the corner further up from the high school for Mary.

Once they were all in the car heading for home, she broke the news.

"I've got a surprise for you all."

"A surprise for me, Mummy?" Emma clapped her hands.

Jacob giggled.

"A surprise for all of you. Are you listening, Mary?"

"What? Oh, yeah." Mary sounded uninterested.

"I'm picking up our new car tomorrow."

Emma squealed. "Oh, goodie. Does it got DDD."

Amanda chuckled. "Sorry, sweetie. No DVD. But there'll be lots more room."

"Aw, that's dumb."

"Emma!" Amanda scowled at her daughter through the specially-placed rear-view mirror.

"Dats dumb," Jacob mimicked his sister.

"Now look what you've done, cheeky."

"Dats dumb," Jacob repeated.

Amanda shook her head. "Why do I bother?" She turned to Mary, sitting beside her in the passenger seat. She was picking at her finger nails and seemed miles away. "What's wrong with you, little miss?"

"Oh, nothing." She replied without lifting her head.

Amanda scrutinised her again. "You know you can talk to me, don't you?"

"Yes."

"Or Sandra. If you feel you can't talk to me, Sandra is a great listener."

"I know."

Amanda sighed. She wished Mary would open up, but she wouldn't force her, hoping she would come around in her own good time.

***

On the way back to the station, Adam groaned.

"What is it, boss?" Frances said, suddenly jolted from her daydream.

"I told Amanda I'd meet her to test drive a new SUV."

"Then go."

"It's too late now."

He waited until he'd parked the car at the station before calling home, worried if he used the car-kit Amanda would give him a dressing down while Frances was listening.

**

Once home, Mary went to her room while Emma and Jacob shared a plate of cookies in front of the TV. Taking advantage of the quiet time, Amanda began peeling the potatoes for dinner.

At 4.30pm the phone rang.

"I'm so sorry, Mand. We've had another double homicide and we're flat tack."

"Don't worry about it." She rolled her eyes knowing full well she was being unfair.

"I'll make it up to you. Can we go tomorrow?"

"No point. Unless you want to drop me off at the car yard on your way to the station."

"What do you mean?"

"I pick the new car up tomorrow."

"You bought it?"

"Yes, I bought it. What did you expect me to do? Walk out of there with nothing?"

"No. I guess not. But listen, babe. I've got to get back to it. I shouldn't be home too late. I'll call you if that changes."

She hung up, feeling a total bitch. She never reacted this way where his work was concerned. What the hell was wrong with her?

She finished the dinner and called Mary down.

Still behaving strangely, Mary slunk down the stairs and took her place at the table.

"How was school today, love?" Amanda asked, placing the food on the table.

Mary shrugged. "Okay."

"Did you do anything fun?"

"Not really. I only like maths and we didn't have that today."

"I don't know who you inherit that from. Maths was my worst subject at school. Your dad's too."

She dropped her eyes at the mention of her dad.

"Are you sad, Mary?"

"Don't be sad, Mary." Emma stabbed a fish finger and took a bite.

Mary smiled at Emma before turning her eyes back to Amanda. "A little."

"Me too. I miss him every single day. But he wouldn't want you to be sad."

She played with her food without taking so much as a bite. "We're doing our family trees in English."

Amanda's breath hitched. "Okay. Is that why you're sad?"

Mary nodded.

Emma squirted tomato ketchup on Jacob's plate.

"No more, Em. He's got enough," Amanda said, taking the bottle from her daughter. She turned back to Mary. "Is it?"

Mary's eyes began filling up. She put her fork down and covered her face.

Amanda got to her feet and placed an arm around her shoulder. "Come with me a minute, hon."

She led Mary through to the lounge knowing Emma and Jacob would be upset if they saw their cousin crying.

"Tell me what's upsetting you?"

"We need photos of our parents and grandparents from when they were little, and I don't have any. All my friends will think I'm a freak."

"They will *not* think you're a freak, and besides, I have a couple of photos of your dad from when he was a little boy."

"You do?" Her eyes lit up.

"And I'm sure we could find a few photographs to pass off as your mum if you want?"

She nodded. "Yes, please."

"We can ask Sandra for some and, in fact, one of the photos I mentioned has mine and your dad's mum on it."

"My grandma?"

Amanda nodded, smiling.

"Is she still alive?"

"I think so. We rarely speak, but the last I heard she lived in Scotland."

"Would I be able to meet her?"

Mary's eyes sparkled for the first time in weeks. And although Amanda had no intention of contacting her selfish, unreliable mother, she didn't want to burst the girl's bubble either.

"I don't know where she is, but I could try and find her, if that's what you want?"

"Yes, please. I love Sandra, but I don't have many real relatives and it would be nice to have another grandmother."

"I'll see what I can do. But don't get your hopes up. I may not be able to find her."

"I won't. Can I see those photos now?"

"They're in a box underneath the stairs, and I promise I'll dig them out once the kids are in bed. Deal?"

"Deal."

"Come on. Let's go and finish your dinner."

They hugged and went back through to the dining room.

*

"Be a darling and load the dishwasher for me, Mary, while I give the monsters a bath."

"Okay," she said, much brighter than she'd been in ages.

Amanda ran a bath while Jacob and Emma bounced on the beds, laughing hysterically. It seemed the more exhausted *she* felt, the more energy *they* seemed to have, and it was only going to get worse once the baby arrived.

Once the kids were bathed, in their pyjamas and tucked up in bed, Amanda wearily trudged down the stairs.

"You ready to look for them photos now, Mary?" she said, popping her head into the empty kitchen. "Mary?" She headed for the lounge, but stopped short and gasped, her hand flying to her mouth.

Mary was sitting on the hallway carpet surrounded by newspaper clippings. Tears streamed down her face and dripped off her chin.

Chapter 14

"Was Amanda angry?" Frances asked as he ended the call.

"Worse than that. She's sulking. I'd rather her shout and scream at me than sulk." He laughed.

"Yikes!" She grinned.

"Anyway you, hop-it."

"But, I..."

"No arguments. Go! We'll see you bright and early in the morning. And besides, I need to tell the others about Steve and I presume you don't want to be present for that?"

She shook her head. "Okay. I'll go just this once. But make it clear to them, I don't want to be treated any—"

"Blah, blah, blah. Go!" He pointed to her car.

She skulked away, and he watched until she drove from the car park.

The rain began just as he reached the station door.

"Any news?" he asked Cal when he entered the office.

"Nothing, boss. Nobody saw or heard a thing. Devon police managed to inform the victim's next of kin and they are on their way over."

"Good."

"I also got hold of Jemima Muldoon, his mother, in Perth. She was horrified, of course, but bizarrely relieved. She's been searching for him for years. The last known address was London when he worked for BP. She's been going out of her mind."

"She didn't look very hard. The name Miles Muldoon isn't common. I'm pretty sure a Google search would have found him easily enough."

"She said she did that. Sent him an email asking if he was her son, but he denied it. She couldn't afford to come over and check him out in person."

"He's a nasty piece of work. Why would anyone put their mother through that?"

"Beats me, boss."

"Anyway, I see everyone's here. Can you call them all together. There's something I need to tell you."

"You're not off back to Manchester are you, boss?"

Adam tutted, shaking his head. "Are you for real?"

"Oh, good. I've been stressing all day."

Adam headed into his office, took off his jacket and dropped his phone on the desk. Cal appeared in the doorway as Adam rummaged in his briefcase for his pills.

"Right when you are, boss. But I can't find Frances. Is she on her way up?"

Adam swigged the pills down with a two-day-old glass of water. "She's gone home." He scratched his chin with both hands, making a rasping sound. "Be right with you, Cal."

They all stood by Cal's desk, whispering amongst themselves. Ginger Dave, the oldest of the team at sixty-three, whose once-red hair was now snow-white, had worked for the department for forty years, and although he had no ambition, he was loyal and hardworking. Les McManus, a quiet yet thorough detective, had worked as a PC for more than twenty years before applying for promotion to homicide eighteen months ago. He was a slender man in his late forties, with thinning brown hair. His side-kick, Julie Sellers, the newest member of the team, had also come to them from uniform and, at only twenty-six, showed a lot of promise.

"Shh-shh." Ginger Dave nodded in Adam's direction and stood upright.

"I need to tell you all something, but you've got to swear not to let it go any further than this room."

"Of course not, boss," Les said.

"It's about Frances. Now, we're all aware how private she is, and there has been a lot of banter about her sexuality over the last few months, but..."

"So she *is* batting for the same team then, boss?" Cal cut in. "It's no biggie, anyway."

"The thing is..." He shook his head. "...thanks, Cal, but, the thing is—Frances is married."

They all smirked at each other, as though surprised.

"I never expected that," Julie said.

"Frances prefers to keep her private life just that—private. But she's agreed for me to explain to you that she married Steve six years ago."

"She's a dark horse," Les said.

"Sadly, soon after their wedding, Steve had a car accident and has been paralysed from the neck down ever since."

They gave a collective gasp.

"That's not all, I'm afraid," he continued. "Frances told me this morning that her husband contracted an incurable infection, and he doesn't have long to live."

"Oh, no!" Julie cried.

"Poor girl," Ginger Dave said, running a hand though his hair.

Cal sat down heavily on his desk, his milk-chocolate skin suddenly pale. He and Frances were close and Adam knew this bombshell would probably affect him the most.

"She had her reasons for not telling any of you."

"Why? What are they? I don't understand how she could come to work day in and day out and not let on something this massive was happening to her." Les almost sounded miffed.

"She didn't want to be treated differently. I told her that wouldn't have happened, but then found myself behaving different with her all day. I've even taken her into two cafes today! Usually, the first few days of an investigation, we eat on the hop, if at all."

"Only because you care. We all care about her. We're like family here," Julie said.

"I know we are, and because of that, work is the only place she could come and be treated normally. I'm not saying I agree, but I do understand."

"So is she taking time off now?"

"No, not yet. She promised once we locate Muldoon she will, but for now she wants to be kept busy."

"How long does he have?" Les was no stranger to death. His wife died the year before after a long and debilitating battle with cancer.

"Not long at all."

"Poor, poor, girl." Julie's eyes brimmed with tears.

"That's exactly what she doesn't want. Now she knows I'm telling you but wants nothing to change, and, believe me, that's difficult. But we need to try our best to honour her wishes. She is going to need us soon enough. I suspect his passing will hit her harder than she thinks."

Everyone nodded in agreement except Cal who hadn't uttered a word.

"You okay, mate?" He'd never seen Cal so serious or quiet before.

He nodded, slowly.

"Don't take it personally, Cal. She wanted to tell us, but the longer she left it, the harder it became."

"I get it. I'm just devastated for her."

"I know you are, mate. We all are. Okay, why don't you all get off home? Be here for a briefing in the morning at eight sharp."

Cal stayed behind as the others packed up their things and headed out the door. He slid off the desk and returned to his seat, his stooped shoulders a dead giveaway to how dejected he felt.

"You alright?" Adam asked.

Cal shrugged. "I feel cheated. Is that selfish?"

Adam barked out a laugh. "I'm glad I'm not the only one feeling like that. But I do know she'd have told you if she could."

Cal looked up, close to tears.

"I went around there today," Adam said. "I met Steve for the first time and the situation is shocking. I honestly don't know how she's managed to stay focused. She's tougher than the lot of us put together. And from what she said, we've kept her sane. The banter and laughs have helped her cope."

"I want to hug her. Can I hug her? Or will she spit the dummy?"

"I'm sure she'll appreciate that. She thinks the world of you, Cal. So don't go beating yourself up about it. None of us sensed what she was going through. You haven't lost your touch."

Calvin was a great assistant, always one step ahead of them in the office, and he mothered them all. He seemed more sensitive and intuitive than most blokes his age.

"Thanks, boss."

Chapter 15

"What the hell do you think you're doing?" Amanda shrieked, dropping to her knees. She began gathering all the mementos and newspaper clippings into a pile and throwing them into the box beside Mary.

Mary didn't say a word. She just stared, horrified, at Amanda.

Amanda's stomach did a loop-de-loop. "This is my private stuff, Mary. I wouldn't go snooping about in your things, would I?"

"Why didn't you tell me?" she whispered.

"Tell you what?" But Amanda knew exactly what she was talking about.

"They molested you."

"You were supposed to be looking for photographs. This is none of your business."

"They molested both you and dad and made you sleep with each other."

There was no point denying it. The newspapers didn't mention her and Andrew by name, but Mary had worked everything out.

"Why would we possibly tell you something like that, Mary? You're a child. Children should be protected from ever having to know this kind of thing even happens."

"Everything makes sense now."

"What does?"

"Why my dad did what he did. I don't blame him now."

"Don't talk like that, Mary. Killing those people made him no better than them. He should have just got on with his life and focused on all the good things. If he had, he'd still be alive today."

"If they hadn't molested him, they would *all* still be alive today. They *caused* it!"

Amanda almost slipped up and said, yes, but *you wouldn't*, but stopped herself just in time. "Look, you're upset. It's a lot to take in. I intended to tell you, but not until you were older."

"Am I the baby?"

"What baby?" Amanda froze and stared at her.

"I'm not stupid. I worked out the dates, and the paper said you were in labour when they found you."

Amanda rapidly shook her head trying to think of something to say.

"Well, am I?"

"The baby was taken from me at birth. I never discovered whether it was a boy or a girl. No, you are *not* my daughter." Saying those words broke her heart, but how could she allow Mary to find out the truth? To discover she was born out of rape and incest, that her father was either her uncle or her grandfather? How messed up was that?

Amanda pushed the box back into the cubbyhole under the stairs and pulled Mary into her arms.

"I'm not a little kid," Mary eventually said through her tears.

"I realise that now, and I promise we can discuss it. Just not today. I think we've both had enough upset for one day, don't you?"

Mary nodded.

The front door swung open and Adam ducked in out of the blustery rain. He slammed the door and shoved his briefcase onto the stairs and turned, startled to see them watching him.

"Oh, hello, you two. What you doing down there?" he said.

They laughed, and Amanda pulled Mary to her once again. "We're putting the world to rights, aren't we, sweetie?"

Mary nodded, smiling through snot and tears.

"Where are the brats?"

"Fed, bathed and both sound asleep for once. I bet you're dying for a cuppa, aren't you?"

"Could murder one, but you two go through to the lounge and I'll bring *you* one. Fancy a hot chocolate, Princess Mary?"

"Yes, please."

They got to their feet and Amanda shoved Mary in the direction of the lounge. "Go on through. I'll be there in a minute."

Once alone, Amanda rummaged around in the box once more and produced three old photographs before following Mary into the lounge.

Mary sat on the sofa and Amanda knelt beside her. She handed Mary the photographs. "These are the only ones left of your dad from our childhood."

She took them, and Amanda's heart nearly broke as she watched the raw emotion play across her face.

"Is this you?" She pointed to the image of Amanda and Andrew.

Amanda nodded and smiled. "The only one of us both together. Even once I found him again we never managed to get another photo taken."

"I look like you."

Amanda's stomach flipped again as she took the offered image from Mary. "Yes. There's a strong family resemblance. Look at our mum, your grandmother. We are all very like her."

Mary scrutinized the photo of her dad at around three or four years old, sitting on her grandmother's knee.

Amanda and Andrew were both very much like their mother with the same blonde hair, pale blue eyes and full lips. However, she hoped Mary wouldn't notice that she looked more like Amanda with the same translucent skin and dark smudges under their eyes.

Mary sighed when she looked at the third photo. It showed Andrew, aged fifteen, taken just before he vanished. The edges of the image were tattier than the others because Amanda had slept with it clenched in her fist for the first few months, convinced her dad and his cronies had disposed of him in some awful way.

"So you've got the start of your family tree now. I'll find a better one of me from when I moved in with Sandra. Then there's Emma and Jacob and the photos of your mum and dad in frames in your bedroom. You can either use the photo of your real grandmother, or Sandra, or even both."

"Would Sandra mind?"

"She'd be delighted. She already thinks of you as her granddaughter."

Adam appeared with two mugs. "Here you go, my gorgeous ladies. What you got there?"

Mary handed the photos to Adam. "I'm doing a family tree at school. Auntie found these of my dad."

"Is that you, Mand?" he asked, a smirk playing at his lips.

"Shut it, you." Amanda shot him a death stare.

"It's cute. I've never seen any photos of you before."

"Sit here, Adam." Mary moved to the other sofa so he could sit beside his wife. "Can I have some photos of you?" she asked.

"Thanks, sweetheart." He placed his cup on the coffee table and sat down. "You want some photos of me?"

Mary nodded.

"Well, I might need to visit my mum if you want one of me as a kid, but it can be arranged."

"Is your mum still alive?"

"Don't say it like that, you cheeky sausage. I'm not that old." He feigned shock and then hurt.

"I didn't mean that." Mary's cheeks flushed.

"Don't you remember meeting her at the wedding?"

"Oh, yeah. The one with the blue hair?"

"We don't mention the blue hair. Goodness knows what got into her to do a thing like that."

"I thought it looked cool. I told Charlotte about it in school."

"Tell you what. It's high time we paid my dear old mother a visit. Do you want to go next weekend if I can get some time off work?"

"Yes, please. All of us?"

Adam nodded. "She'll be in her element to have a tribe of kids to feed and fuss over."

Amanda smiled gratefully at him.

She suddenly felt blessed. Not only had Adam taken her on with all her baggage, but he'd become a wonderful father figure to all the children.

She stroked her stomach as the baby within kicked her hand. "Oh, hello," she said, smiling.

"Is he kicking?" Adam said, placing his hand where hers had been.

The baby gave another huge kick and Adam's eyes lit up. "Blimey, mate! We'll have you playing for England if you keep that up."

"Can I feel?" Mary asked.

"Of course. Come on," Amanda said.

Mary rushed over and dropped to her knees beside the sofa.

Amanda guided her hand and pressed firmly. Everyone waited in silence. "Come on, babba. Say *hi* to your sister."

A strange expression crossed Mary's face.

Amanda suddenly realised her mistake. "Oh, I mean cousin. I'm sorry. It's just that I think of you all as brother and sisters."

Mary smiled and nodded. "Me too." Suddenly Amanda's stomach rolled, and Mary squealed with delight. "I thought it would be like a little kick. That felt like something out of Alien."

"That's what *I* thought when I first felt it," Adam said.

Amanda laughed. "When have you been watching scary movies, missy?"

Mary blushed. "When I stayed at Charlotte's last time. Her mum said it was okay."

Amanda hugged her, and kissed her forehead. "Do you want to help me finish Adam's dinner?"

Mary nodded and helped her to her feet.

"We're going to have to install a crane if you get any bigger," Adam said.

Amanda picked up a cushion and whacked him with it.

"Alright, all right, I give in." He laughed.

Chapter 16

Adam could tell he'd walked in on something heavy but presumed Amanda had given Mary a dressing down for going to her friend's without permission yesterday.

After dinner, he and Amanda settled on the sofa and Mary went to her room.

"So what's happened this time?" He nodded to the seat Mary had vacated.

"Oh, Adam. You'll never guess what she did. I told her I had some photos of Andrew in a box under the stairs, and she only went through all my stuff while I was putting the kids to bed."

"What stuff?"

"All the newspaper clippings from the trial. They didn't name us but they didn't need to. She worked it out. I should never have told her where the boxes were. Never!"

"What did you say?"

"What could I say? She's not stupid, but there's more."

"I don't get you."

"She read the clippings and came up with the million dollar question."

"What do you mean?"

"She asked if she was the baby I gave up for adoption."

"Fuck me, Mand. I hope you convinced her otherwise."

"I think so, but can you imagine my reaction? I almost died on the spot."

"Come here." He pulled her head to his chest. "She must see how ridiculous that is. She already had a Mum and Dad."

"I'm sure you're right. But imagine if she..."

"Shhh, we'll make sure that doesn't happen. I promise."

"I'm sorry, by the way," she said.

"Sorry? What for?"

"I was a grump to you on the phone earlier. I didn't mean it."

"It's all right, and I didn't mean to stand you up. I've had a day from hell."

"Can you tell me about it?"

Adam stroked her hair and kissed the top of her head. "We discovered another double murder—the same guy. A young girl we interviewed yesterday and her dad. Killed in their beds last night."

"Shit, babe. I wish I'd checked the news before I packed a sad."

He laughed and squeezed her shoulder in her ticklish spot.

"Okay, I'm sorry. I'm sorry," she squealed until he stopped. "Go on. I'm listening."

"We found them, me and Frances."

"Her name's Holly. I hate you calling her Frances."

"It's what she wants to be called." He shook his head and rolled his eyes. "I thought you were listening?"

"I am. Go on."

"Well, the killer left his calling card again. It was disgusting."

"You mean…"

He nodded and laughed when she heaved. "We're concerned for his ex. She's not able to lie low. Her dad's in the late stages of cancer and can't be moved."

"Oh, my goodness!"

"The house is under surveillance for a couple of nights, but to be honest we've got no leads. Not really. And then there's Frances—Holly," he corrected himself, making a face at Amanda.

"What's wrong with Holly?"

He rubbed his eyes and sighed. "Her husband's dying."

Amanda gasped. "How? I mean…how?" She sat upright.

"Here's the biggy. He was paralysed in a car accident years ago. Fran—Holly, didn't want to tell us in case we felt sorry for her. But now he's had some complications and has an infection. He's not got long to live."

"Poor Holly! Can we do anything for her?"

"Apparently not. She agreed, after nagging her all day, to take some time off once we find our killer. But the truth is we're no closer to catching him."

He groaned as his phone began ringing from the kitchen.

"Oh, no. What time is it?" she asked as he got to his feet.

"Ten past ten." He strode to the kitchen and was surprised by Cal's name flashing on the display. "What can I do for you, mate?"

"Boss, are you watching the news?"

"No. Why? What's happened?"

"Natasha Barker's only gone and given an exclusive interview—she's slated Miles Muldoon and Sally Kemp."

"For fuck's sake!" He flicked the TV on, but he'd missed it. "I'll have to watch it on catch-up. What did she say?"

"That Sally Kemp drove him to murder—that he was weak and she's the puppet master behind him."

"What a bitch. I'll call Sally now, warn her what's being said. If she doesn't already know, that is."

"Okay, boss. See you in the morning."

Sally sounded concerned when she answered the phone.

"Hey, Sally. DI Stanley here."

"Oh, sorry. I always panic when the phone rings at this hour."

"Yeah, sorry about that. I was calling to see if you watched the news tonight?"

"No. I didn't. Why? Have you caught him?"

"Afraid not. But Natasha Barker has given an exclusive interview blaming you for Muldoon's actions."

"She what? I'll kill her."

"Less of that talk. I'm sure she'll come across as the idiot she clearly is."

"Why would she do this to me? It's been three years for God's sake."

"Exactly. Did you notice a police car out the front?"

"Yes. They've been there for hours. Do I need to feed them or anything?"

"No. That's not necessary. Just tell them if you intend to go out while they're there."

"I'll be going to bed soon. And I must admit, I feel much safer with them there."

He noticed Amanda standing behind him as he hung up.

She stroked his arm. "Do you have to go out?"

"No, thank God. But I'm going to have an early night just in case anything else happens."

Chapter 17

I replay the news interview for the fourth time.

"Bitch!" I roar, swiping the contents of the desk to the floor.

I slam my forehead with the heel of my hand several times and then bite my knuckle until I taste blood.

There is no way I can make rational decisions while surrounded by this red mist. I need to calm down.

After pacing a rut in the carpet, I'm in no doubt what must be done.

Within half an hour, I'm standing outside her house confident the police won't be able to organise themselves this fast. But I don't want to leave it much longer.

The rain has recently stopped leaving massive puddles in the footpath. I take care to step around them as I approach the council house which is just as I remember it—scruffy.

The front gate hangs on one hinge and is in desperate need of a lick of paint. I skulk along the washed out path to the back door. A light is still on inside, but I'm sure it's just the landing light.

Lifting the old wooden bench with one hand, I fumble about underneath and almost squeal with excitement as my fingers nudge and wrap around a key.

With one last scan around me, I open the back door leaving the key in the lock. I wait, listening for any sign of life, either human or of the canine variety. But no sound comes from within.

A police siren begins to wail not too far away, and my heart misses a beat. The wail approaches rapidly before fading away.

I venture inside. My nerves are more on edge than before because I knew the other properties, but I've never been inside this house. I use common sense and touch to help me reach the stairs and, once again, pause.

Still no sound.

Upstairs, I stop on the landing struggling to see a thing.

Once again I battle with myself whether or not to continue or run from the building. I replay the news interview in my mind, and it spurs me on.

The first door on the left is a cluttered airing cupboard. The second is a bathroom.

I hesitate at the next door on the right and place my ear against it. No sound.

The knob turns silently. As the door opens inwards, there is a clicking sound as though it had been recently painted, and the paint is still tacky. I freeze, waiting for movement of any kind. Nothing.

In two strides I'm beside the bed. A chink in the curtain gives me enough light to realise the bed is empty.

I have no doubt this is her room. She just isn't in it.

A car pulls up outside, and I rush to the window just as Natasha steps from a taxi with another woman. They both trot on high heels up the path to the front door.

In sheer panic, I stride to the top of the stairs.

They laugh as they fall inside the house, clearly drunk.

"That guy's face was a picture when he realised you were the one from the news," the other woman gushes.

"Got us another round of drinks, didn't I?" Natasha laughs.

My skin crawls and I shudder.

"Remind me to go out with you the next time you have a spot on primetime TV."

"I might've made it big by then. Perhaps I won't fraternise with you once I'm rich and famous."

By the sounds I could make out, they were in the kitchen.

Used to the dark, I move slowly and check out the other two rooms. One is made up with a single bed, and the other is filled with baby gear. An empty cot stands beside the door and a changing table is under the window. Although I can't see the decor, my guess is the room is decorated with a baby in mind.

That threw me. As far as I knew, Natasha didn't even have a baby. I gently close the door, leaving a tiny gap, and wait.

*

The friend is the first to come upstairs. She puts on the landing light and goes into the single bedroom. I hear her kick her shoes off and the sound of a zip unfastening.

I step into the room that is now fully illuminated from the landing light.

With her back to me, the woman pulls her dress over her head.

I don't make a sound as the turquoise fabric is tossed onto the carpet. She is naked apart from a pair of nude-coloured granny knickers and a bra.

As she turns to face me, she gasps, her hand flying to her mouth.

"Shhh," I whisper, indicating the knife in my hand. "Don't make a sound."

Her breath has quickened and exquisite tears are squeezed from her beady eyes, giving me a thrill. Then, the stench of hot urine puzzles me at first until I notice the puddle at her feet. She's pissing herself.

I'm tingling all over. This could go so wrong, but I'm sexually stimulated by a wet stain in her knickers. My body feels electrically charged, and my nipples stand on end.

I rub myself through my clothing. This wasn't supposed to happen, but my body says otherwise.

I step closer to her and hold one finger to my lips and lift up the knife in my other hand.

She whimpers, causing an involuntary spasm in my crotch.

I grab one of her humungous tits. I'd never seen any as big in the flesh, never mind touch them. I gesture with the knife for her to get on the bed.

Once she's lying down, I slice the bra straps and her massive breasts flop free.

More whimpering.

Feeling delirious, I'm almost too far gone when I hear a sound at the bottom of the stairs.

"Ang? What you doing up there?"

I place the flat of the knife on the woman's lips and shake my head.

Natasha sounds closer. "I've already necked my wine. I'm gonna start on yours next."

I move the knife down to the woman's throat and press my hand over her mouth. Her eyes are wide as she stares at me in utter terror.

With one stroke of the knife, the blood spurts. I don't want to miss one second as the life leaves her amber-coloured eyes, yet I'm aware of Natasha fast approaching.

"I know you're trying to scare me, Ang. But it'll take much more than you jumping out of a cupboard."

I yank a pillow out from under the woman's head and place it over the top of her. In two strides I am behind the door as it begins to open.

"Ha-ha. Very funny," Natasha says, as she enters the room.

"So you want me to pull the pillow off you and then what? Are you wearing my Halloween mask?"

I gently push the door and it silently swings closed again leaving a six inch gap through which the light pours in. I'm standing directly behind Natasha.

"What the...?" she says, as she splashes into the large pee puddle with bare feet. "This isn't funny anymore, Ang. What's this on my carpet?" She yanks the pillow off her friend and drops it.

A soundless scream leaves her lips.

"Scary enough for you?" I say.

Her shoulders tense and she turns slowly.

She freezes, her eyes on stalks.

Then she screams and lunges towards me.

I move sideways much faster than the drunken bitch.

She trips on nothing I can see and sprawls face-down on the carpet before scrambling to her knees and heading for the door.

I aim a well-placed kick to her side and thrill at her scream.

She flips to her back holding her midriff with one hand and trying to reach for my feet with the other. "Please, please don't..."

"Oh, no, you don't, bitch." I stamp on her outstretched wrist pinning it to the floor.

Her bloodcurdling screams send my heart racing. I've never felt so alive. But I'm aware the noise she's making will alert the neighbours or any passers-by. I need to shut her up. And quickly.

I straddle her, sitting on her chest, and notice her breathing is suddenly shallow and laboured.

She is having some kind of panic attack. She stops struggling against me and instead tries to focus on getting enough oxygen into her lungs.

This gives me a delicious moment to inspect her exquisite face.

The light from the landing illuminates the room, but her face is in the brightest strip close to the slightly open doorway.

Her cat-like green-grey eyes are rolling. Her chest heaves with every breath made even more difficult with my weight on her.

Is she having a fit? I'd never witnessed anything as totally thrilling before.

Once again, I feel a stirring between my legs, and I press the fingers of my free hand there.

Natasha seems oblivious of me while her own body struggles to perform the most basic of functions.

I consider grinding my crotch onto her dying face, and the thought alone sends wave after wave of ecstasy pumping into my jeans.

My orgasm makes me groan and shudder.

Then, suddenly repulsed by what only seconds ago had delighted me, I roar and slam the knife into the side of her head directly above the ear.

I know the blade is sharp—I'd spent hours sharpening it myself. But I didn't expect it to slice through a skull with such ease.

The result is instant.

Natasha stops moving. Her eyes freeze mid-stare.

I lean forwards. My face so close to hers, I could lick her. I stare into her dead, unseeing eyes for a while.

Chapter 18

After a chaotic breakfast with the kids, and having to change his shirt at the last minute because of Jacob's jammy fingers, Adam arrived at the station ten minutes late for the briefing.

On the upside, Cal and Frances seemed okay. They were huddled together over their morning coffee at the kitchenette table.

"Right, team, can we do this?" Adam said, heading to the huge whiteboard at the back of the room.

They all congregated behind him, dragging chairs with them.

"Okay. Let's go through the facts. To date we have three murders, and prima facie, all committed by Miles Muldoon."

They nodded, settling down. Les and Julie both scribbled on pads.

"There have been zero sightings of the suspect since Tuesday, the day of the first murder. His fingerprints and DNA were found at the first murder scene, and I'm in no doubt today's results will put him at the second as well."

"Michael Curtis..." He pointed to a grainy image of a grey-haired gentleman. "...a sixty-eight-year-old retired naval officer, suffered sixteen stab wounds to his upper body and head. The blade, one of the neighbour's kitchen knives, had snapped off in his skull. Muldoon's fingerprints were found on the knife handle and crowbar left at the adjoining property belonging to Sally Kemp, his ex-girlfriend. The words, *DIE YOU BITCH*, had been smeared in faeces across her bedroom wall."

"Dirty bastard," Les said.

"We've also had confirmation the blood on the clothing discovered in Muldoon's car boot belonged to Michael Curtis."

"Surprise, surprise," Frances said.

"Indeed." He nodded. "Sally Kemp, some of you may be aware, is the daughter of Charlie Kemp, our ex—Chief Constable."

"I remember little Sally as a girl," Ginger Dave said. "She was beautiful back then with milky white skin and masses of red hair."

Adam nodded. "She's just as beautiful as an adult, but has shitty taste in men, by all accounts. Anyway, Charlie Kemp is in the late stages of cancer, and Sally has taken time off work to help care for him at home."

His eyes involuntarily sought out Frances which caused awkward glances from the others.

Adam coughed and turned back to the board. "We've arranged for a public protection unit to be based at the property for a couple of nights as Mister Kemp can't be moved."

"Good call, boss," Dave said.

"Yeah, but we can't justify blowing the budget on a whim, so we need results ASAP." He turned his back again. "Okay, next up, Lana and Dean Davis." The image taken from Lana's Facebook page looked nothing like the serious young woman they'd met a couple of days ago. "The father and daughter were found still in their sleeping positions in bed, their throats cut ear to ear. Lana is another of Muldoon's ex-girlfriends, and we believe Dean had assaulted Muldoon on Tuesday for mistreating his daughter. A message of YOU DESERVE IT was once again written in faeces on the wall. Lana's mother lives in Devon and should arrive today to identify the bodies. Anything else, Cal?"

Cal got to his feet, and everybody turned to face him.

"Just last night's news. Natasha Barker, yet another ex, gave a doozie of an interview. She slagged off Muldoon and Sally. Clearly, this was a scorned woman hitting back. But she gave a lot of facts away, and we've had several irate phone calls already this morning. Oh, and the DCI is gunning for you, boss."

Adam shrugged. "Thanks, Cal. Frances and I will pay Miss Barker a quick visit this morning although a bit after the fact. The best we can do is ignore it and hope it dies down. Anybody else want to share anything?"

Ginger Dave raised his hand. "I went through Muldoon's phone and work computer, going back four years. I found nothing untoward. Even the small amount of pornography was as vanilla as it gets. This guy was squeaky clean up until Tuesday this week, and he vanished off the face of the earth, if you don't count the murders, of course. He's not touched his bank account or anything, and the five hundred quid he withdrew on Tuesday won't last him long."

"Thanks, Dave. How about you, Les? Julie?"

"We'll be interviewing all the staff at Pinevale Publishing today. They're setting up an interview room for us, unless you've anything else for us to do, boss?"

"I wish I had. If we don't get anywhere today, we'll all be twiddling our thumbs by tomorrow," Adam said.

"There is one thing," Julie said, surprising everyone. She usually stood behind Les and let him do all the talking. "The Sentinel Hotel where Muldoon was staying doesn't have CCTV, but the key card was last used around 6pm on Tuesday."

"Yeah, but it doesn't show what time he left the room, and he didn't take the card out of the power slot," Frances said.

Adam sensed a little competition between the women. Frances had had them all to herself for the past year, and now she had to share them all with a younger and extremely astute woman.

"Yeah, but we know the time of death for the first victim was around 2.00am. Sally received a call from him at 8.15pm and we can safely say he made the call from his hotel room as that was the last call made, and he left the phone behind. If he didn't let himself back into the hotel after 6pm then he had to be there when he made the call."

"Valid point, Julie. Well done."

"So we can scour the CCTV footage from the main roads for any cars approaching the roundabout between 8.15pm and 2.00am," Julie said, clearly pleased with herself.

"Wonderful, and while you're at it, check all the cab firms. Muldoon got from the hotel to the apartments somehow. He could've walked, but then I'm sure somebody would have spotted him." He jumped to his feet. "Right, you lot. We need results today. You ready, Frances?"

*

"How are you today?" he asked, once they were in the car heading to The Bed Superstore.

"I'm okay. Oh, and thanks for talking to the others for me."

"No worries. I presume they were all good this morning?"

"Yes. Cal called me when he got home yesterday which made it easier. They were all lovely today."

"Good. They were all devastated, just so you know. Amanda too."

She smiled, sadly, and nodded. "I know. So what are you going to say to our Ms Barker? How do you want to play this?"

"I'll tell her to go in hiding, give her the wild shites, as Cal would say."

She chuckled. "Yeah, he cracks me up with that."

"She must have known she was jeopardising our investigation. I'd like to throw her in the clink for twenty-one days."

Frances raised her eyebrows, a smile tugging at the corner of her mouth. "A bit severe, don't you think, boss?"

"No more than she deserves, in my opinion. Some people have no regard for others."

"Is something wrong?"

"What do you mean?" he asked, glancing at her, then back to the road.

"You seem tetchy. Has something happened at home?"

He rolled his eyes. "Mary found Amanda's newspaper cuttings about the paedophile ring. Amanda's devastated as you can imagine."

She sucked air in through her teeth.

"And Mary also asked if she was the baby Amanda gave up for adoption."

Frances had discovered Mary was Amanda's actual daughter at the same moment he had. She swore to keep it to herself, and this was the first time they'd mentioned it since that day.

"Yikes! What did Amanda say to that?"

"Denied it, of course. But if it ever gets out, I'd be up shit creek for not reporting it. Mary was kidnapped, for God's sake."

"It won't get out, and if it did, you'd both have to deny it. As far as you all know, Mary is Andrew's daughter."

Adam nodded as he turned into The Bed Superstore carpark. "Yeah, you're right. Nobody would be able to prove that Andrew confessed to Amanda."

"Exactly. Okay, are you ready? You can play bad cop, seeing as you're grumpy today."

"Gee, thanks." He smiled.

Inside, they knocked on the office door, and when nobody answered they strolled up and down the aisles searching for a staff member. There were only two, a large-boned woman deep in discussion with a couple who seemed to be trying out each and every bed in the place, and the nerdy guy from the other day who seemed to be stalking a woman and her two children.

After a few minutes of being ignored, Adam approached the lad.

"Hey, mate. We're looking for Natasha Barker."

He looked over to Adam and then back to his lady, before reluctantly walking towards him. His name badge said *Reuben*. "She's sick I think."

"You think?"

He nodded. "She's not come in. Left us in a right mess since we were already short staffed."

"Did she call in sick?"

He shrugged. "Not to us, she didn't. Maybe head office."

"Thanks." He handed Reuben a card. "Could you ask her to call us when she gets in?"

"Are you thinking what I'm thinking?" Frances mumbled, as they walked away.

"I'll call Cal for her address and get uniform to go around there."

"Why not us?"

"I don't want you walking into yet another massacre. Let someone else do it."

"Bullshit, Adam! This is what I meant about treating me differently. It's not on."

He sighed. "Okay. I'll get the address."

Chapter 19

A burnt out car at the side of the road greeted them as they pulled onto one of the rougher council estates in Pinevale. The solid brick houses were, on the whole, uncared for and run-down.

They parked the car outside number nineteen, and a group of yobs sauntered over to them.

"What you looking for, mister?" the taller of the gang said.

"None of your bloody business. Now hop it."

"They'll probably let your tyres down now," Frances said, once out of earshot.

"Let them. I'll cart their arses off to the nick if they do. See how they like that."

Mud covered the uneven path, and Frances jumped over the worst parts trying to keep her highly polished shoes clean.

Nobody answered their knock, so they walked down the passage between the houses to the rear of the property.

"Ayup," Adam said, reverting back to his northern slang. "What do we have here then?"

He pointed to a key in the lock.

Adam banged his palm on the wired safety glass that filled the top half of the door and listened for any sign of movement inside.

"Open it," Frances said, nodding at the key.

"What if she's in the shower? She'll have a fit!"

"Either you do it, or I will. I've got a bad feeling about this."

He turned the handle and it opened.

A cat made a dash for the open door, startling them both.

Frances screamed and almost toppled over into a puddle. She'd made no secret of the fact she had a cat phobia, but she managed to calm herself relatively quickly.

Adam stepped inside with Frances hot on his heels.

The contents of the house were basic, not very clean and tidy, but there was no sign of anything untoward.

Then the smell hit them.

"Oh, fuck!" Adam said. "Go and call it in, Frances." He wanted to get her out of the way.

"Call what in? Someone might've just taken an extra-large dump in the toilet."

Adam shook his head at his stubborn partner. "Okay, if you insist."

He called out several times as they climbed the stairs. As he reached the top, he saw Natasha lying on her back just inside the bedroom in a pool of blood.

"Now call it in, Frances. Go!" His raised voice finally got through to her, and Frances turned and ran back down the stairs.

There only appeared to be one stab wound to the head from what he could see. Natasha, her face fully made-up, stared with milky-coloured eyes. She was wearing a cerise-pink dress and strappy high-heeled sandals. Her clothing didn't appear touched.

The shit smear across the wall said *GOBBY BITCH*.

As Adam turned to leave, he noticed more blood dripping off the bed and did a double-take.

Another woman, naked except for her underwear, was lying on her back with a gaping wound in her throat. Her large, floppy breasts spilled out of the flesh coloured bra and the straps had been cut. Was Miles escalating his attacks and getting some kind of sexual thrill from his victims?

***

Amanda opened the front door to Sandra, her foster mother. "Is it that time already?" she said, glancing at her watch. "Do you fancy a coffee while I finish preparing dinner?"

"Of course. I'll make it." She hugged and kissed Amanda on the cheek before holding her daughter at arm's length and scrutinising her face. "Are you all right? You're looking a little peaky."

"I'm fine. How are you?" Amanda tactfully switched the conversation back on the older woman knowing she hated being asked the same question.

She shrugged. "What time are you picking up the car?"

"They said any time after eleven."

Sandra filled the kettle while Amanda continued chopping carrots and onions for the slow cooker.

"So what's new?" Sandra sat at the dining table.

"Not a lot. Adam's stressed out over a case he's working on. Plus he discovered Holly's husband is seriously ill and dying."

"Bugger! Poor girl."

Amanda nodded. "She apparently didn't want any special treatment at the station."

"I can understand that. When my Peter got sick and died, I hated the pitying way everybody looked at me.

Amanda had been living in Italy when her foster father passed away.

"Yeah, but at least you had a handful of close friends to lean on. I couldn't imagine dealing with something like this alone."

"She's got family, hasn't she? Her career is important to her. I had a long chat with her at your wedding."

"I'm aware of that, but..."

"We all deal with trauma and death differently, Mand. You know that."

She nodded. Sandra was right. Amanda was well known for suffering trauma-induced black outs, similar to a coma, that could last for weeks. Her shrink convinced her she had a dissociative disorder brought on by her childhood abuse. Thankfully she hadn't had any episodes since being with Adam, even coping well with the death of her only brother.

She threw the last of the vegetables in the slow cooker. "Well, so long as she turns to us if she does need support. I like Holly. She's a decent woman and good partner for Adam. She keeps his feet on the ground." She wiped down the worktop and plugged in the slow cooker before sitting across from Sandra.

"Are you eating properly, love? You don't seem yourself."

"It's Mary. She's been playing up lately, which is understandable, I guess. But then last night, she found the newspaper clippings from my dad's trial."

Sandra winced. "I told you to throw those bloody articles away. Or at the very least, store them at my house. This is what kids do. They rummage."

"I meant to, but I just couldn't face them again."

"You didn't need to face them. You could have just chucked the whole thing in the rubbish."

"I've got other stuff in the box that I want to keep. Besides, the secret's out now. She would have found out eventually anyway, but I wanted to wait until she was a little older. She asked if she was the child I'd given away."

"Jesus, Mand. What did you say?"

"That she definitely wasn't, but I barely got a wink of sleep last night.

"She's clever, that one. I hope she drops it now."

"So do I. Have you nearly finished?" Amanda nodded at Sandra's cup.

Sandra drained the last of her coffee and got to her feet. "Right, you are. Let's be off."

***

Adam headed down the stairs to Frances who was talking on the phone.

He lifted two fingers up and nodded at her.

"Hang on a minute." She turned the phone in to her shoulder. "Sorry, boss?"

"There are two dead bodies. Both women."

Frances gasped and spoke slowly into the phone, "He said there are two dead bodies, both women."

Within the hour, he'd handed the crime scene over to SOCO. The overcast, grey street was suddenly alive with flashing blue lights and uniformed officers.

Cal texted through Natasha's next of kin details, and as they left they bumped into Felix, the medical examiner, dressed in his best golfing attire.

"Busy on a course, were you, Felix?" Adam laughed.

"Ho-ho. Very funny. There's no let up with this bloody guy, is there?"

"No. He's prolific all right. Although, he may have done you a favour, I suspect the heavens are about to open." Adam patted the older man on the shoulder. "We're just off, mate. Can you give us a shout with approximate times of death etcetera—just the usual. We've got the thankless task of informing the parents."

"Yep. Someone's got to do it, unfortunately."

They made it to the car just as large drops of rain began to fall.

Once inside, Adam turned on the engine, flicked the wipers on full pelt, and cranked up the heater. After a few minutes, he dialled Sally's number, letting it go through to the loud speaker while he put the car in drive and headed across town.

"Hello?" Once again the woman seemed wary of who was on the other end of the phone. Adam was used to this reaction as his number came up *withheld*.

"Sally, DI Stanley. How was your evening?"

"Fine. I had an early night and slept like a baby. I did feel a little sorry for your man in the car though. It was freezing. I took him out a flask of tea before I went to bed."

A flash of lightning lit up the sky.

"That's nice of you, and I'm sure gratefully received. I've got some bad news, I'm afraid."

"More bad news? What now?"

Startled by a crash of thunder that sounded as though it was directly above them, he gripped the steering wheel and turned to look at Frances who held onto her seat and stared at the road ahead.

"Detective?" Sally said.

"There've been another two murders. Natasha Barker and another unknown woman. The same MO as before, so..."

"So, it was Miles again?" She sounded shaken up and close to tears.

"It looks that way, yes."

"What's wrong with him? He's completely off his rocker!"

"I know how frightened you must be, but we have another car booked for tonight, so don't fret. Just stay indoors, if that's possible, and call me if you're concerned about anything."

"Thanks, detective. I will do."

Chapter 20

The GPS directed them to another rough part of town. Seven high-rise concrete blocks of flats loomed above them.

The rain had eased off, but when Adam opened his door, he could still hear the trickling as the water made its way through the drains and gutters.

"We're looking for Pendleton Court," he said, reading his phone.

"That one there." Frances pointed to the second building in the row. "What number is it?"

"Eight-one-nine. That will be the eighth floor."

"Oh, sweet joy. Yet another elevator ride from hell."

"You could always wait down here," he suggested, tongue in cheek.

"Piss off!"

They ran through the light rain to the main door. He got there first and held it open for her to enter. A stench of stale urine and vomit hit them.

The only colour in the dark, grey foyer was the masses of graffiti on every single surface.

"Seems this is your lucky day." He nodded at the tape and the *out of order* sign that covered the lift doors.

Frances groaned, shaking her head, and trudged towards the stairs.

Two flights up and they came across a man lying on the concrete, his head beside a pool of yellow puke.

"Classy bloke." Adam held his hand out and helped Frances step over him.

Barely able to breathe as they reached the eighth floor, they had to take a few minutes in order to compose themselves.

Flat eight-one-nine stood out from the others. A brightly coloured welcome mat lay outside the door, and a hanging basket, filled with artificial flowers, was padlocked to the wall-holder.

Adam raised his hand to knock just as the door swung inwards. A man dressed in a long grey overcoat, matching blue woollen hat and scarf, and pushing a shopping bag on wheels, appeared. He gasped and clutched his chest when he saw them.

"Sorry to startle you, sir. We're looking for a Mrs Joan Barker. Do we have the correct address?"

"Yes. But she's not been called that for almost ten years. She's Joan Morris now."

Adam nodded. "My apologies. Are you Mr Morris?"

"I am. What's this about?"

They pulled out their ID. "I'm DI Stanley and this is my colleague DS Frances. May we come in, sir?"

"Now's not a good time. Can you come back later? I'm just going to the supermarket."

"I'm afraid not, Mr Morris. Is your wife home? We need to speak with her, urgently."

"She is, but she's unwell. Can't you just tell me what's wrong?"

"It concerns her daughter, Natasha. Can we come in, please, sir? It shouldn't take more than a few minutes."

He angrily yanked the shopping bag back inside. "Come in then, but be warned. Joan won't like it."

He led them inside the tiny square hallway and through a door opposite.

"I thought you went to the shop," a woman cried out as the man entered.

"We have visitors, Joanie," he said, in a hushed voice.

"No! Don't let them in. I'm not up to seeing anybody today."

Adam stepped into the large, artificially lit living room and noticed the heavy curtains were all drawn.

"Who are you?" the woman screeched. "Get out! Get out of my home. Now!"

"Mrs Morris. My name is Detective Inspector Adam Stanley, and this is my colleague Detective Sergeant Holly Frances." He spoke slowly and clearly, hoping to calm the woman.

Mrs Morris jumped to her feet and climbed on top of the sofa when Frances entered the room. "Out! Tell them, Bill. Tell them to go."

Adam turned to her husband. "We need to speak to your wife, Bill. Can I call you Bill?"

Bill nodded.

"Is there anything you can do to calm her down for a sec?"

"I'll try." He shrugged and approached his wife, hands outstretched as though she were a rabid dog. "It's okay, Joanie. Let them tell you why they're here, and we will clean everything once they leave. I promise."

She gripped her husband's hand and allowed him to pull her back down to a sitting position.

"We're here about your daughter, Natasha," Adam continued.

"That girl's nothing but a fucking problem. What's she done this time?" Joan spat.

"Actually, Mrs Morris. You daughter was found dead this morning," Frances said.

Adam expected screams, but the woman bent her head, inspecting her hands. "We will need somebody to identify the body, of course, but we are quite certain it's her."

Mrs Morris silently got to her feet and walked through a door to the side of her.

Adam raised his eyebrows at Frances before glancing back to the sofa. "Do you want to go and check on your wife, Bill?"

He shook his head. "Best not. She'll let me know when she's ready to talk. Sorry. Take a seat."

Adam sat in the only other chair and Frances leaned on the arm of it, beside him.

"Can you tell me who would want to harm Tash? She's a lovely girl," Bill asked, sadly.

"I'm guessing you didn't see the local news last night?" Adam said.

"No."

"Well, Natasha gave them an interview about an ex-boyfriend who's currently wanted for murder."

"And he killed her too?"

"It certainly seems that way. A friend of hers who was staying at the house was also a victim. Do you know any of Natasha's friends?" Adam felt his phone buzz in his pocket.

"She never comes here anymore. Since Joanie's illness took a turn for the worst, the kids are never in touch. Joseph called around to tell us of his wedding, but Joanie wouldn't allow his fiancée to set foot inside the flat. As you can imagine, he left soon after."

"As I already mentioned, somebody will need to identify your step daughter's body in the next few days. I guess, considering the circumstances, that task will fall to you."

Bill nodded.

"I believe Joseph, Natasha's brother, is overseas at the moment?"

"Yes. He's still on his honeymoon and isn't due back for weeks."

"Is there any way you can contact him?"

"No. Another one of Joanie's phobias is we aren't allowed a phone or television in the house. She even makes me shave off all my hair." He removed his hat showing a smooth head. He had no eyebrows either.

"Has anybody examined your wife, Bill?" Frances asked.

"How can they? She won't leave the flat, and won't allow anybody in. We're stuck. To be honest, I'd have left her years ago, but how can I? She needs me. I'm as much of a prisoner to this illness as she is."

"I think we need to report this, Bill. You understand that, don't you?" she said.

Tears spilled from his eyes when he nodded. "Everything's got out of hand. It started with a fear of dirt. Going out into the corridor freaked her out, but I could see why, it was filthy. Then, if she saw any dust motes floating in the sunshine, she'd go berserk and insist we clean the flat from top to bottom. That's the reason we never open the curtains any more."

"Bill, this can't go on. Obviously we are here over something totally different today, but if you like, I'll arrange for Joanie to be assessed by a professional. If it goes untreated this will only escalate. I can promise you that."

"Yes, okay then. I'm aware something needs to be done."

Adam uncrossed his legs and sat forward on his seat. "Bill, we'll need a way to contact you. Do you talk to any of your neighbours?"

"Yes. The young woman next door is friendly, and I always hear her phone ringing."

"Great. Could you go and ask for her number?"

When Bill left, Adam got to his feet. "It's stifling hot in here. I need some fresh air."

Frances made a face as she wafted her hand in front of her. "The heating must be on full."

Bill returned with a phone number. "Here you go. She said she's home most days, so there shouldn't be an issue getting hold of me."

"We'll be off now then, Bill," Frances said, handing him her card.

"I'll walk down with you. I still need to do the shopping."

"Will Joan be all right?"

"She will have taken a pill. I probably won't see her until tonight, now." He grabbed his shopping trolley and led them out to the corridor.

"It's out of order," Adam said, when he stopped at the lift.

"Just the ground floor lift is broken. We can get out on the first floor and walk down one flight."

Frances made a face at Adam.

"Well, how was I to know?"

"Did you walk up the whole way?" Bill smiled.

She nodded. "Yes, and I don't recommend it."

They travelled down in silence, and once outside they watched the old man shuffle away, pulling his bag behind him.

"Well, that was an experience," Adam said.

"I know. How the hell did it get so out of hand?"

Adam shook his head. "Beats me. But she must have seen a doctor because he said she takes pills."

"True. That doctor deserves to be struck off."

Adam dug in his pocket and pulled out his phone. "Cal's been ringing," he said, returning the call.

"Hey, boss. I have the details of the second victim."

"Go on."

"Angela Smith, a thirty-five year old mother of two. Should I send Les and Julie to inform the husband?"

"No. We're free now so we can go."

"Okay, boss. I'll text you the address."

Chapter 21

The home of Angela Smith was a far cry from the rough council estate where she spent her last night on earth. It always made him think about the *what if* scenario when things like this happened to a person.

If Natasha had kept her opinions to herself, at least until Muldoon was caught and behind bars, she and her friend would today be going about their business just like everybody else. But life didn't work like that.

"You okay, Frances?" His partner had been silent for the entire fifteen-minute journey.

"Yes. I'm thinking about Mr Morris. What an awful way to live."

"I know, shocking. What's more shocking to me though, is how he let it get so bad before asking for help."

"Are we here?" She glanced up and scanned the street.

"Yep. Are you ready to do this?"

"As I'll ever be."

"Listen, if this is too much for you, I'll understand. As I've already told you, I would much rather you take this time off to spend with Steve."

"I'm fine," she snapped.

"Okay, keep your hair on. Let's do this, and then we can stop for a cuppa somewhere."

A dark-haired, wiry man answered the door, holding an infant who, Adam guessed, was around eighteen months old.

"Mr Smith?"

The man nodded pulling the child even closer to him.

"I'm DI Stanley and this is my colleague, DS Frances, can we—"

"That was quick! Come on in." He walked away leaving them with their mouths agape.

Adam glanced at Frances.

She shrugged and followed the man inside.

The modest house seemed homely and well cared for. Messages of love hung from every wall, from heart-shaped carvings to paintings and written love declarations.

In one corner of the lounge hung several pink heart-shaped balloons secured with a ribbon fastened to the frame of a wedding photograph.

"Sit, sit. I dug out a couple of recent photographs of my Angie." He nodded to the coffee table which had three close-up images of his wife lined up.

They sat side by side on the sofa opposite him.

"And she was wearing a brown skirt and cream coloured Tshirt when I last saw her, but I presume she took something else to wear considering she planned going to the pub."

Adam cleared his throat. "Mr Smith, it seems we are at cross-purposes here."

"Call me Ben."

Adam nodded. "Ben, I'm assuming you've called the station regarding the disappearance of your wife."

He glanced from Adam to Frances, a bewildered expression on his face. "Yes, that's right. Isn't that why you're here?"

Frances shuffled to the edge of the oversized sofa and glanced at Adam for silent approval.

He nodded, relieved she wanted to take the lead.

"Is there anybody who could take the child for a short time, Ben?"

His forehead crinkled. "My mum lives on the next street, but why?"

"Could you call her, please?"

He staggered to his feet and reached for the landline handset beside the television. He pressed a few numbers and Adam heard the ringing tone from across the room.

"Hello-oo?" an elderly female voice said.

"Mum, can you come over? The police are here. Something's wrong."

"But..."

"Just come, Mum. I need you." He hung up.

Frances' knee began twitching up and down.

"You okay?" Adam mouthed.

She shrugged him off and smiled as Ben returned to his seat. "How old's the baby?"

"She's fifteen months."

"She's a big girl. What's her name?"

"Charmaine." He flapped his hand impatiently. "Listen, I need to know what's wrong. Can't you just tell me, please?"

Frances smiled apologetically. "Best we wait a few more minutes."

He got up again and plonked the baby down amongst a pile of toys and reached for an electronic cigarette.

"I could do with a real one, right now." He took a deep drag of the pen-like object, and smoky vapours escaped his mouth.

Seconds later, the front door slammed open and a woman, who appeared to be in her late sixties, rushed in.

The man reached for her hands and pulled her down beside him on the lounge chair. "This is my mother, Vera."

Vera stared at Adam and Frances. "Ben! What's happened?"

He shook his head. "They haven't told me yet."

Frances watched the little girl as she played with her toys. Adam took that as his cue to take the lead.

"There's no easy way to tell you this, Ben. But..." He cleared his throat. "...we found your wife's body this morning."

"Her body?" he asked, flatly.

"She's dead, I'm afraid."

The inhuman wails that belched out of Ben made Adam's stomach churn.

The baby began to scream, and Frances looked to Vera who was ineffectively trying to comfort her son.

Frances lifted the child into her arms, gently cooing and calming her.

The child wriggled, wanting only to get to her daddy.

After a few minutes Ben noticed, and, easing away from his mother, held his arms out for his little daughter.

Frances didn't need much encouragement and immediately handed the child over.

They waited for the initial shock to sink in, knowing they would be bombarded with questions.

Ben eventually handed the baby to his mother and got to his feet. After pacing the room several times, he turned to them, pleading with his eyes. "Are you sure it's her?"

"We will need a formal identification, Ben. But we are quite certain it is your wife. Where did you think she was?"

"She went out with her friend, Tash, whose boyfriend was working away and she needed a shoulder to cry on. I wanted to put my foot down, but Angie hadn't had a night out since before the baby was born and I caved. I knew she'd have a skinful, and we couldn't afford taxis, so she planned to get her head down there and come home early this morning. When she didn't arrive, I knew something terrible must've happened. She would never miss taking little Dane to school."

"Dane?" Frances asked.

"Our son. He's six. We always drive him to school. He goes to Pinevale West, but she had the car, so Mum had to take him. What happened? Did she crash?"

Adam glanced at Frances who nodded.

"She was murdered, Ben."

"No! Why? It can't be her. Who would want to harm my Ang? She loves everyone." He gave several vigorous shakes of his head.

"We think she was just in the wrong place at the wrong time," Frances said. "As far as we're aware, Natasha was the main target, and Angela must've got in the way. I'm so very sorry."

"Do either of you work, Ben?" Adam asked.

"Yes. We work together as wedding planners. Angela promotes the fact we are so happy and have the perfect marriage to snare the clients. They always want what we have..." He shook his head.

Frances sighed.

Adam's heart broke for them both. He knew what despair they were both facing in the coming months.

"How well did you know Natasha Barker?" Frances asked.

"I didn't. Not really. She was a friend of Angela's from before we met, but I didn't like her very much, to be honest. And I think the feeling may have been mutual as she never called around here when I was home. Maybe if I'd been a little more tolerant of her, Angie would have felt she could invite her to stay here last night instead of going there."

"You can't blame yourself, Ben. Nobody could have predicted what would happen. When Natasha gave an interview to the press last night, we never for one minute expected she would be targeted herself. Not so soon anyway."

"So she brought this on herself and dragged my Angie into it?"

"It seems so, sir. I'm terribly sorry."

Ben's mother had sat silently listening as she comforted the baby who, against all odds, now slept soundly in her arms. Adam almost welled up as he glanced at the child's dainty features, the sweep of her long eyelashes lying on her upper cheeks. She was oblivious as to what had happened. Yet he had no doubt the effects would stay with her for the rest of her life.

He gave Frances the nod to wrap it all up, and soon after, they left Ben on the doorstep sobbing his eyes out.

"You okay?" Adam opened the car.

"Will you stop asking me that?" She climbed into the passenger seat and waited for him to slide in beside her. "No! If truth be told, I'm not okay, but I'm coping. Yes, I find it difficult to see the pain and heartache death brings to a family. And it's doubly hard knowing I'm going to have to deal with it too, in the not too distance future. But honestly, this is much better than the alternative."

"I get it. Of course, I do. But it doesn't stop me from worrying about you."

"I know. Now, did you promise me a sarny before?"

"Yep. But you're not having the luxury of stopping in an upmarket diner. Oh, no, young lady. You can grab a snack on the run like every other copper worth their salt. Do you hear me?"

"Loud and clear, boss." She laughed. "And thanks. I need you to work my arse to the bone."

"Be careful what you wish for." He wriggled his eyebrows at her as he put the key in the ignition and started the car.

"Bring it on. I'm up for a challenge."

Chapter 22

They grabbed a handful of sandwiches from the bakery and took them to the station.

"So what's happening?" Adam asked when they arrived back.

Cal dove into the bag and snaffled a ham salad roll. "The same as before. Nobody saw a thing. The adjoining neighbour thought she might have heard a scream, but she was asleep and hasn't a clue of the time."

"How's Julie getting on with the CCTV footage?"

The main roads in and out of Pinevale town centre were the only ones covered by CCTV, but he figured it must be worth a shot.

"Nothing yet. The roundabout by the hotel showed a late model Land Rover Discovery and a green Volkswagen Passat within the time frame. But none of them flagged up anything of interest."

"Oh, well." Adam unwrapped a chicken and stuffing sandwich on granary bread and took a huge bite. He was famished.

He filled Cal in on their day so far while Frances took her sandwich to her desk.

"It's looking bad, hey, boss?" Cal said, mid-bite.

"I hope something comes to light soon, or we're done for. I've been giving DCI Williamson the runaround since yesterday, but he'll want to collar me today for an update and no doubt a bollocking." Adam threw the last of the sandwich to the desk, not hungry anymore.

"How do they expect results when there's nothing to go on, boss? Even releasing Muldoon's image on the news produced very few calls, and the ones we did receive were from obvious nut jobs."

Adam nodded. "They don't see it like that. They want results at head office otherwise they'll threaten to send in the big boys."

"Well, good luck to them. Surely they know by now, if *you* can't find them, no-one can."

Adam smiled. "Thanks for the vote of confidence, Cal."

***

Frances nibbled on her sandwich and proceeded to check her emails. She kept one ear on what Adam and Cal were saying and agreed the shit *would* land at Adam's feet before too long.

Their superiors weren't interested in reasons or excuses, only results. The unreasonable way they piled on the pressure meant some dubious officers would put anybody in the frame rather than admit they couldn't crack a particular case.

But they *knew* the killer in this case—they just couldn't bloody well find him.

"Frances," Adam called over as he headed to his office. "You and Cal may as well take the weekend off unless something else turns up, in which case, I'll call you. It's pointless us all sitting around twiddling our thumbs, and, no doubt, Les and Julie will be around as usual."

Her first instinct was to bite his head off again, eager to drum into him she wanted no special treatment. Then she realised he would have done the same last weekend and the one before if there was nothing happening. She needed to stop being so touchy. "You sure?" she said, instead.

"Certain. But don't go off gallivanting. If anything comes to light, you'll have to get your backsides in here quick smart."

"Let's hope Muldoon doesn't strike again tonight. He's not missed a night since this killing spree began," Cal said.

"Good point, although I hope there aren't many people left for him to want dead," Frances said.

Adam paused, fingering the doorframe of his office. "Who knows what's going on in his head? He may well start popping off everyone he's ever argued with. He's certainly not in his right mind."

The rest of the afternoon passed in a flash. Adam was summoned to meet with the DCI at police headquarters in London. Frances stayed behind to catch up on some overdue paperwork.

Cal got the call confirming that the faecal matter all came from the same person, surprise, surprise. And the results of the autopsies for Lana and Dean Davis provided nothing new, except to confirm the time of death for both was between 2.00am and 4.00am on Thursday.

Ginger Dave, Les, and Julie all returned to the station before heading off for the day. Julie and Les confirmed they intended to be around for the weekend as usual.

Frances waited until Cal began climbing into his bike leathers, and, after packing her things away, walked out with him to the car park.

"How are things at home?" Cal asked.

"Not good. A few of Steve's workmates were due to visit today. To say their goodbyes."

Cal stifled a gasp. "Sorry," he said. "It just sounds so dreadful—knowing you're about to die."

"I think he must have guessed, but we haven't told him outright. How could we?"

Cal shook his head. "You amaze me. I haven't a clue how you're coping with something as massive as this."

"Who says I am. I think I'm on autopilot, going through the motions so I don't crack up."

"If you ever need..."

She nodded and squeezed his arm before turning towards her two-door Rav 4. "Call me if anything else occurs. I'll be right in."

"I will, I promise." Cal put on his helmet and straddled his scooter.

Frances laughed. "You know how gay you look on that thing?" she called over to him.

He shouted something back but the helmet muffled the words.

She waved and jumped in her car.

Once Cal had driven off, she let the happy façade fall away taking her smile and sturdy posture with it. She felt her entire body slump at the prospect of what lay ahead.

Guilty pangs forced her to turn the key and point the car in the direction of home. Then, she got guilty pangs for the fact that the guilty pangs were the only reason she was heading home at all.

The house was silent when she let herself in which was a surprise. Val was usually fluttering about in the kitchen at this time of day. She blamed her Irish background for the fact she always made mountains of food every single day even though most of it went to waste.

The sound of music coming from Steve's room sent chills through her body. Dragging heavy feet, she braced herself at the door and took a deep breath in anticipation of what she was about to find.

As she opened the door, she gasped at the sight before her. Steve, sitting up in his bed, was smiling as he listened to the album his mother played on the antique record player. The record player had been boxed away in a cupboard under the stairs. They'd once had plans to set up the room they now used for Steve's bedroom as a studio.

Val was sitting back in the armchair beside him, her eyes closed, as she sang along to the scratchy-sounding oldie.

"Hey, babe," Steve said, when he spotted her in the doorway.

She fixed a smile on her face and rushed to his side. "Someone looks happy. Are you feeling better?"

"When Devon and James came over today, we got talking about music. I asked Mum to drag this lot out."

"Can I get you a nice cup of tea, Holly, love?" Val said.

"No, I'll do it. You're enjoying yourself, which is lovely to see. I should have got the camera."

Steve held his finger up, the only thing he could move now. "No camera."

"I know. I won't," she said, gripping his hand. "I'll make everyone a cuppa, and you can tell me about your visitors."

She reached the kitchen on jelly legs, and the tears poured down her cheeks. She'd actually thought the music meant he'd died. But the worst of it was a small part of her wished he had.

She would never admit to feeling like this. How could she? Nobody would understand. But she'd watched cancer ravage her dad's body over three years. Her mum had been no use leaving Holly to care for him. Then when Holly was seventeen, she got up one morning to discover her mother had left in the night taking Holly's eight-year-old brother with her. This sent her dad's illness into a nosedive.

She hated her mum with a passion because of it, but now, after all this time, she understood why she left. Not that she intended to do the same, but she loathed the feeling of being trapped.

When she first married Steve, he was the love of her life—so funny and quirky. They had big plans and dreams of starting a family as soon as Steve's web design company took off.

She never once planned for his catheter emptying routine or feeding schedule. Why would she? He'd been a fit and healthy man before the accident. But as soon as it happened, everybody looked to her to pick up the slack.

Steve spent the first few months in hospital, and she dreaded him coming home. He could move one hand at that stage, and they adapted his wheelchair so he could power it himself. Big wow! The rest was up to her.

Val lived on the Isle of Wight, and when she suggested she move in with them for a while to help Holly cried with relief.

It wasn't as if she no longer loved her husband. She did. But she couldn't face caring for another invalid. She didn't have the energy to do it all over again.

The house was converted to include a wheelchair-friendly shower room, and they added an extension, giving Val her own living area. That was almost six years ago.

Holly had heard many stories and jokes about the mother-in-law from hell, but Val was nothing like that. She didn't know how she'd have coped without her.

Tea made, she went back to Steve's room as they were clearing the albums away.

"Have you had enough, love?" Holly said, holding Steve's cup in front of his face so he could reach the straw.

He sipped and then shoved it away with his chin and began to cough.

She placed the cup on the nightstand. "You okay?"

He nodded. "I've chosen my funeral song."

Holly's stomach slammed to the floor. She looked at Val who shrugged sadly.

"Don't talk like that, Steve," she finally mumbled.

"Aren't you gonna ask me what it is?"

"I don't want to talk about it."

He moved his finger rapidly meaning for her to look at him.

She did.

His lovely hazel eyes brimmed with unshed tears. "It's okay, babe. We need to talk about it and it's okay."

She couldn't believe, after just voicing to Cal that he didn't know, here he was talking about his funeral. Sometimes the universe played games. She was certain of it.

She gripped his hand again and lifted it to her mouth. She tried to hold back her own tears, but the buggers still came, running hot and fast down her face. She nodded, their eyes glued to each other.

"Lou Reed, *Perfect Day*."

"I think I know the one you mean," she managed. Her stomach bounced with suppressed sobs and she felt as though her body was about to turn in on itself.

"Don't cry...my angel," Steve said. "Didn't mean to upset you. But the lyrics say everything."

Holly nodded, unable to speak at that moment.

He continued, his voice slurring with exhaustion. "I know how hard it's been on you...especially after...your dad, but fortunately for me, you hung around."

She hugged his neck and kissed him hard as wave after wave of emotion flooded through her.

"However shitty things...got for me, I had you...by...my side. You keep...me hanging on, my love. But, I'm tired now. So tired. And...I need you to know...how much you mean to me."

Chapter 23

Holly couldn't speak. Long-suppressed tears flowed freely causing a wet patch on the blue cotton duvet. Pain gripped her to the core, making it difficult to breathe.

Val sobbed and left the room.

Holly let her go.

Steve moved his finger again. "We talked...a few minutes ago." he said. "She needs...time to...process...everything. Stay with me. I need you. Just us."

Holly was a wreck. Once the floodgates were open, there seemed to be no closing them again. She stroked Steve's gaunt face. The doctors warned he wouldn't live much longer, but she'd thought they were mistaken. Looking at him now, she knew they were right. Her heart compressed painfully.

She climbed onto the bed beside him and wrapped her arms around his head. He closed his eyes and slept, a faint smile on his face.

Val returned a while later. "Your dinner's ready," she whispered.

Holly nodded, slid off the bed, carefully placed her husband's head down on the pillow, and followed Val into the kitchen.

Hugging her mother-in-law, she asked, "Are you okay?"

"It came out of the blue. I had no way of warning you."

"At least we're aware of his wishes now. We both witness his suffering every single day. The stench of his rotting flesh, and the nurses' reaction, upsets him every time they change his dressing. Watching him like this breaks my heart. I hope, for his sake…"

Val rubbed her eyes. "He had a good day today, laughing and joking with his old friends. And for a time I allowed myself to believe that maybe he was getting better, although I know it's quite common to perk up a few hours before taking a turn for the worse."

Holly nodded. All the crying had left her feeling drained beyond belief.

"Sit down, lovey. I've made a pan of corned-beef hash. We're going to need to keep our strength up for this next stage."

She did as instructed, the same way she did every single night after work. She doubted she would have eaten a thing the past few months if Val wasn't there standing over her, making sure she didn't get sick too.

Steve hadn't been able to eat for weeks, being fed via a tube that went up his nose and directly into his stomach. The nurses trained Val how to check the tube was in place before feeding him twice a day, but apart from the odd sip of tea, he struggled to swallow.

With a heavy heart, Holly dreaded the future.

***

Adam's meeting with Detective Chief Inspector Williamson went better than expected. Only once did he insinuate they might need another team brought in. This was the problem with working in a small station. Everyone outside of the station thought they must sit around twiddling their thumbs waiting for the perpetrators to walk in the door with a giant red arrow above their heads. But he got out of it relatively unscathed after promising, if they'd got no further by next week, he would personally ask the DCI to intervene.

Muldoon was bound to slip up sooner or later.

*

As Adam left HQ he checked his messages. Cal had left several, the last being that everyone had left the station for the day, so he headed for home. Any paperwork would wait until the morning seeing as he'd volunteered himself to do the weekend shift.

A flash, new cherry-red Nissan X-trail was parked on the street in place of Amanda's old blue Toyota.

Adam let himself in to a quiet house, and found Sandra and Mary doing a jigsaw on the carpet in the lounge. "Hello, ladies. Where are the others?"

"Amanda's watching Mary Poppins with the kiddies," Sandra said. "Unless they've all fallen asleep. They're very quiet."

Adam laughed and headed through to the family room.

Amanda sat on the small sofa sandwiched between Emma and Jacob who were engrossed in the TV.

"Hello, you," Amanda sat forward and paused the movie.

"Aww!" both kids complained.

Amanda shook her head and pressed *play*. She got to her feet to kiss him. "I didn't expect you back for ages yet."

"I got off early. It's been another full-on day."

"You must be shattered, poor baby. Come here." She pulled him into her arms.

"If you grow much bigger, I'll need to kiss you from the next room." He put his hands on either side of the bump.

"Tell me about it. I was never this big with the others."

"Maybe we're having twins?" He gasped and bit his bottom lip in mock horror.

She placed her hands on top of his. "Shut up, you. I mean it. If there's more than one shacked up in here, *you're* looking after them, and *I'm* going back to work."

"Do you have twins, Mummy?" Emma asked.

"See what you've done now. She misses nothing." Amanda shook her head in disapproval, but laughter sparkled in her eyes.

"I like the flash new car. Maybe we can go for a drive if Sandra's staying for a while?"

"I'm sure we can. Sandra's cooking for us tonight, so we can go now if you like?"

He grabbed the keys and told Amanda he would wait at the car.

As soon as he opened the car door, he breathed in the brand new smell. Adjusting the driver's seat, he climbed in, impressed by the plush leather seats and seriously cool dash.

"It's got a built-in GPS and hands-free system," Amanda said, as she climbed in beside him.

"You chose well. It looks spot on. Does it have seven seats?"

"Yes. They're optional. They're stored in the boot if not needed."

"I guess for just you and the kids, five seats are plenty and you'll need the boot space for all the baby gear you'll be carting about."

"Yes, but Emma already had a sulk on the way home from school because she wanted to sit in the back."

"Why couldn't she?"

"Promise you won't laugh." She half-closed her eyes in shame.

"What've you done?"

"Nothing! I just couldn't work out how to lift the seats out."

Adam barked out a laugh, shaking his head.

She swatted at his shoulder. "Shut up, big head."

"Why am I a big head?" he said, still laughing.

"Because you'll work it out in a flash. Sandra and I were stumped."

"Don't worry. I'll have a look at it when we get back. Where shall we go?"

"I don't mind, but I do need to pick a few things up from the supermarket before we come back."

He drove out of the cul-de-sac and headed out of town to the motorway. He was more than impressed with the car and knew that within the first few minutes, but he enjoyed spending time just the two of them, so he drove further than he intended.

He eventually did a u-turn and headed back to Pinevale.

"How was Holly today?" Amanda asked.

"She seems fine. We've had a crazy, emotional day, having to break the news to several people that a family member's been murdered. It wrenches at my heartstrings at the best of times, but I know it got to her today. The poor woman is coping remarkably well, but for how long is anybody's guess."

"I don't know how you do it. I would be a basket case."

"That's what I think might happen to Frances if she doesn't slow down and take some time out for her and her husband."

"Would it help if I was to talk to her?"

He shrugged. "It might. She's got a lot of respect for you, and you are of the female persuasion after all."

"So nice of you to notice." She smiled.

"You know what I mean." He turned into the supermarket car park. "You got the list?"

"Yep. You don't have to come in. I'll be in and out in a sec."

"What? And waste time alone with my beautiful wife?"

"Hardly alone," she said, eyeballing the mass of Friday night shoppers.

"Come on." He ran around the car and opened her door. "I'll be your escort and push your shopping trolley. How can you pass up on an offer like that?" He squiggled his fingers into her ribs as he nuzzled at her neck.

"So long as you keep your hands firmly on the trolley," she giggled, ducking out of his embrace.

"Spoilsport."

They walked, hand in hand, towards the store.

"We should get Sandra to have the kids for a weekend before bubs is born and maybe go for a mini break."

"Where to? I'm not going anywhere if I need to get into a bikini! Look at me! I look like a Womble."

"You're beautiful! Just carrying my baby, that's all. I wouldn't care if we were surrounded by bikini clad supermodels, I'd only have eyes for you."

"Aw, you're so sweet. But the answer's still no."

"Come here, my little Womble." He put his arms around her and kissed the top of her head.

"Sod, off, you cheeky bugger. Go grab a trolley and be quick. Mush!" She laughed and flicked his behind as he walked towards the trolley bay.

Chapter 24

I feel elated as I go about my usual business, still no closer to being picked up. The detectives are nigh on useless, which has spurred me on even more.

Being swept along the aisle by a crowd of shoppers, I feel anonymous and inconspicuous. I finger the knife in my pocket. If I chose to, I could take a few of them out right now. But that's not my style. I don't go for frenzied terror attacks. I prefer to look deep in the eyes of my victims and thrill at each and every stage of their suffering, from the initial shock to the realisation of their impending fate.

As I round the corner, I stop in my tracks causing a few of the shoppers behind me to curse and suck their teeth as they manoeuvre their trolleys around me.

I stare at the detective standing at the checkout pawing at the pregnant blonde by his side. He is totally oblivious to me, and I am empowered. If I were reckless, I'd consider getting into the queue behind him. But I'm not done yet. In fact, this is just the beginning.

I shove my basket down at another checkout and mumble something about leaving my money at home. I head outside.

Minutes later, they leave the store, hand in hand, and get into a shiny new car. Keeping some distance between us, I follow them to their ordinary looking house, in an ordinary looking street.

I smile. Now let the fun begin.

**

They had a great evening seated around the dining table as a family for the first time in ages. Even Mary seemed much more settled after her talk with Amanda.

Sandra left around 10.00pm, and, after waving her off, Adam made a couple of trips upstairs carrying two sleeping children off the sofa. On his way back down the second time, he passed Mary on the stairs.

"Are you off to bed, love?"

"Yes. Night, night, Adam."

"Goodnight, sweetheart. Sorry I can't make our trip this weekend, but I'll call Mum and see how we're all fixed for next week, if you like?"

"Cool. Thanks."

He found Amanda emptying the dishwasher.

"You go and put your feet up, babe. I'll do that."

"I'm fine, honestly. You go and put the TV on. I'll be through in a sec."

"Are you sure?"

"Positive. Go on."

He went through to the lounge and, as he was closing the curtains, he noticed a movement from out near the car. He lifted the lace curtain and gasped. A person, dressed in black, was standing at the front of the car doing something to the windscreen.

"The cheeky..." He raced to the front door and out up the path. But there was nobody around by the time he reached the street. He walked up and down cursing the feeble street lights.

Amanda appeared in the doorway. "What's wrong?" she called in a hushed voice.

"There was someone hanging around the car a minute ago." He walked back towards the car and wrinkled his nose as a familiar stench wafted his way. "What the...?"

"What? What is it?" Amanda padded barefoot down the path.

"Go back to the house." He blocked her way and ushered her back inside.

"Tell me, Adam. What is it?"

"Stay here. I'll tell you in a minute." He grabbed his phone off the table and a sandwich bag from the drawer. "Go and get me a couple of cotton buds from the bathroom, Mand," he said, as he pulled a bowl out from under the sink and began filling it with hot soapy water.

"I wish you'd tell me what's going on." She flounced from the room and stomped upstairs to the bathroom.

He met her in the hall as he carried the bowl of hot water through. Balancing the bowl on the hall table, he took the cotton buds from her and wrapped them in a tissue, then placed the tissue in the sandwich bag.

Amanda chewed her lip, her brow wrinkled.

"Don't worry, Mand." He bent forwards and kissed the tip of her nose. "Go and watch TV. I won't be a minute."

At the car, he placed the bowl on the bonnet and took out the sandwich bag. After taking several photographs, he ran the tips of the cotton buds through the faeces smeared on the windscreen, wrapped them in the tissue and shoved it all back in the bag.

Using a scrubbing brush, he set to work cleaning the windscreen message. NICE CAR. The bastard was taunting him. Worse still, he now knew where he lived!

***

Holly and Val took turns to sit with Steve throughout the night. He was awake, on and off. But as the night turned to morning, his breathing became shallow and a strange rattling began in his throat.

"What's going on?" Holly asked, as she appeared in the doorway to take over.

Val shook her head, her eyes full of unshed tears. "I don't know. I was about to shout you. He's awake but not awake, if that makes sense."

"What should we do? Are the nurses due soon?"

"Not for a few more hours. We could call them, though."

"Maybe call the doctor, instead," Holly said.

Val nodded. "I'll do that now."

They swapped places, and Holly leaned over her husband and kissed his cheek. "Don't worry, sweetheart. We'll make sure you feel better soon."

Steve's eyes opened briefly before closing again. The rattle sounded like someone was sucking up the dregs of a cup through a straw, and it terrified her. No matter how much she tried to block the memories of her father's death, she remembered the noise well. The Macmillan nurse told her it was known as the death rattle.

Val returned and pulled Holly to one side. "Doctor Ing will be here shortly."

Holly nodded, and gripped the older woman's arm. Their eyes held, saying much more than words ever could.

Val sighed. "He said this probably means…"

"I know. I've heard it before." She closed her eyes tightly trying to find some strength to deal with the next few days. "What time is it?"

"Nearly six o'clock. The nurses should be here by nine," Val said.

"Too early to phone Adam. I need to take time off work."

"Good idea, lovey. I'll make us a nice cup of tea."

"Thanks, Val."

Chapter 25

Adam arrived at the station a few minutes before eight and Les and Julie came in together soon after.

"Do you have much on today?" Adam asked.

"Not much, apart from tidying up some paperwork and preparing ourselves for court," Les said. "The Jenkins trial starts Wednesday, you remember? The woman who was thrown out of the moving car?"

"Great. Then, after that, maybe you can help build a profile for Muldoon. I could do with you going through every little detail with fresh eyes. Find out if he had another Facebook or an Instagram account, anything at all."

"Has something else happened?" Julie eyed him, a worried expression on her face.

"You could say that." He walked to the printer and handed her the photographs he'd taken last night.

"Whose car's this?"

"Ours. Mine and Amanda's"

"Far out, boss."

Les got off his chair and looked at the images. "He knows where you live?"

"Clearly. And more worryingly, he's taunting me with it. So what does that tell you?"

"He's a cocky shit, is what it tells me." Les fumed.

"He is, that. And he obviously feels confident we're nowhere near catching him. We must be missing something."

His phone rang and he looked at the screen. "It's Frances. I need to take this." He strode to his office and accepted the call. "Can't help yourself, can you, missus?" he teased.

"Adam."

The tone of her voice gave him the chills.

"Are you okay?"

"No. I need time off."

"Of course, take as long as you need. Is Steve…?"

"He's had a bad night. The doctor's just left. It won't be long now."

"Oh, fuck, Holly. I'm truly sorry. You need anything, anything at all, you ask."

"I know."

He hung up, feeling the weight of helplessness settle in the middle of his chest. He picked up the phone again and dialled.

"Cal, Frances called. Bad news, I'm afraid."

He gasped. "Has he died?"

"Not far off. She won't be in for a while. I thought you'd want to know. I'll tell the others shortly."

"Thanks for calling. Any developments with the case?"

"No more homicides, but he left a shitty message for me on Amanda's new car last night."

"I'm coming in."

"There's no need."

"Well, all I'm doing is dossing around the house. I may as well come in for a couple of hours, at least."

"Please yourself, but don't feel you need to."

***

After the doctor left, Holly took herself off for a shower leaving Val to sit with Steve. In the bedroom, she made the call to Adam, and, after actually voicing the situation, she crumpled into a ball on the bed and sobbed.

If she packed a few things, she could be on the other side of Pinevale within fifteen minutes. She wouldn't have to watch her darling husband take his last breath or see the total devastation on Val's face as she lost her only son.

But, no matter how strong the desire was to flee, the need to stay close and help Steve on his final journey won hands-down. So, she sat upright on the bed and gave herself a mental shake. She could do this—she owed it to them to be in control and make her husband as comfortable as possible.

She showered, changed and returned to his side with a newfound strength.

"Why don't you go and take a shower, Val?"

She shook her head. "I don't want to. What if...?"

"He'll wait for you, won't you Stevie?"

Steve moved his eyes although the lids didn't open this time, not even for a second.

"See? You go and freshen up. She's beginning to pong, isn't she, Steve?"

Steve's eyes moved again.

"There you go. He agrees with me."

Val smiled sadly. "Okay, you pair of bullies. I'll be back in two ticks."

Holly sat beside the bed and stroked Steve's hair, mumbling words of love into his ear.

Ten minutes later, Val returned with her wet hair scraped back off her face. Her eyes were red from crying, but she'd changed into a freshly laundered dress and did appear more in control.

"The nurses are here." Val bobbed back into the hall to answer the door.

Steve seemed to stiffen at her words, and she realised he was still aware of everything. "Don't worry, baby, I won't let them change you, not today." His reply was more rapid eye movement.

Susan, the cute blonde nurse, who tended Steve's sores daily, breezed into the room. Although petite, she more than made up for it in the strength department.

Her bungling, yet extremely loveable sidekick, Neil, entered close behind.

"Val tells me Steve isn't himself today!" Susan's booming voice cut through the silence of the room and had Steve's eyes flickering wildly.

"No, he's not. And we don't need you today. I'm sorry, Susan. Can you come back tomorrow?" Holly said, in a no-nonsense tone.

"Can I just have a quick look at the bed pad? If the sores are oozing, which they will be, we can possibly just replace the bed pads, underneath him."

Holly looked at Steve. His eyes had stopped their dance. "Susan's going to replace the bed pad, Steve. Don't worry, she won't touch the dressing." He moved his eyes gently in response.

"Okay, but keep it to the bare minimum, I don't want him distressed today."

"Fair, enough." She lifted the bedclothes.

The rotten stench hit the room, and Holly, whose stomach had never been very strong, gagged. "I'll go and put the kettle on," she said, rushing for the door.

She found Val busily brewing a pot of tea in the kitchen.

"You beat me to it," Holly said.

"I can't be in there when they do their thing. I usually go outside if he cries. I hate it."

"I know, and I've told them not to do his dressings today, although the stink that came from the bed tells me they desperately need changing. But I can't allow them to put him through it, not today."

"Good call, so what are they doing?"

"Changing the absorbent bed pads. If he's still with us tomorrow, they'll have no choice but to change the lot, but from what the doctor said he probably won't see out the rest of the day."

Holly didn't think about the effect her words would have on her mother-in-law until Val bent double and crumpled to the tiles. Her face wore an expression of total anguish.

Horrified, Holly dropped to her side concerned when the older woman didn't appear to be breathing. "Val, I'm sorry, Val."

Val finally took a deep breath in. They held each other, both sobbing, until the two nurses appeared at the kitchen doorway.

Holly uncurled herself and helped Val to her feet. "I'm sorry," she said. "We had a bit of a melt-down."

"Understandable." Susan helped get Val seated at the dining table.

"Have you finished?" Holly asked the nurse, as she handed Val a paper towel and proceeded to pour hot water into the teapot.

"Yes. He wasn't disturbed too much. There is a big change in him since yesterday," Susan said.

"Did you hear the rattle?" Holly placed the teapot on the table and reached into the cupboard for the cups.

Susan nodded.

"When the doctor came out this morning, he said if Steve seems to be in discomfort then he'd order a suction machine to remove the excess fluid from his throat." Holly sat beside Val and poured four cups.

"To be honest, the suctioning would cause him more discomfort than the pooling itself. The sound is often much more upsetting to us than it is to the patient." Susan took the cup off Holly and scooped two heaped sugars into it.

"That's what we thought. Didn't we, Val?"

Val nodded seeming a little more in control.

"Are you still happy to care for him? We could arrange for him to go into a hospice for the final stage if that would be easier?" Joanne frowned.

Holly shook her head. "He's going nowhere. We're doing fine."

Val agreed.

"I'm not suggesting for one minute that you haven't done a wonderful job. But this stage is the hardest on the family, even though it's easiest for the patient."

"He's not been fully conscious since last night," Holly said, "but he's still awake. His eyes move when you speak to him."

"There's a chance he won't wake again. He'll drift off into a deep sleep and then he should pass peacefully. Neil will administer his morphine once Steve's had time to settle down."

"I couldn't extract anything from his stomach this morning," Val suddenly said. "Sorry, I meant to tell you. But with everything else, it just slipped my mind."

"No problem." Susan glanced at Neil who headed back to Steve's room.

When he returned he was carrying the feeding tube.

Val gasped. "Is that...?"

"You were right. It had come loose," Neil said softly.

"Are you going to replace it?" Val sounded a little irate once again.

Susan placed her hand on Val's arm. "We won't replace it now, Val. There's no point."

"But what if he gets hungry? It's not fair."

Neil got to his feet. "I'm going to call Doctor Ing and ask him if we can up the morphine dose. Steve won't feel anything, I promise you."

"I'm sorry. I need to get back in there." Holly jumped to her feet and rushed from the room.

Chapter 26

Adam scratched his head irritably. They'd trawled through every bit of evidence several times, yet nothing had come to light.

Picking up his notes, he walked into the main office and pulled a chair up to Cal's desk. "So tell me. Who is Miles Muldoon?"

Cal cleared his throat and pushed his keyboard away. "He's a hardworking, extremely private individual. He doesn't drink, except for the occasional glass of wine with dinner, doesn't do drugs, and doesn't have any real friends out of work."

"What about his work life?"

Cal shrugged. "He's ambitious, always striving for perfection and recognition."

"Exactly, which is why this random behaviour doesn't make any sense. What else?"

"Last seen by Lana and her dad on Tuesday around 5.30pm after which he withdrew £500 in cash, the maximum allowed. CCTV footage, from the ATM he used, confirmed he arrived there alone at 5.45pm. He let himself back into the hotel room at 6.00pm. Sally Kemp received the last known communication from him at 8.15pm, and she said he was very angry with her.

"After that, it's a mystery. He left the hotel leaving behind his car, his phone and his wallet. We don't know how he got to Sally's apartment or anywhere else."

Adam tapped a pen on his teeth. "Has anybody checked if there were any stolen cars in the area that night?"

"I sent a request out, but I don't recall getting a reply. I'll check in a minute, boss."

"What else?"

The team were used to him going through cases like this. He would often have light bulb moments as he listened to them verbalise what he might have read several times.

Cal checked his notes. "Nobody saw or heard anything during any of the attacks. I suspect the first murder was a catalyst. If Michael Curtis disturbed him ransacking Sally's apartment, then maybe he acted in blind fury. The others could be a case of in-for-a-penny, in-for-a-pound. He's already in trouble, so he may as well make everybody pay before he's banged up for the foreseeable."

"Your theory would explain why one of Sally's kitchen knives was used in Michael's attack. The blade snapped in the old man's skull, so Muldoon made sure he had a weapon fit for purpose after that and acquired some kind of hunting knife."

The desk phone rang and Cal reached for the handset. "Okay, I'll tell him." He hung up. "Boss, Sally Kemp's here to see you."

Adam groaned. "We need to set up some sort of cover for tonight. Can you arrange it?"

"Did you speak to the DCI about it yesterday?" Cal asked.

"I mentioned it, and he wanted me to send him all the updated case notes which I've done. Do you want to bring Ms Kemp up while I call him?"

Cal breathed an exaggerated sigh of relief and got to his feet.

"Pussy!" Adam laughed, heading to his office.

The DCI didn't answer so he left a message. Chances were, with it being the weekend, he wouldn't get back to him in time. Adam made the decision to arrange for two more nights' surveillance.

After calling the department, he quickly read the surveillance reports. On both nights, Sally had presented the officer with a flask of tea and soon after the upstairs lights had gone out. Other than the nurse, nobody had left or entered the property.

DCI Williamson would probably say it was a total waste of their resources, but he couldn't chance it. Sally was the only other person they knew that had upset Muldoon. In fact, she'd caused the initial outrage that put him in this position. No. He suspected her crazy ex wouldn't just leave it at that, and neither would he.

"Knock, knock." Sally, looking exquisite in a bottle-green jumpsuit, popped her head into his office.

"Ah, come in, Sally. Take a seat. I did intend to call you this afternoon. I managed to arrange another two nights of surveillance."

"Phew!" she said, sitting down opposite him. "I didn't tell my dad what's going on—he's too sick. But I was dreading having to move him into a hospice, his worst nightmare, by the way." She gathered her mass of red curls into her hand and brought all her hair forwards over her right shoulder.

Adam noticed the colour of the jumpsuit made her green eyes stand out more than usual.

She smiled at him seductively.

Flustered, he cleared his throat. "Hopefully it won't come to that. I don't suppose he's tried to contact you?"

She shook her head rapidly. "No."

"Any unexplained occurrences? Silent phone calls? Anything at all?"

"Absolutely nothing. He could've left the country already."

"No, he hasn't. He left his calling card on my car last night."

"His calling card?"

"A message smeared in faeces on the windscreen. We haven't had the lab report back yet, but it's got to be him. The excrement detail hasn't been released to the public at this stage."

"That's disgusting. And worrying too. Was your car outside the station?"

"It was parked outside my house."

Her hand flew to her mouth. "How did he find your address?"

"I've got no idea, but yes, it is worrying. Especially given the fact I have a heavily pregnant wife and three children at home."

He wouldn't normally divulge so much information about himself, but he wanted Sally to appreciate that he was a happily married man.

***

At 5.22pm Steve took his last breath.

Holly and Val were sitting on either side of the bed, each holding one of his hands. Both of them stared at him, holding their own breath as they willed him to take another, but silently praying he wouldn't.

After a minute, Val said, "Is he...?" and gulped.

Holly got to her feet and placed a hand on his throat, searching for a pulse. She shook her head. "He's gone."

An anguished cry came from her mother-in-law.

Holly couldn't go to comfort her. All the air seemed to be sucked from her body, and she felt physical pain in her solar plexus. He was dead. Her husband was dead. Although she knew it was coming, had done for weeks, it still managed to totally shock her. She'd never see his radiant smile or twinkling eyes again. Ever.

She didn't know how long she stayed in that position, with his head in her arms, but the pillow was sodden by the time she moved.

"I'd best call the doctor," she whispered to Val.

Chapter 27

Once Sally had left, they spent the rest of the afternoon going over and over the evidence to date.

"We must be missing something." Les leaned back in his chair.

"Believe me, Les. If there was any way of finding him with the evidence already discovered, he'd be locked up by now." Adam got to his feet and stretched each muscle in his six-foot-four-inch body. "We can only hope he tries something else soon and slips up somehow."

Les yawned and also stretched. The yawn went through the rest of them like a Mexican wave.

Adam slammed the flat of his hand on the desk. "I'm so wild with myself for not moving faster last night. I'm the only one who's ever seen him in action, and the bastard got away."

"I'm sure you moved faster than most. He had a head start on you. That's all," Cal said, popping a gummy dinosaur in his mouth.

Adam pushed the chair back under the desk. "Come on. I'll buy you all a pint, and we can call it a day."

They grabbed their jackets and personal items and headed to *The Crown and Badger* on the opposite corner. The pub was notorious for being full of coppers, so no scallies or scumbags came within a mile of the place.

He shouted them a round of drinks and also paid for another on the quiet. He had a cola, which they all thought had something else in it, but they never got to know what as he never stayed for more than one.

"Cheers, boss." Cal raised his glass before taking a deep swig of lager.

"You're welcome, Cal. I appreciate your hard work and loyalty, although you really should've stayed home today."

"To be honest, boss, what else would I do? I don't have a family like you."

"I know, but still..."

"I'll be in tomorrow, too, so why don't you spend the day with your lovely wife and kiddies?"

Adam shook his head and sighed. "I can't take time off while we have a crazed killer on the loose."

"But there's nothing to do, boss. Take the time with your family and come at it with fresh eyes on Monday."

"Are you sure? If anything happens, anything at all, call me."

Cal gave a three-fingered salute. "Scout's honour."

"I'll be off then. You've all got another drink in the pumps, but don't go getting trashed and blaming me."

"As if we would, boss." Les laughed, clinking his glass on Julie's outstretched one.

Shaking his head, Adam flicked a beer mat at them and got up to leave.

As he walked to the car, he dialled home. Amanda answered.

"Hey, Mand, fancy a trip to my mother's tomorrow?"

"Aren't you working?"

"Cal's going to cover. Don't say anything to the kids yet. I need to check Mum's going to be home."

Hanging up, he dialled his mother's number.

She took longer to answer and seemed a little vague as though she'd been sleeping.

"Hey, Mum, it's me."

"Adam? Is that you?"

He chuckled. "Is there anyone else who calls you Mum?"

"Don't be cheeky, Adam. I wasn't expecting to hear from you."

He felt a pang of guilt. He didn't call her nearly enough.

"Are you home tomorrow?"

"Of course, I'm home. Where else would I be?"

"Good, because we're coming for a visit."

"All of you?"

"All of us. Do you think you could handle us?"

"Oh, Adam. That'll be lovely. I'll need to go shopping and buy something in for the children."

"I don't want you to go to any trouble, so we'll bring everything to make us all a sandwich for lunch and snacks and stuff."

"That won't do. On a Sunday? I never cook a roast for myself, but I'd never live it down if I allow you to eat a sandwich for Sunday lunch."

Adam sighed deeply. His mother was old school and inflexible with certain traditions. "But we're coming to see you, Mum. Not have you fuss around in the kitchen, waiting on us hand and foot."

Stopping on the corner, Adam waited for an old man on a bike to pass. Then he walked diagonally across the road to the station car park.

His mother continued. "I'll have it all prepared for when you get here. What time will you be leaving home, son?"

"We'll aim for 8.00am, but I'll call you as we set off."

"Oooh, I'm looking forward to seeing you all. I'll hardly sleep a wink tonight."

Adam chuckled. "Me too, Mum. I've missed you."

As he hung up, his phone rang immediately. His stomach dropped when he read the display. "Frances? Are you okay?"

"He's gone," Frances said, in a breathy voice.

"Oh, no. Oh, shit! I mean, I'm so sorry, Holly. Is there anything I can do?"

"No. Just tell the others please."

"Consider it done. And if you need to get away, our house will be empty tomorrow. I won't set the alarm, and I'll leave a spare key under the patio pot in the back garden."

"I might just take you up on that, boss."

"Do! I mean it. I've been there, remember. Shitloads of well-wishers will come out of the woodwork, and you'll have to force yourself to smile when it's the last thing you want to do."

"You've just described the last hour to a tee."

"The offer's there. I'll call you tomorrow, and if you need to talk, don't hesitate."

"Thanks, boss."

He got in his car and drove to the pub, parking on double yellow lines. He ran inside and found them all where he'd left them. They looked up, puzzled.

"Hey, boss. I thought you'd gone," Cal said. A worried expression crossed his face.

"I had, but I've just received some bad news, I'm afraid. Frances' husband, Steve, has passed away."

"Shoot! That was quick," Julie said.

Adam nodded. "Will one of you let Ginger Dave know?"

"Yeah, I'll do it, boss." Cal pulled his phone from his pocket.

"I've gotta go. I'm illegally parked. We've decided to visit my mum in Manchester tomorrow. I'll have my phone on me if you need me for anything."

***

I watch as the detective and his workmates leave the station and head to the pub. Not one of the docile bastards notices me.

I hang around in the cold. I even think about entering at one point, but that's too blatant, even for me.

After around twenty minutes, the detective leaves alone. Once outside, he calls somebody on the phone.

I peek around the corner, but he's oblivious of me down the side of the pub. I listen as he arranges to visit his mum. How touching.

I keep my distance as I follow catching every word the careless prick says.

He stops at the road and waits, turning slightly, his phone pressed firmly to his ear, and I freeze. If he turns a little more, he'll catch me in his peripheral vision.

But he doesn't.

Once a scruffy old codger passes on his bike, he crosses the road, and I hang back. When he enters the car park, I run across the road keeping on the outside of the station fence.

I reach him. We are no more than six feet from each other on either side of the fence, and a thrill passes through me as I hear him say he'll leave a key for the house under a pot.

I smile and scurry towards my car excited about tomorrow.

Chapter 28

I watch the performance from the safety of my car as the detective tries to organise his family and get them all into the vehicle.

The little boy, the youngest child, proves to be the least trouble of them all. He and his father sit out in the car for twenty minutes while the pregnant woman and her daughters faff about, in and out.

I duck as they drive past me at 8.45am. I'm dressed in black with a cap pulled down low and don't think he will recognise me, but I'd rather not chance it.

I sit and wait before making my move just in case they've forgotten something and double back. At 9.30am, I start the car and move it closer to the house.

The street is deserted, but, on the off chance any of the neighbours are watching, I walk from the car and through the gate with confidence and purpose as though I am meant to be there.

Around the back, there is a decent sized patio with a wooden table and chairs, a plain, hedge-bordered lawn and a garden shed standing in the far corner. Two green ceramic pots filled with dead bedding plant twigs, are on either side of the door. Tipping the first one up, I find nothing beneath it. A feeling of doom descends on me. What if he forgot to leave the key after all?

I tip the second pot, and my fingers brush against something metallic. Smiling again, I pull the key out.

The door opens into a spacious kitchen-dining area.

I glance around the homely room taking in the remains of a chaotic breakfast for a family with young children. The sink is piled high with dishes, and an untouched cup of tea sits on the worktop. I touch the cup. The contents are still warm which gives me another thrill.

I take my time, looking at everything. I open drawers making sure I don't leave any sign I've been through them.

Down the hall, I come to a neat and tidy lounge room. Two identical brown leather sofas and a single beige chair fill the small space. A smallish TV in the corner indicates the detective and his pretty wife are not ruled by having the biggest and the best of everything. I'm impressed.

I peruse the bookshelf that is light on actual literature unless you count the shelf of children's books, a few cookery books and an encyclopaedia.

The other shelves are filled with DVDs, mostly children's, and the odd boxed set. I presume the Inspector

Morse, Prime Suspect, and A Touch of Frost belong to the resident detective. The Cold Feet, Doctor Quinn and several romances clearly belong to the woman of the house.

But I'm bored. I don't see anything that could give me any real insight into what goes on in the detective's mind.

I head up the staircase and look in each of the four bedrooms. I can tell by the décor which room belongs to which child, and a vulgar amount of possessions fill each of them.

The parents' room is sparse in comparison, and immaculate. A king-sized bed takes up the bulk of the space, draped in a luxurious, white bedspread. The room is decorated in mainly beige tones with a splash of red in the light shades, wall art and cushions. Dark wooden bedside cabinets and matching drawer units are dotted around the room and a fitted wardrobe takes up the entire wall opposite the bed.

I sit down and open the top drawer of the bedside cabinet closest to the door. Definitely not the detective's side unless he is into lacy lingerie. The contents of the bottom drawer makes me chuckle. I pull out the pink dildo and bring it to my nose, inhaling deeply, but all I can smell is rubber. I stand it on top of the cabinet and close the drawer.

The top drawer on the other side of the bed holds socks and white cotton trunks. Moving them to one side, I find a man's leather strapped watch, a couple of batteries and some loose change. As I tidy the drawer up, I feel something bulky in a pair of socks. Unfolding them, a bottle of sleeping pills fall out. They have Adam John Stanley printed on the label. I raise my eyebrows. So the detective struggles sleeping. Interesting. I slip the bottle into my pocket.

The bottom drawer has a selection of neckties and cufflinks. Nothing seedy. No stroke magazines, or anything to tell me more about the man who's every waking moment over the past week have been, no doubt, filled with thoughts of finding me.

I lie on his side of the bed, snuggling my head down into the pillow. Although not obviously dirty, my boots leave black marks on the bedspread, a touch I am thrilled with although it was entirely accidental.

After a few minutes, I venture into the only bathroom in the house.

This is the one room that hasn't been recently redecorated. An old, white-painted, wooden wall cupboard is above the sink, and inside several jars of lotions and potions fill the top shelf.

I find nothing of interest, but I have business to do in this room. I shove the door closed, out of habit more than anything, and undo the button of my trousers.

***

As soon as the word was out, the phone didn't stop ringing. Several more local well-wishers brought food. There was enough casserole and lasagne in the fridge to feed the street. However, neither Holly nor Val could face a bite.

Val had been a rock. Once the initial shock had worn off, she rallied around and organised everything from bagging up the excess medication for the nurses to contacting the hospital to collect the bed and equipment loaned from them.

They had made copious amounts of tea. Every time someone knocked on the door, one of them filled the kettle and it started all over again.

Holly felt like a spare part. She couldn't face helping with the practical jobs and longed instead to take Adam up on his offer to hole herself up in his house for the day, but she couldn't leave Val. Plus, the tide of people wouldn't just go away. If they didn't deal with them now, they would keep coming and phoning until they did.

"Fancy another cuppa, lovey?" Val asked, standing in the doorway of the lounge.

"Is it possible to drown yourself in tea?"

Val smiled. "Feels a bit like that, doesn't it? I'm looking for any excuse to keep myself busy."

"Come and sit down." Holly patted the seat beside her. "Take five minutes before the next round of visitors."

Val threw the tea towel she was holding onto the coffee table and slumped down beside her. "I'm surprised how many friends he had," she said.

"Had is the correct tense and not because he's died. Most of the people who showed up today haven't been near him since his accident. It annoys me when they act all heartbroken and tearful when they've not seen him for more than six years."

"It's always the way, I'm afraid."

"I don't know how you keep it up, to be honest. I'd have shut the curtains and taken the phone off the hook hours ago."

"Well, if that's what you want. I don't want to take over, lovey. This is your house after all."

"No, don't be daft. Unless you want to hide from the world too. We could curl up on the sofa together and watch chick flicks."

"What the heck's a chick flick?"

Holly smiled. "Never mind. I was joking."

The doorbell rang.

Holly rolled her eyes and groaned. "I'll put the kettle on while you get the door."

"You're a good girl. Steve won the jackpot when he married you."

"You're not so bad yourself, Mrs Eff."

They hugged as the doorbell chimed again.

Chapter 29

They arrived in Manchester just before 1.00pm. Jacob had fallen asleep just ten minutes before and was grouchy when Adam took him out of the car seat.

"Wow! Nice car."

Startled, he turned quickly to see his lovely old mum standing behind him. "Hello, you." He bent and kissed her on the lips, noticing how well she looked.

The blue hair had gone, replaced by perfectly styled, dark grey curls. She even wore lipstick, some of which now coated his lips. He pressed them together, wanting to wipe the greasy film off, but Jacob lay half-asleep in his arms.

Amanda came around the car with Emma and Mary, and they were off, squealing and talking ten to the dozen.

Adam left them all to it, and carried Jacob inside. He got prickles over his entire body as he smelled the familiar scent of home.

After lying Jacob down on the sofa, he followed his nose through to the kitchen where he spied a large roast beef resting underneath a tea towel. His stomach growled. He loved his mother's roast dinners. Picking at the edge of the beef, he pulled a piece away and snaffled it into his mouth.

"Caught you," his mum said, suddenly behind him once again.

He laughed, covering his mouth while he chewed. "This is divine."

"Good. There's plenty. I hope the kids are good eaters."

"You're looking well, Mum." He put his arm around her shoulders and they headed back through to the lounge.

"Thanks, son. I thought I'd make an effort. I can't remember the last time I had anyone around for dinner."

Jacob, now playing with his cars on the carpet by the fireplace, smiled as they entered. "Hi, Gammar," he said.

Amanda and Emma, sitting together on the sofa, burst out laughing at him.

Jacob rarely spoke. He could speak, when it suited him, but mostly he chose not to. Hearing him call Adam's mum Gammar had them all cracking up.

"I don't understand," the old woman said.

Adam rubbed her shoulder. "He just said, *Hi Gammar,* to you."

"To me? He called me Grandma?"

Adam nodded.

She walked over to Jacob and kissed him on the head. "Hi, sweet boy." Then she perched on the arm of the chair.

Adam sat beside Amanda. "Where's Mary?"

"She's gone up to the bathroom. She'll be down in a minute," Amanda said.

"That reminds me, Mum. Can I show Mary some of our old photos after lunch? She's doing a family tree at school."

She put her hand to her chest dramatically. "If I can remember where I put them."

"Aren't they still in the bedding box in your bedroom?"

"Oh, yes. Probably. I haven't looked in there for years." She got to her feet. "I hope you're all starving. Everything's more or less ready to dish up."

"Can I help you, Nelly?" Amanda jumped up.

"You could set the table if you don't mind."

"Can I help?" Emma said, following her mother.

Mary entered the room as the others left it.

"Did you live here when you were little?" she asked Adam.

"No. I lived in a few different places after Dad died. We moved here when I was around twelve or thirteen."

"Do you still have a bedroom here?"

Adam nodded. "Last time I checked."

"Can I see?"

He nodded. "Jacob, do you want to come with us to see my old bedroom? We may even find some of my old toys."

Jacob didn't need asking twice.

Adam led them both up the stairs to his room.

He'd left home when he was seventeen, yet it was still exactly as he'd left it all those years ago. Posters of *The Manic Street Preachers* and *REM* covered every spare wall surface. His old navy-blue duvet cover that had army tanks all over it still lay on the single white-painted wooden bed. There wasn't a speck of dust anywhere, which didn't surprise him. His mum always cleaned and changed the bedding in the spare bedroom, and nobody ever slept in there as far as he knew.

"What's this?" Mary asked, examining the hi-fi system.

"My old CD player." He pointed to the stack of CDs beside it."

"Does this mean you could only listen to music in your room?"

He pulled a storage box out from the wardrobe and took the lid off for Jacob, who squealed with delight when he spotted all the superhero figures, tubs of Lego and jigsaws.

Adam chuckled at his reaction then turned back to Mary.

"Yes, that's right. Although I did have a Walkman a bit later on."

"A what?" She screwed her face up comically.

"Hang on, I'll show you. It must still be here, somewhere." He rummaged through a few drawers until he found his old faithful Walkman. "Here you go. My portable CD player."

"It's massive."

He nodded. "I guess it is compared to today's gadgets. But it was *state of the art* at the time." He shoved it back into the drawer.

"Who's this?"

He gasped when he saw the framed photo she held up, of him and Sarah sitting on a blanket in the back garden, laughing.

He took it from her and traced a finger over the image. That day seemed like a lifetime ago. Remembering Mary, he smiled and placed the frame back down on the chest of drawers.

"She was my wife."

Mary gasped. "Does Amanda know?"

Jacob, momentarily disturbed from the box of goodies, looked around at them before turning back to the box.

Adam smiled. "Of course she knows. Sarah died before I moved to London."

"What did she die of?"

"She was hit by a car. She died instantly."

"Like my dad?"

"Yes. Exactly like your dad." He stroked her fine blonde hair and tucked it behind her ear. "Come on. I bet lunch is almost ready. Help me carry this lot down for Jakey."

Between them they carried the box downstairs, and Amanda met them in the hallway.

"I was just coming to find you lot. Lunch is ready."

Mary smiled at Adam.

"See? What did I tell you?" He wiggled his eyebrows at her. "I swear sometimes I'm psychic."

Amanda laughed and ushered them all through to the dining room.

As usual, his mum had prepared a mountain of food, and they all made a supreme effort to devour it all. There was much laughter and frivolity and Adam made a promise to himself to do this more often—it was good for all of them.

After lunch, Amanda and Mary loaded the dishwasher while Adam took Emma and Jacob back through to the lounge to play with the box of toys.

"I forgot about that lot. You could take it home with you if you have room." His mum struggled to get onto her knees beside the children. "I may need a hand getting up," she laughed.

Watching his mum with the kids brought back some happy memories of his childhood. Before his dad had died, she used to build Lego with him too. After the death of his father, however, things changed rapidly. It was understandable, she must have been devastated, but he didn't understand it back then. He was only eight. Not only was his beloved father gone, it felt as though he'd lost his mother too.

Things didn't get better either. Soon after, they shifted from their home, because his mum couldn't afford the rent, and moved into a dilapidated block of flats on the outskirts of Manchester.

Four years later, his mum met Vernon at church. Vernon was a God-fearing man and proposed to his mother after only a few weeks. He promised them the world. After the wedding, they moved in with him, and at first they all got along well. But Vernon, an ex-army man, had definite ideas of how a twelve-year-old boy should behave and began to terrorize him.

Vernon seemed to brainwash Adam's mother, convincing her anything he did was for Adam's own good. So she turned a blind eye to the abuse of her only son.

Of course, Adam rebelled, and as he got older the abuse went from physical beatings to more mental torture. If Adam did anything to piss Vernon off, he would restrict the boy's meals. His mother was petrified of her husband at this stage and was always trying to appease him in some way.

When Adam began to steal food from his schoolmates, one of his teachers got involved and he eventually told her everything.

The next few days were a blur. He remembered making a statement to the police. His mum was also interviewed and the next thing he knew, Vernon moved out.

Although he was never charged, Vernon made a deal with Adam's mum—if they promised to keep quiet about everything, he would sign over the house in the divorce settlement.

His mum had become introverted and a nervous wreck since meeting Vernon, but she didn't believe in divorce, and she stopped attending church because of her humiliation. But she slowly regained her confidence and began to make friends again.

He smiled as he watched her now. She was such a lovely woman and desperately wanted a more hands-on role in their lives.

Chapter 30

Adam went up to his mother's room to find the photo albums, and when Mary came through from the kitchen he had them all ready for her.

Mary sat in-between him and Amanda on the sofa, and he placed the first album on her knee.

Within minutes, both Mary and Amanda were in fits of laughter, pointing at images of a young Adam in a pair of short-shorts that showcased his knobbly knees.

"It's not that funny!" he said, defensively.

"Oh, yes, it is," they squealed together.

Each turn of the page brought about more cackles, and he eventually got to his feet. "If you don't mind, I might pop by the station and catch up with a few old mates."

Amanda nodded, still grinning.

He rolled his eyes at her then left.

It seemed strange to be back at his old workplace and he was surprised to find Matt, his ex-partner and ex-brother-in-law, in his office.

"Hey, buddy!" Matt jumped up from his desk and gave Adam a man-hug.

"Got time for a cuppa?"

"For you, anytime."

They walked through to the staff kitchen and Matt poured them both a coffee.

Adam cringed as he sipped the bitter blend. "Some things never change."

"Putrid, isn't it? But marginally better than nothing. So what are you doing here?"

"I brought the kids to visit the old lady. How about you? I thought you'd probably be off out with the family today."

"Too busy. We're chocca around here."

"How's Carole and the girls?"

"Carole's fine, but she's booked in for a hysterectomy next week. Women's problems."

"Bummer. You weren't planning any more kids, were you?"

"No. I don't think so, but as soon as you're told you can't, it makes you question everything."

"It does. I had a similar scare recently when I found a lump in my gonads."

"Shit, buddy. That's heavy. Are you alright?"

He shrugged. "To be honest, the swelling hasn't been nearly as bad the past couple of days. But the first night, the *what-ifs* did play on my mind quite a bit."

"They're bound to, buddy. But I'm sure you'll be fine. Lots of people find lumps and, nine times out of ten, it's nothing to worry about."

Adam nodded and drained the last of the coffee. "I'd better let you return to your work. Do you fancy catching up properly one weekend? We could meet halfway with the women and kids."

"I would love that. Maybe after Amanda has the baby and then Carole can get her baby fix at the same time."

"Sounds perfect. Say *hi* to them for me."

Apart from the guy on reception, Adam didn't bump into anyone else he recognised, and, after a quick trawl around his old stomping ground, he drove back home.

His mother was still on the carpet with the kids. This time they were attempting to do a jigsaw, but bossy Emma kept pulling the pieces apart.

"Emma! Don't be such a spoilsport!" Adam shook his head.

"I don't mind, sweetheart. She's having fun, and that's the main thing."

"Where are the girls?"

"Here, help me up." She held her hand out and he pulled her to her feet. "They went upstairs. Mary wanted to show Amanda your old room."

He rolled his eyes. "She's fascinated with family and the past."

His Mum shrugged one shoulder. "Stands to reason, really. By all accounts, the poor thing's had an uncertain time of it lately. She should be settling down by now, though."

"She is, I think. She just has the odd wobble, nothing major."

Amanda and Mary came into the room.

"Oh, I didn't know you were back." Amanda kissed him. "Did you manage to meet up with some of your old mates?"

"Just Matt. I didn't recognise anyone else."

"Is he okay?"

"Yeah, I think so. I would've arranged to catch up with them later, but we should head off soon. We've still got a long drive home."

"Shall I make you a cuppa before you go?" his mum asked.

"That would be lovely, Mum. I need something to wash away the nasty taste of the station coffee."

Half an hour later, they'd packed up the car and said their goodbyes, promising to send for her once the baby was born. She tried to disguise the tears that filled her eyes, blaming them on the wind. But he knew she was lonely and promised to call her soon.

As they pulled onto the motorway, Amanda turned to him. "I don't know why your mum doesn't sell up and come and live near us," she said. "She's got nothing keeping her here."

"I don't think she would. Maybe when she comes over for a visit we can show her around. See if we can convince her."

"She must be so lonely."

He nodded. "She is. I need to make an effort to come over more often."

The journey back to London wasn't as bad as he'd expected. The children had fallen asleep within ten minutes and Amanda wasn't too far behind them.

They arrived home just after 10.30pm. He carried Jacob in and up the stairs to the bathroom. "Do a wee-wee, young man, and you can go straight to bed," he said.

As Adam lifted the lid on the toilet, he froze. A humungous turd filled the bowl. "What the..." His first instinct was to flush, but he could tell there was no way the mound was going down without a fight.

Jacob began doing a dance, holding on to his privates.

"Oh, sorry, son. Hang on." He pulled Jacob's pants down and lifted him up to the sink. "Do it in there, the toilet is broken."

"Adam!" Amanda gave him a look of reproach when she suddenly appeared behind him holding Emma's hand. "What's that stink?"

"The toilet's blocked. This'll have to do unless you would prefer it all over the floor."

Amanda did a double take at him. "Okay, don't bite my head off."

"I'm sorry, love. But it was an emergency."

He put Jacob down and washed the sink.

"Emma, can you wait a second while I look for Jacob's old potty." Amanda eyeballed him as if to say, that's what *you should* have done.

But he didn't care. He had bigger things on his mind, namely how to get rid of the massive shite in the toilet.

He bumped into Mary as he stepped onto the landing. "The toilet's blocked, sweetheart. Shall I knock next door and see if you can use theirs for now?"

Her face fell. Mary wasn't the type to go broadcasting to all and sundry she needed the loo.

"Hang on a tic." He smiled. "Amanda?"

"I'm in here."

He followed the sound of her voice to their room. She was standing still, her back to him. "We might have to take the kids to Sandra's. We can't expect them to pee in the bloody sink till we can call a plumber out."

She didn't say anything.

"Amanda?"

She turned slowly, her mouth open and her eyes wide in shock.

"What is it?"

She held out her hand holding the sex toy, a gift off her friends from her hen night.

He shook his head. "What? I don't understand."

"Did you take this out of my drawer?"

"Did I hell! I never go in your drawers."

"And look at this." She pointed at the bed.

Two dirty black marks were on his side of the usually-immaculate bedspread, and his pillow was flattened and had a hollow made by a head.

"What the..." he said again, scratching his head.

"Mum, I need to do wee-wees," Emma called from the bathroom.

"Right, I'm coming now," she shouted, stepping towards the door.

Prickles formed at the base of his skull. "Get the kids in the car. We're taking them to Sandra's."

"But—"

"No arguments, Amanda. Kids in the car, now!"

Her mouth fell open as terror filled her eyes.

He nodded, stroking her hair, then he headed back onto the landing. "Right, Jakey. Trousers back on. We're going for another adventure."

"Yes-ss," he said.

"Can you hang on for the toilet until Grandma's house?" he asked Mary.

She nodded.

"Go as you are. We'll bring you back for your school stuff in the morning."

Chapter 31

After dropping the kids off, Amanda got back into the car with a face like thunder. "So, what's wrong? Who's been in our house?"

Adam shrugged. "I left the key out for Frances, but I can't imagine *her* being responsible."

"No way. She wouldn't rummage through our bedroom and climb on our bed with filthy feet."

"I know but..." He put the car in drive and pulled away from the kerb.

"But what? Do you really think she could have done all that? Oh, and let's not forget, blocking the toilet up with the biggest mound of shit I've ever seen."

"Of course not. But who else knew where to find the key? Or that I didn't set the alarm, for that matter? It doesn't make sense."

"Call her."

"And say what?"

"Ask her. Because if it wasn't her, we need to find out who the fuck's been in our house."

"Okay, calm down. I'll call."

He dialled Frances' mobile, and her sleepy voice came over the loudspeaker.

Adam glanced at the clock and winced, 11.25pm. "Sorry to wake you, Frances. It's only me."

"Has there been another?"

"Another what?"

"Homicide. Why else would you be calling me at this hour?"

"Oh, no. Not that I'm aware, anyway. I'm just getting back from Manchester."

"Did you have a nice time?"

"Yeah, lovely, thanks. Listen. Did you manage to escape to our house today?"

"No. I wanted to, and I appreciate the offer, but I couldn't leave Val in the end. Why?"

"Did you tell anyone else about the key by any chance?"

"You're pulling my leg, aren't you? Why would I tell anybody how to access your house?" Her voice raised an octave.

"Because, I think Muldoon has been at my house."

"Fuck! I'm on my way over."

The line went dead.

"What the hell was that all about? Who's Muldoon when he's at home?" Amanda said.

"He's the man we've been looking for all week."

"The murderer? You think a fucking murderer let himself into my house and rifled through my things?" she yelled.

"Shhh! Calm down, Amanda." He turned onto their street and pulled over. "I'm not saying I'm right, but he knows where we live."

"How could he? Why would you say that?" She still sounded furious, and he didn't blame her.

"He left a message in shit on the car windscreen."

"That's what you were doing the other night? Why the hell would he target you?"

"Haven't a clue, love. Listen, why don't you go back to Sandra's? I'll sort the house out, and you can bring the kids back in the morning."

"Are you sure?"

"Of course I'm sure. Just give me the keys so I can let myself in, and then you shoot off."

"What if he comes back?"

"He won't, and even if he did what good would *you* be? If you fell over you wouldn't be able to get up again."

"Shut up, cheeky." She shoved him playfully. "I'm serious. What if he does come back? Maybe you should come to Sandra's too?"

"I'll be fine. I promise."

He ran to open the front door and then brought the keys back. Amanda was already in the driver's seat.

Leaning through the open window, he kissed his wife on the lips. "See you in the morning."

He watched her drive off before going back inside. The thought that someone had been through their stuff made him feel violated, but the fact their intruder was probably a crazed killer terrified him. What if the next time he decided to pay them a visit Amanda was home alone, or worse still home with the kids?

In the kitchen, he saw nothing out of place. In fact, the entire place was extra tidy.

He had been the first in the car that morning, but he didn't think Amanda would've had time to clean the breakfast dishes, never mind the whole kitchen.

He picked up the dishcloth which had been folded neatly over the tap. Amanda always hung it on a bar in the cupboard under the sink. The same with the tea towel that now lay folded in two on the edge of the sink, instead of over the oven door handle.

He opened the cupboard and gasped. The shelves had been reorganised. Someone was seriously messing with his mind.

Every single cupboard and drawer was the same. Nothing like the disorganised chaos he would usually find.

On first inspection, the lounge didn't look any different, but being a kid-free zone the room generally stayed tidy. Then he noticed the DVD's on the bookcase had been reorganised in alphabetical order rather than the haphazard way they were normally filed.

He needed to call this in and get the place dusted for fingerprints. As he pulled his phone from his pocket, someone hammered on the window causing him to stiffen.

He whirled around, relaxed, and let out a long sigh.

Frances pointed at the front door, and he nodded.

"So what's he done?" she said, as soon as she stepped inside.

He exhaled and shook his head. "More than I first thought. But it sounds bloody stupid, to be honest."

"What does?" She followed him into the kitchen.

"Look around. What do you see?"

She began scanning the room looking at every single item, a frown on her face. "Nothing."

"Look in the cupboard." He indicated the main food cupboard. "Use this." He opened the cupboard under the sink and handed her a rubber glove.

She pulled the glove on and opened the door, shaking her head. "What am I missing?"

"What if I told you that when we left home this morning this place looked as though a bomb had gone off?"

"Eh! So you mean..."

He nodded as the penny dropped, and, putting on the matching glove, he opened several more drawers and cupboards. "Someone has given the whole house a spring clean."

"And you're complaining! Maybe you should send them around to mine."

"I think it was Muldoon."

She snorted. "No way. Someone cleaned your house and you automatically think a serial killer is to blame. Maybe Sandra came over."

He shook his head. "See, I told you it sounded stupid, but I know he did it. He came here the other night and smeared a shitty message on the windscreen of our new car.

"Really? What did the message say?"

"It said NICE CAR. Amanda had only picked it up that day. And that's not all. Come and look at this." He led her upstairs and into the bathroom. He gestured towards the toilet as though presenting a prize. "Ta-da."

She lifted the seat before letting it slam closed again. "Oh, the dirty..." She pressed her hand to her mouth and spun from the room.

"Sorry, but there was no explaining that lot. You had to see for yourself. Most people would say maybe one of the kids went to the loo before we left home this morning. But looking at that lot, what would you say now?"

"I'd say, thanks for thinking *I* was capable of that fucking lot!"

Suddenly laughing, he bent double and allowed it to burst from him. Tears flowed down his cheeks as he struggled to breathe.

Frances was also laughing, the silent kind of laughter causing her to exhale only, and her whole body to shake uncontrollably. She gripped the banister, bending her body over the top of it, her legs crossed as though she needed to pee.

It took ages before he was able to talk. Standing upright, he wiped his eyes on the sleeve of his jersey. "I didn't think you'd done it." He set off laughing again, sounding like an old chain-smoker.

"Yes, you did!" Frances pulled herself together first. She was breathing heavily as though she'd just run a marathon. "We'd best call the station. This is serious."

"I know." Adam forced himself to get a grip.

"Shall I call them?"

He nodded, exhausted all of a sudden. "Let me show you this first." In his bedroom, he showed her the dirt on the bed and the sex toy on the bedside cabinet.

"Ooh, whatever floats your boat, I s'pose!"

Adam rolled his eyes. "Grow up."

She sniggered and walked around the bed to Adam's side and peered at his pillow. "There are a few longish, dark hairs on there. Longer than yours, I mean."

He opened the wardrobe and was once again shocked by the orderliness, something that neither he nor Amanda possessed. "The bastard has been through everything. Had his mitts on every last item of our clothing."

"It must have taken hours. I hate this kind of job. Why would somebody choose to do it if they didn't have to?"

"To give me a brain-fuck. Why else?"

"I'll stay here with you until they've taken evidence, and then I insist you come home with me for the night."

"What would your mother-in-law say?"

"She won't say a thing. And besides, she could do with a laugh like you've just given me. I didn't think I'd ever laugh again."

Adam felt his stomach twitch again and had to force himself to continue. "Go and call them then. I'll get rid of the dildo. It's not important to the case, and they'll have a field day with it down at the station."

He picked up the sex toy, carried it downstairs and threw it into the bin. Frances' voice carried through from the hallway. A few minutes later she joined him in the kitchen.

"I'm sorry to have dragged you out," he said.

"I can't tell you how happy I am that you did. Not that I wanted this to happen, of course."

"Yeah, but..."

"*And, before you say anything,* I'm away from work, aren't I? Helping a mate out isn't classed as work."

"I appreciate it, either way." He nodded at her phone. "How long will they be?"

"They're going to rush it through, hopefully not too long."

He opened the fridge. "Fancy a bottle of beer from my incredibly tidy fridge?"

"I'd love one."

Chapter 32

I smile as I imagine the detective and his perfect family arriving home. I wish I could see the expression on his face when the truth dawns. In my head, it plays out perfectly.

They arrive home. Notice all the kitchen has been cleaned up and silently thank their friend. They have a cuppa—isn't that the first thing anyone does after a day out? Then, once the kids are tired, they go upstairs to get them ready for bed and BOOM! Shitfest!

I laugh aloud at the thought. DI Stanley must be going out of his tiny mind right now.

I open the box beside me on the sofa and pull out all the newspaper clippings. The contents are clearly important to the loved-up couple, but why?

As I read on, I realise Amanda Stanley AKA child #1 was the victim of her disgusting father's paedophile ring.

"Well, well, well." I push the box to one side and reach for my laptop.

Searching the internet for Dennis Kidd, the name of the paedophile in the articles, I'm surprised by the amount of recent entries, considering the newspaper clippings were from years ago.

According to Google, Dennis Kidd was murdered along with another couple of his sicko mates by his son, Andrew Pitt. Detective Adam Stanley was the arresting officer.

"Bingo!"

I continue reading. In a later article, Andrew was also killed after escaping from prison where he was on remand for the murders.

I have no doubt Amanda Stanley is Andrew's sister and fellow victim, but for some reason, nothing is coming up when I search for Amanda Pitt or Amanda Kidd.

Reading more of the articles, I see child #1 was in the throes of labour when the authorities discovered the abuse.

I think back to their older daughter, Mary. Her name was on some of the artwork in her bedroom. She's the right age to be Amanda's oldest daughter and looks the image of her. But according to the internet, Andrew's daughter was also called Mary, and she'd gone to live with her aunt after the murders. Does this mean DI Stanley is playing daddy to the product of child abuse and incest?

And, if the girl is in fact the child Amanda had given up for adoption, how the hell did she end up living as Andrew's daughter?

A delicious thrill runs through my veins.

In a last ditch effort to find something more about Amanda, I type their home address. Moments later, I punch the air above me as I read all about Amanda Flynn's interior design business.

A search for Amanda Flynn tells me how happily married she is to a man called Michael Flynn. Together, they have two children, Emma and Jacob. There is no mention of an older child.

This new information confirms my suspicions. Amanda Stanley-Flynn-Kidd, or whatever she was called, was sexually abused as a child and had a baby born of incest, which she gave up for adoption as soon as it was born. Andrew Pitt-Kidd, Amanda's brother, vanished aged fifteen and turned up years later with a child who looked the double of his sister, and she just so happened to be the exact age of Amanda's adopted child.

One final sweep of the internet for 'adopted girl is kidnapped', brings up an undeniable image of a young, three-year-old Mary.

I wonder if the detective knows his wife is harbouring an abducted child.

***

It was 4.00am before the forensics team finished their sweep of the place.

Once a sample of the faeces had been taken, Adam had the disgusting task of fishing the rest of it out of the toilet bowl and dumping it into a plastic bucket which he sent off with the team for disposal.

Afterwards, he and Frances cleaned the entire bathroom down, stripped the beds, and wiped the surfaces which were covered in fingerprint powder.

"Amanda will probably want to wash the clothes again," Frances said. "But she'll sort it out herself. At least it looks better than it did."

"Yeah, it is. And thanks. I owe you big time."

She put her arm through his. "Come on. Let's go to mine for a bit of shut-eye."

"I could stay here. It's not as if he'll come back." A thought suddenly occurred to him. "The key!" He rushed out of the back door and lifted the patio pot. The key had gone.

"That settles it. You're coming back with me. You can arrange for the locks to be changed tomorrow."

He bolted the back door from the inside, set the alarm and followed Frances out to the street. Once in his Mondeo, he followed Frances home. They parked outside on the street.

As they approached the house, the front door opened and Frances' mother-in-law came outside in her fluffy blue dressing gown and slippers. She put her hand on her chest dramatically. "Holly! I've been beside myself. Why did you run out like that?"

"That would be my fault, Mrs Frances."

"Oh, hello, Adam. Please call me Val. She just took off in the middle of the night and didn't even take her phone." She pulled Frances into her arms. "Are you alright, lovey?"

"I'm fine. Adam needed me, and I thought you were asleep."

"Are you alright, Adam?"

"I'm fine, thanks. I had an intruder in my house today, that's all."

Val gasped. "Oh, no. Did they take anything?"

"Not really. They left plenty." He grinned.

Val shook her head in confusion.

"It's not very nice. I'm sure Holly will explain later." He smiled. "Amanda's taken the kids to stay with her mother for the night and Fran—sorry, Holly said I could sleep on your sofa, if that's alright?"

"Of course it is, lovey. Come on in."

He was bone tired and followed Frances and Val through to the neat and tidy lounge.

"Can I just say how terribly sorry I was to hear about your son?"

"Thanks, lovey. Do you need anything? A glass of water? Tea?"

"To be honest, I'd rather just get my head down. I'm shattered."

"I'll find you a blanket," Holly said, rushing from the room.

Val pulled all the cushions off the sofa. "It pulls out into a bed. Can you help me?"

"You don't have to go to any trouble." Adam jumped forwards and took over from her. "I would've just crashed on top."

"Nonsense."

Holly reappeared, her arms filled with blankets and pillows, and the two women made up the bed.

"Now, if you need anything, help yourself," Frances said as they left the room.

He took off his trousers and crawled into bed. Although exhausted, he didn't think he'd sleep with the way his thoughts were whirring around his head. But the next thing he knew, Frances shook him awake.

"Wakey, wakey, lazy bones."

He sat up quickly and rubbed his eyes. "I'd swear you'd only left the room two minutes ago," he said.

"So you slept, I take it."

Adam grunted.

"There's a cup of Rosy-Lee here for you." She placed the cup on the carpet by the sofa. "Come through to the kitchen once you're up to a grilling."

"A grilling?"

"Yeah, and I don't mean of the bacon kind." She laughed at his puzzled expression. "Val wants to know everything."

He sniggered. "I'll be through in a sec."

He got dressed, folded the bed away and strolled through to the kitchen. "Morning ladies," he said, sounding brighter than he felt.

"I've just finished telling Val about our local psycho killer."

"I'm horrified he's been inside your house," Val said.

"He's ballsy. I'll give him that." He pulled out a stool and perched on it beside the breakfast bar.

"Can I make you some breakfast, lovey? Bacon and eggs, toast?"

"No thanks, Val. I need to go home. Amanda will be bringing the kids back to get them ready for school." He swigged at his tea.

"I was thinking. I could come in today for a couple of hours?" Frances said.

"No. No way." He shook his head, his lips in a firm line. "You need this time at home. Work will still be there after Steve's funeral. Tell her, Val."

"To be honest, Holly doesn't know how to sit around moping. If she feels up to it, maybe a couple of hours at work will do her good."

"Are you sure you don't mind?" Frances put her arm around the older woman's shoulders.

"Of course I don't mind. We've got an appointment with the funeral director this morning, and after that you may as well help to catch the nutter who seems fixated with your boss."

Adam got to his feet. "Well, if you're sure. I won't stand in your way. See you at the station later, then."

He drank the last of his tea and placed the cup in the sink.

Chapter 33

Amanda's car was parked up outside the house when he arrived.

"Where've you been, and what the heck's gone on here?" she demanded, as soon as he opened the front door.

"Long story. Where are the kids?"

"Upstairs, getting ready. I'm glad to see you managed to unblock the toilet."

He blew out his cheeks and nodded. "And I'm glad you weren't here to witness it, you'd still be chucking up now."

"I can imagine. But who cleaned the kitchen? They've done an amazing job."

"The intruder. I found this when I came home last night."

"You're kidding?"

"Nope. He's even rearranged our wardrobes."

"What lunatic breaks into someone's house to clean up?"

"A deranged one. I stripped the beds. If you can't manage to wash and dry the sheets, I'll take them to the laundry later."

"No. I'll do them. I feel strange now, though. Do you think he'll come back?"

He shrugged. "I hope not. But, he took the back door key, so I'll arrange for someone to come out and change all the locks. To be on the safe side."

"Where did you go?"

"I got a couple of hours' shut-eye on Frances' sofa. She insisted once she knew he had the key."

"Good."

"Oh, and you might find some fingerprint powder around the place. We cleaned afterwards, but there's a chance we missed some."

"I want to throw out all the food in the fridge. Do you think he's done something to it?" she said.

He shrugged. "I didn't think about that. Just use your own judgment." He kissed the top of her head. "I'm going for a shower. I need to get my skates on and head to the station."

*

The team, minus Frances, were at the station when he arrived.

"Right, we've had some further development."

They all stopped what they were doing and gathered round him.

"Miles Muldoon entered my house yesterday."

"What the hell!" Cal said.

"He went through every drawer and cupboard, rearranging each. He's taunting me. He also left a pile of shit in my toilet."

"This guy is repulsive!" Julie said, disgusted.

"He sure is. Anyway, I had the place swept for fingerprints, DNA etc. But I'm in no doubt this was our guy."

"How did he gain access?" Ginger Dave rubbed his head with his knuckles.

"I left a key under the plant pot for Frances. She said she might go around if she needed some space. So I didn't set the alarm or anything. How he found this out, I have no idea."

"This is getting creepy now. I've never heard of anything like it." Julie shuddered.

Les rubbed her arm. "It's highly unusual, but we'll get him. He's too cocky, and he's bound to slip up sooner or later."

"Let's hope he does. I'd die on the spot if anybody went through my house." Julie sighed.

"Cal, could you arrange for a locksmith to change all the locks at my house? The bastard took the key with him."

"Will do, boss."

The others dispersed while Adam printed off several images he'd taken of his house and added them to the board.

"That's not normal!" Cal said, coming up behind him. "What kind of monster can fill a bowl with turd, like that?"

"I've got no idea. It looks like he's saved all his waste up for a month." Adam shook his head as though trying to dislodge the memory. "I had to pull the lot out with my hands. It wouldn't flush away."

"Whoa, boss!" Cal gagged.

Adam chuckled. "How do you think I felt? Oh, and Frances intends to come in later, just for a couple of hours."

"Are you sure she's up to it?"

"She insisted. I'll take her for a drive out, maybe visit Sally Kemp and Catherine Bailey, give them an update."

Cal answered the internal phone as it rang. "Okay, hang on a minute." He held the handset to his chest. "Someone's left an envelope for you downstairs."

"Okay, I'll run down now."

PC Ryan Duncan held an envelope up for Adam when he got down to the front desk.

"Oh, cheers, Dunc. Who dropped it off?"

"I don't know. I just found it sitting there." He pointed to the side of the counter.

"That's odd."

"Not really, we've been flat tack already this morning. They may have got tired of waiting."

"No problem. Thanks, mate."

Adam opened the envelope as he jogged up the stairs back to the office, but stopped in his tracks as he pulled out the contents. His stomach dropped.

Stuffing the papers back into the envelope, he marched through the open area to his office and slammed the door. Once he was safely behind his desk, he opened the envelope again.

Several sheets of paper were folded together. The top sheet showed an image of a little girl eating an ice-cream. But, it was the caption that caused his blood to run cold.

Could Mary Pitt be the missing toddler, Bella Sullivan?

Page after page of newspaper articles followed with details of Dennis Kidd's trial and subsequent murder. The mention of Child #1 had been highlighted in yellow and the words *this is Amanda* written in ink at the side of the paper. The article also mentioned a baby born of incest, which was highlighted too, and the words *this is Mary* written beside it, in carefully printed handwriting.

More articles showed Andrew's arrest and death, and stated his daughter had gone to live with her aunt. *Mary and Amanda* had been written, in the same handwriting, beside it.

Finally, there were clippings of the original abduction of three-year-old Bella Sullivan.

He picked up the phone and dialled his wife. She answered almost immediately.

"Amanda. We have a problem."

Chapter 34

Amanda almost flaked out on the spot. Nobody knew she was Child #1. The police had been careful to keep her name out of the news.

When Andrew came back on the scene, he confessed to Amanda he had kidnapped Mary from her abusive, drug-addicted, adoptive parents. He told her how he took the child to France with fake documents. He returned a couple of years later, met and married Judith who treated Mary as her own. But Judith became sick which, when added to the news of their dad's release, caused Andrew to flip out and murder their childhood abusers one by one.

Poor Mary had had to deal with the death of her mother at the same time her father went missing, and Amanda didn't want to add to the girl's distress. How could an eleven-year-old girl cope with the knowledge she was born of such awful circumstances, so Amanda made the decision to keep Andrew's confession to herself.

After Adam arrested Andrew, she worried her brother's mental state might drop her in the poop, so she eventually confided the truth to Adam, which was overheard by Holly and Sandra. Only four of them in the whole world knew the truth, and she would trust each of them with her life.

How could somebody else work out the truth?

"So, what are they demanding?" Amanda said.

"They haven't, yet."

"This can't be happening, Adam. We can't allow Mary to discover the truth. It'll ruin her. She's already been through much more than she should've."

"Well, at this stage nobody else knows about the letter. We just need to wait and see what happens from here."

"I don't want you losing your job. If push comes to shove, I'll say I told nobody," she said.

"If push comes to shove, we act shocked. How can they prove Andrew told you?" Adam argued.

"Why would they send this evidence to you and not your boss?"

"To mess with my mind. Amanda, check the cupboard under the stairs. I think this might be the handiwork of Miles Muldoon again."

She reached the cupboard in a couple of strides and stared at an empty space instead of the treasured box she'd kept there. She gasped. "Oh, no, Adam. He's taken the box."

"That explains everything, then. He's found everything he needed in that fucking box."

She couldn't talk. Her mind was in chaos. "I—I'm sorry, Adam," she eventually uttered.

"No, I'm sorry. I shouldn't have snapped at you. When I get my hands on Muldoon, God help him. I'll call you later."

She hung up, and sat down on the sofa in a daze.

Then she hit redial. "Can you come over, Sandra? I need you urgently."

***

When Frances turned up, Adam called her into his office.

Cal, who'd been standing with her, opened his mouth to speak but Adam cut him off. "Not now, Cal." He slammed the office door.

"What was that all about?" Frances asked.

"Sit down."

He walked around the desk and shoved the envelope towards her. "Look at this."

She gasped, her eyes racing over the pages. "How?"

"Somebody left this for me in reception today."

"Who?"

"Good question. It just appeared on the counter."

"Can't we look at the CCTV?"

"I don't want to make a scene. If I do then everyone will ask what's in the envelope and I can't allow that to happen."

"Fuck. Any idea who would do this?"

"It was Muldoon. He took a box belonging to Amanda that had all her childhood details in it. I haven't a clue how he connected it to Mary, but he did."

"This is terrible. What are you gonna do about it?"

"I can't do anything right now. I have to hope his taunting is just aimed at me. Proving he's a better detective than I am, maybe?"

Frances bit her lip. "What the hell is wrong with this maniac?"

Cal tapped on the door. His closed face told Adam he was offended with him for snapping at him earlier.

"Put that lot away," he said to Frances. "Come in, Cal."

The usually bubbly young man now spoke with tight lips. "DCI Williamson is on the phone."

"Okay, I'll take it. Put him through."

Cal stomped back to his desk. Moments later Adam's desk phone rang.

"Good morning, sir."

"Stanley, we need to talk."

"If it's about the extra surveillance on Sally Kemp's house, I tried to call you, sir, but—"

"It's not, although I'm instructing you to cancel that with immediate effect."

"What is it, then?"

"I need to meet with you urgently. I have several meetings I can't get out of, but I can fit you in at three this afternoon."

"As you know, I'm actually in the middle of an urgent case at the moment, sir. Can you tell me what it is you need to see me about?"

"Just be here. 3.00pm on the dot."

"Will do, sir."

"What was that all about?" Frances asked, once he'd hung up.

"He puffed his mouth out and shook his head. "I've got no bloody idea. I've been summoned to HQ at three o'clock." He rubbed his face with both hands. "I'll be glad when today's over, I can tell you that much."

Frances smiled, uncomfortably.

He pushed his seat back. "Come on. Let's go for a drive. Someone must know more than they're telling us."

He walked out of his office just as Cal hung up the phone. "There were no useable fingerprints collected from your house, boss. But the hair and the faeces are a match for Muldoon."

"Thanks, Cal. And I'm sorry about before. This case is getting under my skin." He smiled awkwardly.

Cal shrugged, his face tight and inexpressive. "It's fine. Don't worry about it."

Adam rolled his eyes as he turned back to Frances. "Okay, we're off to see Sally Kemp and Catherine Bailey. Call me if anything else comes up."

As they left the building, Adam turned to Frances. "How did the meeting with the funeral director go?"

"Okay, I think. I'm crap at that kind of thing so Val took over. I don't care what kind of casket he has. Nothing will bring him back."

"I know, but some people find that kind of thing a comfort."

"I guess. This is something Val needs to do for her son. Whatever she wants is fine by me."

As they approached the car, Adam pressed the key fob to open it. "That's very selfless of you, Frances. I'm sure it means a lot to Val. When is the funeral?"

"Next Tuesday at 11.00am. Do you think you can make it?"

"Of course, I can make it. I may not have known Steve very well, but I'll be there for you."

"Thanks, Adam."

Chapter 35

They arrived at the Kemp household a few minutes later.

Sally opened the door with tears in her eyes. "Come in, come in. I was about to call you, detective. I just found an envelope that had been shoved through the door."

Adam raised his eyebrows at Frances and stepped inside the entrance hall. He followed a visibly shaken Sally through to the lounge.

She handed him an envelope that looked similar to the one he'd received. His heart thrashed about in his chest as he opened it up.

He found two photographs inside, and Adam breathed a sigh of relief that they had nothing to do with Mary.

An image showed a man lying in bed, with Sally sitting on a chair beside him. On closer inspection, he could tell the photograph had been taken through a diamond-leaded window.

"Is this your dad?"

She nodded. "Taken from outside Daddy's bedroom last night."

"Are you sure the photos were taken last night?"

"I'm positive," she snapped, gasping for breath. "Look at the blouse I'm wearing. I only bought it a couple of days ago. I wore it for the first time yesterday."

In the second image, Sally stood over her father, wiping his mouth.

Adam replaced the images in the envelope and handed it to Frances. "We'll need to take these with us."

Sally nodded.

"Did you notice one of our cars outside last night?" Frances asked.

"Yes. Just after these photos were taken, I took the officer a flask of tea before going to bed. I didn't see anything, but I reckon he was still there. He could've fucking attacked me." Her tone escalated with every word spoken, and she gripped Frances' outstretched hand.

"Okay, okay. Calm down," Frances said. "He didn't hurt you, and, like you said, he could have if he wanted to."

Sally nodded.

"It's strange the officer didn't see him though. Is your father's room at the back of the house?"

Sally nodded. "Yes. There are two windows, but the angle of this photograph means he took it from the side window."

"Can you show us before we go?"

"Yes. I would prefer you didn't go inside his room."

"From outside will do for now."

"Okay. Oh, I'm sorry I didn't even ask you what you're here for."

Frances looked at Adam to take it from there.

"We have bad news, I'm afraid. The DCI cancelled the surveillance."

"Really? So Miles could just walk in here and slice us to ribbons for all you care?"

"That's not entirely fair. It's not up to me, Sally. But like Detective Frances said, if he wanted to, he would've done it already."

"I hope you're right."

"But we're no closer to finding him although he's been taunting us all weekend, and now he's doing the same to you. Can you think of anybody at all who might be hiding him?"

"Honestly, I can't. He wasn't that close to anybody except me, and of course Lana. Albeit briefly."

"Hopefully he'll slip up before too long." Adam turned to leave. "Can you show us to your father's window?"

They walked out the front door and down the left-hand side of the detached house.

"He took the photo from here." Sally pointed to a narrow diamond-leaded window.

Adam glanced through it at the frail man in the bed. He didn't appear to have moved since the photograph was taken.

A chubby, dark-haired nurse, sitting beside him, turned to see what they were up to. Sally waved at her, and she smiled and turned to face her patient again.

"Look." Frances crouched down beside the square of soil below the window.

A clear set of men's size nine or ten footprints faced the window.

Adam took a number of photographs on his phone. "I'll get someone over to take an impression of these prints, too." He put the phone back in his pocket.

"Okay, thanks, detectives. I know I sounded petulant in there, but I truly appreciate your vigilance and I'm sure you'll catch Miles soon."

Adam wasn't so sure.

*

At the gym, the receptionist told them Catherine Bailey had taken some time off work, so they drove to Catherine's brother's house opposite the park.

Two small girls played with a tea set in the front garden beside the scruffy caravan that, considering the flat tyres with weeds growing through the wheels and the back half of the caravan, must have been there for years.

"Hello, young ladies. Is your mummy home?"

The girls jumped to their feet and ran inside without saying a word.

Catherine Bailey appeared at the front door, wiping her hands on a towel. "Oh, hi. I hope it's good news."

"I'm afraid not. We know Miles is still in the area, but he's proving very difficult to pin down. We wondered if you'd experienced any unexplained occurrences. Anything at all?"

"Not that I know of. But there are five adults and three kids staying in this tiny house. I don't know if I'd recognise any unexplained occurrences if I fell over them. I want to go home and get back to work. What do you think?"

"I think it's safer if you stay here for a while longer. I'm sure we'll catch up with him soon."

"I'll give it two more days and then I'm going home. If I stay here much longer, you might have another murder to investigate."

Adam smiled. "I'll keep you informed of any developments, Catherine. In the meantime, have you had a chance to think of anybody, no matter how vague, who might help to hide Miles?"

"No. I'm sorry. He didn't have many friends like I've already said. All he did was work when we were together."

"Okay. If you think of anything at all, I'd appreciate you getting in touch."

"Without a doubt. I want him caught more than anybody. Believe me."

They called in to Pinevale Publishing on their way back to the station. The young receptionist, with the drawn on eyebrows, recognised them as they entered.

"Ah, detectives. I was just thinking about you."

"Intriguing. And why's that?"

"I've been telling my boss, Julia Rothwell, about all the developments."

"Is she here, then?"

"Afraid not, sorry. She's gone out to meet with a client."

"Has she heard anything from Miles, do you know?"

"No, nothing. She's as baffled as we are."

"And I suppose you've heard nothing either?"

She shook her head. Her fine blonde hair shimmied. "Sorry."

They turned to leave.

"Oh, detective," she called. "Do you know when Lana's funeral is being held?"

Adam shook his head. "I've not heard anything, I'm sorry. I'll ask my assistant to find out."

"I'd appreciate that. Thanks."

Adam nodded and they headed for the door.

He turned to Frances as they approached the car. "I feel like we're just kicking tyres. We've got absolutely nothing to go on."

"We know who it is. The fact he's in hiding isn't our fault and someone has got to know where he is. His face is plastered all over the news, so surely it's just a matter of time before somebody recognises him."

***

Amanda burst into tears when she opened the front door.

"Hey, hey. What's happened?" Sandra rushed in, dropped her bag and coat in the hall, and pulled Amanda into her arms.

After a couple of minutes, Sandra stepped back and scanned the younger woman's face. "Are you going to tell me what's wrong?"

Amanda shook her head and nodded to the kitchen. "There's someone here, changing the locks. Let's go in the lounge."

She closed the door and told Sandra about the envelope Adam had received.

"Blimey. What a mess," she said.

"What if he tells someone else? What if they take her off us? The poor girl will be distraught."

"Now, come on. We don't know it'll come to that. You're just getting yourself in a state over nothing."

"How can you say it's nothing? If Adam's bosses find out, he could lose his job."

"You know what I mean. Nobody's been told yet, except Adam. Adam thinks there's a good chance Muldoon won't tell anybody else. You've got to hope he's right. But getting worked up about it won't help anybody."

"I know you're right. I just can't help it. The more I try to protect poor Mary, the more trouble seems to be thrown her way."

"She's tougher than she looks that one. She'll be alright, whatever comes of this."

"I hope you're right. She asked me the other day if I was her mum and I lied to her face. If she finds out, she'll never trust me again."

"But, like Adam said, you'd have to say you didn't know. As far as you know, Mary is Andrew's daughter. Say it."

"Mary is Andrew's daughter."

"Good girl. It's important you stick to that version. You've too much to lose otherwise.

Chapter 36

Adam arrived at HQ with plenty of time to spare, but the DCI was running late. He gave an exaggerated sigh and sat outside the office to wait.

Over twenty minutes later, DCI Williamson rushed out of the lift carrying his briefcase and jacket. When he spotted Adam, he looked at his watch and hurried into his office.

"Come on in, Stanley. I've got another meeting in ten minutes, so we'll need to be quick."

Suits me, Adam thought. He always felt like a naughty schoolboy being called to the headmaster's office when the DCI summoned him.

Once they were both seated, Adam launched into a detailed report of the last couple of days.

DCI Williamson held his hand up stopping Adam mid-sentence. "Interesting as this all sounds, Stanley, I didn't get you here to discuss the case."

"You haven't? Then why *am* I here?"

He opened the top drawer beside him and brought out an envelope identical to the ones he and Sally had received. Adam's stomach dropped to his boots.

"When I arrived this morning, I found this on my desk." He plopped the envelope down in front of Adam.

Adam reached for it trying to keep his hands from shaking. His boss watched him closely while he pulled the papers out. They were identical to the ones he'd received that morning.

"What the hell?" Adam said, frowning as he gave an Oscar-winning performance.

"Exactly my reaction when I first read it. But looking into the case, I discovered a child called Bella Sullivan was indeed abducted aged three years old. Her parents adopted her as a newborn. A couple of days after your wife gave birth to her baby, in fact."

Adam wiped his forehead with the back of his hand and battled with what his next move would be. Come clean, or lie through his teeth?

"But you know this, don't you, Stanley?"

"Erm..." He shook his head. "I don't..."

"Oh, sure you do. Your wife must've told you that Mary's her firstborn child."

Adam sat upright in his chair. "I'm sorry, sir. But this is the first I've heard about it. As far as Amanda and I are aware, Mary is her brother's child. Her mother, Judith, died of acute MS."

"There is no record of Judith Pitt ever giving birth. And in any case, Mary was five years old when Andrew met her."

"News to me, sir. I'm astonished, to be honest. Who sent this information to you?"

"I haven't a clue. But unfortunately I'm going to have to pass it on to the authorities to investigate." He pushed his chair back and got to his feet. "Now, if you don't mind, I need to get to my next meeting."

Dazed, Adam also got to his feet. "Where does this nonsense leave Mary?"

"I'd say that's something you'll need to take up with the social workers. I've given you a heads up, so I advise you to use the information wisely. But, in my opinion, you may be best to explain everything to Mary, just in case. Otherwise I'm sure this will come as one hell of a shock to her."

"As it has to me, sir." He left the office and calmly walked to the lift. Once on the ground floor he ran to the car as though his arse was on fire and pulled out his phone. He dialled his home number.

"Amanda, you're never gonna guess what's happened."

"What?" She sounded irate and close to snapping.

"The bastard's only sent the stuff about Mary to the DCI. I'm sorry, babe, but he's passing it over to the authorities."

***

"What the hell does that mean?" Amanda had an instant urge to vomit.

Sitting at the dining table, Emma and Jacob giggled at her bad language. She slammed down their colouring books and crayons. They'd just arrived back from the school run. Mary had stayed behind to help with the after school club. Her friend's mother promised to drop her off later.

"Your guess is as good as mine," Adam said. "I suppose they'll delve into Mary's birth certificate details and try to trace her *supposed* natural mother in France."

Sandra came downstairs from the bathroom, a frown fixed on her face.

Amanda sighed. "But there is no such person."

"I know that, and, when they find that out, the shit will well and truly hit the fan."

"Will they take her away from us? Because they can't! I'm still her only living relative, whichever way they look at it, unless you count our useless mother." Tears fell from her eyes, and she turned away from the kids.

Sandra jumped in and distracted them while Amanda headed for the lounge.

"Don't fret, Mand. I'm sure everything will work out in the end. It's not as if *we've* done anything wrong, is it?"

"But what about Mary?"

"They will want to do a DNA test soon, no doubt. You need to accept this is going to come out. And Mary will cope. She's a tough cookie. You'll see."

"Can we tell her soon? I'd rather she hears the truth from us."

"We'll tell her together, later."

As Amanda hung up, a griping pain in her stomach made her double over. She sucked the air in over her teeth as she rubbed the base of her bump.

After a couple of minutes, she wiped her eyes and joined the others.

Sandra eyeballed her questioningly when she entered.

She glanced at the kids busily colouring at the table and, with a nod of her head, indicated Sandra follow her to the kitchen sink.

"What's wrong?"

"Adam's DCI knows about Mary."

Sandra covered her mouth with her hand.

"Like you said earlier, we've all got to act dumb. But, would you lie if they question you?"

"Of course, I'll lie. You know I don't condone lying, but in this case there's no other option."

Amanda winced as another griping pain ripped through her.

"What is it, love? What's wrong?"

"Just a twinge. Baby must be pressing on a nerve."

"Go and put your feet up."

Amanda made as though to protest, but Sandra shot her down before she had a chance.

"You were up half the night worrying about Adam. You know I love looking after you all."

Amanda nodded and headed back to the door. "I'll just snatch ten minutes rest until this twinge goes away. I feel quite breathless."

"Shall I run you a bath? It may help relieve the discomfort, and warm water is supposed to aid in repositioning unborn babies."

"You know, I'd love a nice soak in the tub, but I'll run it. Thanks, Sandra."

She waddled upstairs cradling the underside of the bump. The baby was pressing down hard into her pelvis.

She turned the taps on, tossed in a vanilla scented bath bomb, and waited for the bath to fill before stripping off her blouse, leggings and underwear.

Stepping into the fragrant water, she suddenly groaned and leaned heavily on the side of the tub as the pain grumbled across her stomach again. She'd had Braxton Hicks contractions with each of her other babies, but she couldn't remember them being so intense.

Once the pain subsided, she sank into the yummy smelling foam and closed her eyes. Savouring the warmth as the water filled her ears, she took a deep breath and ducked her head underneath, shutting out the world for a few seconds.

Moments later, she sat up straight and put her hand on her stomach, as another wave of pain approached. The whole bump tightened under her fingers and the intensity stopped her from breathing. They were getting worse. Something felt wrong.

Amanda quickly washed herself and got to her feet. As she reached for a towel, a sudden rush of water ran down her legs. She gasped and looked into the tub to check if it was just bath water, but the foam concealed all trace.

After patting herself dry, she headed to her bedroom and threw on a smock dress. She wadded a towel up in her underwear because fluid leaked from her with every step. After running a brush through her wet hair, she plodded down the stairs.

Sandra looked up from the table where the children were feasting on sausage and mash.

"My waters just broke!"

"Shoot! I'll call Adam."

Chapter 37

As Adam took the slip-road off the motorway heading for Pinevale, his phone rang.

"You need to come quick," Sandra said, in a panicked voice. "Amanda's in labour."

"She can't be. She's not due for weeks yet."

"Tell that to the little one when he gets here. Hurry."

"I'll be there in five minutes."

He hung up and slammed his hands on the steering wheel. Fuming, he blamed Amanda's premature labour on Miles-fucking-Muldoon. He'd get the crazy bastard off the street if it was the last thing he did.

Amanda walked down the path towards him as he pulled up.

As he got out, she suddenly doubled up and winced. He waited a few moments until the contraction passed, before helping her into the car.

"Here, put this on the seat," Sandra said, running ahead of them with a towel.

"Thanks, Sandra." Amanda panted. "Can you ring the hospital? Warn them we're coming."

"Of course." She turned to Adam. "Call me as soon as you know anything."

He nodded. "I will."

"Oh, and Mary should be home soon," Amanda called before closing her door.

"Don't worry about the kiddies. Just go." Sandra waved them off.

"I'm scared, Adam," Amanda said, as they turned the corner. "The baby's not due for another six weeks. What if..."

"Don't stress, Mand. They perform miracles these days."

Her hand shot out and gripped the fabric on his arm as another contraction washed over her.

Trying to keep calm, he blew out steadily controlled breath. He couldn't allow her to see how shit-scared he was.

He parked in a disabled space right at the hospital entrance and practically carried his wife inside.

Once Amanda was transferred to a bed, a young, brunette midwife strapped a baby monitor to her stomach and they all exhaled with relief when a steady thudding sounded from the speakers.

"Will he be okay?" Amanda asked.

"He's a little early, but he sounds nice and strong."

The examination of Amanda's cervix showed her to be seven centimetres dilated.

"Won't be long now, Mummy. He's an impatient little thing. I'll arrange for some Entronox."

"Entronox?" Amanda was confused.

"It's also known as gas and air. I'm sure you would have been offered it with your last children."

She nodded. "Yes. I wanted Pethidine too, but is there time?"

"Maybe not. Pethidine takes around thirty minutes to work, and baby is likely to arrive before then."

Amanda, clearly in pain, looked at Adam. She reached for his hand as another contraction began.

Adam held onto her and turned to the midwife for guidance.

"I'll get the gas, but start to pant through the contraction. It will help," she said.

Adam put one knee on the chair by the bed and crouched down next to his wife. "You can do it. Pant, baby. Pant." He began puffing out his breath in short bursts.

Each contraction seemed to double in intensity, and within twenty minutes Amanda was ready to push.

Adam stayed by her side feeling totally helpless.

Amanda's screams escalated within minutes. She dug her nails into his hand and held on with a vice grip, bringing tears to his eyes. She asked him to wipe her face with a face-cloth, then ripped the cloth from his fingers and launched it across the room.

His beautiful wife resembled someone possessed, and yet the midwife didn't bat an eyelid.

When they lifted the tiny dark-haired baby, he couldn't believe the range of emotions that coursed through him.

"It's a boy," the midwife said, tears glinting in her smiling eyes.

"You've done it, Mand. We've got a little boy."

She began to cry.

Adam cradled her head in his arms as the midwife whisked their baby away to the far side of the room.

He thought his heart would break while they waited for him to make a sound. When the first cry erupted, tears streamed down his face. He kissed Amanda tenderly.

The midwife wrapped the baby in a blanket and placed him in a Perspex crib. Another nurse wheeled the crib away.

"Where are they taking him?" he asked the midwife.

"Baby's lungs aren't properly developed yet, and he's very little, just four-and-a-half pounds. They're taking him to the Neonatal Unit to be on the safe side."

***

I pace the floor wishing I could be out there witnessing the wrath my cleverly placed correspondence must have caused. But I need to stay home for now.

The bang of a car door outside startles me, and I rush to the window more on edge than usual. I peer out into the darkness, and by the illumination of a streetlight I watch a man in a green, knitted jersey tuck a file under his arm and walk up the neighbour's path.

"Idiot," I mutter.

My stomach growls and I realise I haven't eaten a thing all day. I trudge through to the kitchen checking out the contents of the fridge before slamming the door in temper.

I settle on a can of baked beans and shove four slices of stale bread in the toaster. Pulling out two plates, one ceramic and one plastic, I proceed to prepare my speciality—beans on toast.

I take the plastic plate downstairs into the basement. Heading to the back of the room, I put the plate down while I open the hatch in the centre of another door. This room had been used in the past as a music studio, but evidence of that time is long gone.

"Grub's up," I say, sliding the plate inside the opening.

I hear shuffling sounds from within the room, and I slam the hatch closed before heading back upstairs.

As I step into the hallway, Dana Morgan, the fucking nosy nurse, is hanging around in the kitchen doorway. I hadn't even heard her arrive.

Her eyes dart from me to the basement door suspiciously.

"What do you want, Dana? I'm busy."

"Nothing." She shoves past me and struts through the door opposite.

I eat my food with gusto. Although nervous, I'm excited by what I plan to do later on this evening.

As I wash up the dishes and make a pot of tea, a thought occurs to me, and I smile. Taking a china cup and saucer from the glass cabinet, I fill it with the weak brew, topping it off with a drop of milk and carry it through the door Dana had vanished through.

"Knock, knock," I say, walking straight in. "I made you a cup of tea. Don't say I never give you anything."

The fat nurse jumps to her feet and takes the cup from me. "Oh, lovely. Thanks."

"How's the patient?" I ask.

"Sleeping deeply. Has he been like this all day?" Dana says.

"Yes. But that's a good thing, isn't it?" I ask, bending over the supine body of my father. "At least he's not in any pain, if he's sleeping."

"Exactly."

I kiss his warm, leathery cheek. "Hey, Daddy. It's me, Sally. Are you awake?

***

Adam arrived home to an empty house.

A scribbled note from Sandra, saying she'd taken the kids to her house and asking him to call when he got in, was propped up beside a plate of spaghetti bolognese on the kitchen table.

He nuked the food, took it through to the lounge, and ate in front of the TV. He felt exhausted, emotional, and fucking angry at Muldoon. If anything happened to his baby, he wouldn't be responsible for his actions when they caught the cocky bastard.

He'd left Amanda sleeping soundly in the hospital after spending a couple of hours beside the incubator watching the rise and fall of their baby boy's chest. The nurses said he had a good chance, only needing special care until his lungs were stronger.

He glanced at his watch, almost 11.00pm. Too late to call Sandra. He would have an early night and speak to her in the morning.

He kicked off his shoes and put his feet up, pulling a blanket off the back of the sofa. He would stay where he was for now.

Chapter 38

I glance at Dana, sipping on her tea like a fucking queen bee, and I smile. My fingertips stroke the outline of the blade through the material of my trousers and I walk around the bed, stopping just behind the nosy nurse. Once out of sight, I slide the knife from my pocket and hold it behind my back.

Dana drains her cup and leans forward to place it on the table beside her.

"Here. I'll take that," I say, brightly.

She turns, holding the crockery out to me, and her smile freezes as her eyes rest on the knife.

"And you can take this."

With one fluid movement, the blade tears through the soft double-chin, going deep, all the way to the handle.

It seems as though time slows as the cup and saucer fly through the air. The saucer lands with a clatter on the occasional table beside her. The cup smashes on the floor.

Dana's eyes, bright at first, stare accusingly at me before the lids flutter and close.

I giggle, glancing at my father to make sure the commotion hasn't disturbed him. He's still out of it.

I assist Dana down onto the carpet with the knife still stuck in her neck. When I pull the blade away, I jump back as blood squirts from the gaping wound soaking the walls and the carpet and even the stark white sheets on my father's bed.

I admire my handiwork for a few minutes until the ferocious pumping blood soon settles to a pitiful spurt and then a dribble. I'm certain Dana's heart has stopped beating.

I approach my father, the man I used to look up to and adore, and I kiss his cheek before swiping the blade across his throat.

His eyes open for a split second and then close again as his life's blood oozes away.

In the utility room, I wash my hands and the blood-covered knife under the tap. I strip off my clothes. Although they're not totally covered in blood, even a hint of their spattered DNA on me would cause suspicion, and that was the last thing I wanted. After shoving my clothing into the machine, I put it on a boil wash before jumping in the shower.

Singing at the top of my voice.

Dun-dun-dun, another one bites the dust.

Dun-dun-dun, another one bites the dust.
And another one's gone and another one's gone,
Another one bites the dust.
Hey, I'm gonna get you too, another one bites the dust.

I laugh and laugh.

Once I'm dry, I pad up the stairs to my bedroom where I choose a classy white silk trouser suit for my next performance, something that will showcase the scene beautifully.

Thrilled, I style my hair and apply my makeup as though I'm going out for a night on the town. A pair of low-heeled strappy gold-coloured sandals finishes off the outfit. Perfect.

Back in the utility room, I pick up the knife from the draining board and wipe it carefully. I rummage through the laundry and grab a pair of my dad's casual trousers and a T-shirt. I head back down to the basement.

Opening the door of the studio, I smile at the pathetic state of the man curled on the mattress on the tiled floor. He shields his eyes from the light.

"Get up," I snap.

He slowly rolls onto all fours and groans as he gets to his feet.

"Out here now. Any funny business, and you'll know about it."

He shuffles forwards wafting a putrid stench with him.

I screw my face up in disgust. "You've filled the fucking pot again. You knock me sick. Do you know that?"

Still he makes no sound, but shrinks away from my harsh voice lifting his arm to cover any blows that may head his way.

I sneer at the snivelling weak bastard. My dad brought me up with the view a man should be strong and tough. Not like this weak-willed piece of piss in front of me.

"Get out here."

He watches me warily and does as I ask, not once taking his eyes off the knife.

"Here!" I throw my dad's clothing at him. "Put them on."

Once dressed, I shove him towards the stairs. "Walk!" I yell.

He stumbles then rights himself, taking slow shuffling steps.

I push the tip of the blade against the back of his neck. "Move, you fucking idiot."

He cries out and climbs up the steps a little faster, shaking and blubbering uncontrollably.

I smile, more than a little excited by what is to come. My entire body tingles in anticipation.

When we reach the hallway he trips and shoots across the floor in a heap.

I place a well-aimed kick at his stomach. He groans and retches, firing partially chewed beans and soggy clumps of toast all over the immaculate cream carpet.

I roar, close to losing it there and then, but stop myself in time.

"Get up!" I kick him in the pants, shoving him further forwards, and his face smears through the vomit. "Getup!" I scream.

"Sally, please. Tap-tap."

I laugh at his attempt to trick me into thinking this could be blamed on a sex game. "We're way beyond your fucking safe-word, Miles."

For the past two years, he had lived as my submissive until he took a liberty and tried to leave me for that skanky, wimpy bitch, Lana. It began as a joke, a little excitement to spice up our bordering-on-boring sex life. And it developed from there. At work, he was still my superior, but as soon as we arrived home, I would take charge, often locking him up in a box like a dog.

The night he called me, after Lana had dumped his sorry arse, he begged me to take him back. I told him to leave the hotel and all his belongings, bringing only the money he'd withdrawn for the mortgage, and walk to the main road where I would pick him up.

He didn't question it. We'd often role-played and re-enacted scenes from movies, and I knew he'd think I'd forgiven him.

He went along with everything. Coming to Daddy's house had thrown him briefly, but still he entered and allowed me to lead him down to the basement. He obeyed my instructions to strip his clothes off, and he stepped willingly into the soundproof studio.

He even continued to believe it was all part of his punishment, and, as usual, I would release him the next morning in time for work. His face had been a picture when he realised I intended to hold him prisoner indefinitely.

I cleaned the shit pot out every day, one handed, holding the knife to his throat with the other hand.

I kept the stinking excrement in double zippered plastic bags and inside a plastic container.

I even took several of his hairs to place here and there around the crime scenes and voila, the perfect murder.

My father used to discuss his cases with me and gloat about how they'd been solved, so using this information I was always careful to cover my own hair with a shower cap as well as a hoodie. And I always wore gloves. Besides, who would ever suspect me of carrying out such grisly murders?

Miles half-crawls, half-staggers into the kitchen. As he reaches the sink, he turns to face me. "Sally, please." His voice is hoarse and scratchy. "I've learned my lesson. I'll never—"

"Save it." I step towards him and plunge the blade into the centre of his chest.

He looks down at the knife handle, confusion crossing his face, then back at me. He stumbles forward, his arms reaching out in front of him, before dropping to his knees. Moments later, he body-slams onto the white Italian tiles. A beautiful crimson pool spreads butterfly-like around him.

The rich, metallic scent fills my nostrils and I sigh before pulling out my phone.

***

The ringing droned on and on into his brain, but he couldn't understand why it wouldn't stop. Feeling exhausted and bone-weary, he eventually forced his eyes open and reached to the coffee table for his phone.

"Stanley," he croaked.

The screams on the other end of the phone had him on his feet in a split-second. "Amanda?" Totally disorientated, he grabbed his keys and headed out the front door still believing something was wrong with their baby.

"It's Sally. I've killed him! I've killed Miles! Please come."

As he sped to the outskirts of town, he called for back-up and an ambulance to meet him at the property. He parked just outside the gate. All the downstairs rooms were lit from within.

The front door flew open, and Sally ran from the house covered in blood screaming like a maniac.

He gripped her by the shoulders trying to see where the blood was coming from. "Are you injured, Sally?"

She shook her head, her mouth opening and closing wildly.

"Calm down, Sally. Is he inside?"

She nodded pulling away from him as he stepped closer to the house. "No, no! I can't go back in there." Her legs gave out on her, and she fainted almost landing at his feet, but he caught her in time.

Lifting her into his arms, he carried her to his car and eased her into the passenger seat. He removed his jacket and tucked it around her. "Stay there, I'm going in."

He followed Sally's bloody footprints through to the kitchen. There he discovered the body of a man lying face down on the floor. Considering the amount of blood he'd lost, Adam didn't expect him to be alive, but he checked for a pulse anyway. Nothing.

Before leaving, he decided to check on Sally's father. He was horrified by what he found. The dead body of a nurse lay beside the bed. A deep knife wound in her neck had clearly severed the carotid artery given the force and range of the blood splatter.

At first Adam thought Charlie Kemp had been covered in the nurse's blood until, on closer inspection, he realised the old man had also suffered a fatal knife wound to the throat.

Three dead bodies, but thankfully the killer was one of them.

Hearing sirens approach, he stepped outside to greet them.

Chapter 39

Adam led the SOCO team to the bodies and, a short time later, he returned to Sally who was still in his car.

"We need to get you checked out," he said. "An ambulance is waiting to take you to the hospital."

Sally stared at him with bulging eyes. "No, please. I don't want to go in an ambulance. Please don't make me."

"Hey, hey. I understand you're scared, but Miles is gone now. He can't hurt you anymore."

She needed to calm down before he could attempt to question her.

His heart went out to the trembling wreck before him. She no longer looked like the incredible beauty he'd met less than a week ago. Her gently-teased curls now looked as though they had been backcombed by a bunch of hormonal monkeys.

She rocked back and forth, whimpering and blubbering. She clapped her hands to her ears and flinched at every sound she heard outside of the car.

"I'll tell you what. If you don't mind waiting here, I'll take you to the hospital myself. Is that okay?" He spoke slowly, hoping the words would register.

She nodded, curling into a foetal position, her eyes shut tight.

"I'll be back as soon as I can. Is there anything you need from the house?"

She shook her head, staring down at her bloody hands.

"What about your keys and purse?"

Her eyes darted back to him. "My handbag and keys."

He locked the car and dashed back to the house which had been cordoned off with tape already. He went inside looking for Sally's things. He found them in her bedroom.

The Scenes of Crime Officers wasted no time. They methodically went about their business.

Not wanting to get under their feet, Adam waited outside the front door until Felix, the medical examiner, arrived a short time later.

"Sorry to call you out so late, Felix. But you'll be pleased when I tell you one of the victims is our killer."

Felix looked gaunt and grey. "Thank Christ for that. I was just contemplating retirement on the way over. I think I'm getting too old for this lark."

"You? Too old? Never." He patted the older man on the shoulder and escorted him inside.

Soon after, he returned to his car.

Sally jumped up, her posture rigid, and her eyes wild.

"It's alright, just me. I'm taking you to the hospital, remember?"

She nodded, her whole body trembling.

He shoved the handbag beside her and ran around to the driver's side. "Can you put your seatbelt on, Sally?"

She slowly clicked the belt in place.

The ambulance officer at the scene had called ahead, so a doctor was waiting for them when they arrived.

They took her into a private room and examined her, confirming what Adam already suspected—she was uninjured but suffering from shock.

They arranged to admit her and took her upstairs to a ward.

Adam stayed until she seemed calm enough to talk. He was careful what he said, not wanting to set her off again.

"Can you tell me briefly what happened tonight, Sally?"

Instant tears filled her eyes. "After the nurse arrived at eight o'clock, I made some beans on toast for my dinner, then went up to my room. I lay on the bed dozing for a while. Maybe I even slept. I can't remember." Her eyes flashed panic.

"That's okay. Take your time." His softened voice seemed to assure her, and she nodded.

"I ran a bath. I couldn't tell you the time, sorry. I didn't look at the clock."

"What happened then?"

"I soaked in the bath, reading my book. Afterwards, I got dressed and came back downstairs planning to say goodnight to Daddy." She took a deep breath and began to tremble again.

"He can't hurt you anymore, remember?" He placed his hand on her arm, and she grabbed his fingers and held them tight.

"Miles appeared from nowhere. He seemed different, crazed somehow..." She squeezed her eyes tight.

"Go on."

"Then I noticed the knife in his hand. I tried to run, but he grabbed my hair," she squeaked, and huge tears rolled down her face. "I couldn't help it. I vomited on the carpet in the hall."

Adam handed her a fresh tissue.

She took it gratefully and wiped her face before continuing. "He let go of me. He hated things like that. When I stood back up I jumped away from him..."

She stopped crying. Her words seemed to be giving her strength.

"That's when he lunged for me, slipping on my vomit." She took several rasping breaths, her eyes shut tight.

"You're alright. Look at me, Sally." He stroked her hand trying to encourage her to calm down.

She opened her eyes and stared into his.

He nodded, and she too nodded her head.

"What happened next?" he asked, gently.

"He crashed down and the knife went skittering across the kitchen floor. We raced to get it. But I was on my feet. He wasn't..." She shook her head and drew in several deep breaths.

"You got there first?"

"I had no time to think. It was him or me. I shoved the knife towards him, but I didn't intend to kill him." Her pleading eyes begged him to believe her.

"Go on," he said.

Sally rubbed her eyes as if trying to erase the vision. "It was like slow motion. He just fell to his knees, his arms outstretched, still trying to grab hold of me. Then he dropped to the floor."

Her body tremors returned and once again Adam tried to reassure her.

"All that blood. I knew he must be dead. The nightmare was finally over. I got the phone and called you right away. I didn't know about Daddy and Dana. I went in and found them after I called you."

Huge sobs wracked her body. "Poor Daddy. He was dying anyway. Why would he butcher him like that?"

"I've no idea why he did half of the things he did this past week, Sally. But I need to thank you. If you hadn't found the courage to put an end to him, I guarantee he would've gone on to kill you. And goodness knows how many others."

*

Before leaving the hospital, Adam found himself back at the baby unit. He watched through the outer window as the efficient nurses fussed over the precious infants in their care, weighing soiled nappies, closely monitoring and recording each change. From his position, he could hear the beeps of the highly calibrated machines that were keeping each one of the babies alive.

Baby Stanley had his name printed on a colourful card hanging on the side of his incubator. Although teeny, he wasn't the smallest baby in the unit, which Adam found encouraging. Naked, apart from a miniscule nappy, the scrawny, wrinkled little person, with his shock of black hair and face like ET, was the most beautiful creature he'd ever laid eyes on.

An immense sadness hung over him. Not normally religious, he found himself praying to God that his perfectly formed son would make it through the next few days.

Baby was being fed by a drip for now, but they wanted Amanda to begin expressing milk for when she could feed him properly.

Startled by a sudden movement at his side, he turned to see Amanda still dressed in her nightie. She had darker circles than usual under her eyes.

She slid her hand in his. "Hey, you. I thought you'd gone home hours ago."

"I did. Then I was called out." He put his arm around her and kissed the top of her head.

"Another murder?"

He nodded. "Three. One of them is Miles Muldoon, though. So at least he won't be killing anyone else."

She lifted her chin, her nostrils flaring. "I know it isn't very Christian of me to say so, but I'm glad he's dead. His vicious meddling caused me to go into early labour, and could cause Mary to be taken from us. To be honest, if he wasn't dead, I would be tempted to kill him myself."

He pulled her into his arms. "I feel the same. But he's not worth our anger. There's a little boy who needs all our attention right now."

She nodded. "I know. Let's go in?"

"In a minute. Have you thought of names?" he asked.

She nodded again. "I've been thinking about nothing else since he was born." Her eyes filled with tears as she looked up at him.

"What? What is it?"

"Just say if you don't want to and I'll understand. But I thought, maybe, Andrew?"

He wiped her tears away with his thumb, cupped her face, and kissed her softly on the lips. "I love it," he whispered.

"You do?"

He nodded. "It's perfect. Now let's go and see the nurses and ask them to add our son's name to his file.

Chapter 40

After spending a few minutes with the baby, Adam left for home swinging by the station briefly. He slid into bed, and set the alarm for 10.00am. That would give him three hours sleep. But no sooner had he closed his eyes when the shrill, peep-peep-peep, startled him awake. "Not again," he groaned.

He'd left the details of the night's events on Cal's desk, and knew Cal would inform the rest of the team. But he had some loose ends he needed to tie up, and he also wanted to check up on Sally. Then he planned to have a bit of time off with his family.

He showered and got dressed feeling more human than he had in days. As he opened the front door, two official-looking women walked down the path towards him.

"Mr Stanley?" said the older of the two. She had a pinched, thin face. Her brown hair was heavily streaked with grey and pulled into a tight knot. She wore an unflattering, pale-yellow trouser suit.

"Yes."

"Cordelia Brampton, Social Services. This is my colleague Debra Meadows."

The younger woman smiled, her face softened making her appear much friendlier and more approachable than her companion.

"This isn't a good time, I'm afraid. My wife had a baby last night and he's six weeks prem."

"Oh, I'm sorry. We won't keep you long. It's your wife we need to speak to, anyway. When will she be home?"

"I can't say. Hopefully in the next few days, but that's purely a guess." He smiled at the harsh-looking one, trying to get on her good side.

"But you do know why we're here?" she said.

"My boss received some information yesterday about how Mary, my wife's niece, may well be the daughter she put up for adoption years ago." He shook his head as though he disbelieved the whole thing.

"Yes, that's correct. This is a very delicate situation, as I'm sure you can imagine. May we come in for a moment?"

He glanced at his watch before nodding. "If you're quick. I also had several homicides last night and need to head back to the station."

"Oh, are you investigating *them*?" the younger woman said, in awe. "We were just listening to it on the radio on the way over."

"Yes, I am. Awful business." He beckoned them in and led them through to the lounge. Quickly picking up the plate from the floor beside the sofa and folding the blanket, he smiled apologetically.

The women sat side by side on one of the sofas and he perched on the arm of the chair. "So what will happen if there's any truth in the allegation?"

"We're not certain. It will depend greatly on how your wife feels about the situation. She gave the child up for adoption for reasons other than being too young, I believe?"

"Yes. That's correct. But Mary is part of our family now, and we'd like it to remain that way."

They both nodded.

"Well, that certainly makes our decision easier right now. If you're agreeable to Mary remaining with you while the investigation is conducted, we're happy to approve it."

"Of course we are. Mary will be devastated if she discovers there's a chance Judith and Andrew may not be her parents. She's been through so much as it is. We'd prefer she's not told any of this unless we find it's true. I mean, nobody even knows where this information came from in the first place. It could be a load of old codswallop for all we know."

"Yes, it could, but where children are concerned, we've got no choice but to look into each and every claim."

"Of course, I understand that. But I just want to stress to you how damaging this could be for Mary. She lost her mother and then found out her father, a man she adored, was on the run for murdering three people." He paused, hoping his words were striking a chord with them.

The younger woman hung off his every word, and tears filled her eyes.

Her friend didn't show any emotion. She took a deep breath and nodded. "Yes. That must have been terrible for her."

"Yeah, but that wasn't all. When, months later, her father was eventually caught, he escaped and snatched Mary. In his crazed state, he locked her in a wardrobe before he was fatally struck by a car. We found her in the nick of time. She was in a terrible state."

"We've read the file, Mr Stanley. And, believe me, we don't want the child to suffer any more than you do," the older woman said.

"I know. But I just want to reiterate, Mary is part of our family now. We love her and she loves us. If this information holds any truth whatsoever, she would still be in her rightful place, with us."

"Duly noted, sir. But unfortunately we don't make those decisions. We'll keep you informed of any developments in the meantime. That's all we can do." She got to her feet, and her young colleague followed suit.

He walked them to the door. "Thanks. I appreciate you're in a delicate position."

The older woman handed him her card. "We'll need to speak to Amanda. Please call us as soon as she feels up to it."

"Of course."

*

He called the hospital and was told Sally had discharged herself in the early hours. Then he tried Sally's mobile, but it went straight to voicemail. He left a message for her to call him.

Leaving the house, he called Frances on the way to the station.

"Hey, it's me."

"You must be like the cat that got the cream this morning," she said.

"You've heard, then?"

"Cal called me, but it's all over the news anyway. How did it go with the DCI?"

"Oh, shit. I meant to call you. A lot has happened since then. The DCI summoned me because Muldoon sent him the same information about Mary."

"Oh, no! What did you say?"

"I told him it was a load of rubbish, but of course he had to pass the information on."

"Fuck! I'm so sorry, boss."

"But that's not all. Amanda went into labour after I broke the news to her. She gave birth to a baby boy an hour or two later."

She gasped. "Oh, wow. I didn't think she was due for ages."

"She wasn't. She still had six weeks to go, but the baby's fine. He's in the Special Care Unit, they think he'll be okay."

"Thank God for that! Did you tell Cal?"

"To be honest, with everything else that went on last night, I didn't think to tell him. I'm on my way in now though."

"So am I. I'll meet you there. At least I can help you wrap everything up."

"Okay. See you soon."

He hung up and called Sandra.

"Hi. It's me. Just checking in."

"Adam, I was hoping you'd call. How's Amanda and the bubs?"

"When I left the hospital around six this morning, they were both fine. I'm heading to the station and then I'll pop back there to check on them. Did the kids get off okay this morning?"

"Yes, they were all little angels. Mary was a great help though. She had them up and dressed while I was making breakfast."

"Oh good. I don't have a clue where my day's going to take me. Will you be able to pick them up and take them back to yours again?"

"Of course. I planned to anyway."

"You're a Godsend. Do you know that?"

Sandra chuckled. "Give over, you little sweet talker. Listen, I wouldn't mind popping in to visit Amanda and the wee baby myself later, if you think she's up to it?"

"She'd love to see you. If you get there before me, tell her I shouldn't be too long."

"Will do."

Except for Sandra and his mum, he'd informed nobody of the baby's arrival. He would need to take some time out later and ring around everybody.

Chapter 41

A cute blue teddy and half a dozen balloons tied with blue ribbon were the first things he noticed when he walked into the office.

He laughed, surprised Frances had arrived before him.

"I'll buy something special for the baby as soon as I can," she gushed.

"Congratulations, boss." Cal handed him a huge cigar.

Delighted, Adam took the fragrant sausage-shaped object from him and chewed on it like Groucho Marx. "Thanks, mate. Is it Cuban?"

Cal nodded. "I only buy the very best. Did you know Cuban cigars are rolled between the thighs of virgins?"

Adam belched out a laugh. "Well, thanks for the thought—I think." He hugged them both before taking his briefcase through to his office.

"And what a fab result for the case." Cal was suddenly standing behind him at the door.

"Yeah, fantastic. Shame about Charlie Kemp and his nurse, though."

Cal shrugged. "I know, but at least the crazy bastard got his comeuppance."

"I suppose. Anyway, I plan to take a few days off now the case is closed and my son has put in an appearance."

"Great idea, boss."

Adam stepped towards his office then paused. "Oh, by the way, Cal, were the nurse's family informed?"

"Les and Julie went there first thing this morning. She lived with her grown up daughter."

"Okay, good." He followed Cal back out into the main office. "Anybody heard from Sally today?"

"No, nothing."

Adam sucked his teeth, thoughtfully. "She discharged herself earlier. I don't suppose she would go back to her dad's house until the place is cleaned up. The nurse bled out like a fountain. Plus the SOCO team were still at the scene when we left."

"Nasty. Maybe she went to her apartment?"

"I guess so. I'll swing by later."

His phone rang and he ducked back into his office for his mobile.

"Stanley, Felix here. Once again, well done wrapping up the case. This Muldoon fellow kept me busier than I've been in a long while."

"Cheers, mate. Yes, I'm aware it interrupted your golf on more than one occasion." Adam laughed.

"Now, now. You watch your tongue, young man, or I won't tell you what I called about."

"Okay, I'll be quiet. Go on, what is it?"

"Can you spare me a few minutes? There's something I want to show you."

Surprised, Adam scratched his head. "Yeah, but can't you tell me over the phone?"

"Easier to show you, if you don't mind?"

"Okay, I'll come over now."

He walked into the main office as Ginger Dave arrived. "Well done, boss. You got him."

"I can't take the credit for this one, Dave. It was down to Sally Kemp."

"Well, bloody good result. And what's all this?" He tugged the ribbon causing the balloons to bounce. "Did your missus have the baby?"

Adam smiled and nodded. "A little boy. But he's too early and will possibly be in hospital for a while."

"Congratulations! Are we doing a whip-round?" he asked the others.

Cal nodded. "Frances will be."

"Thanks, Dave. Right, folks, Felix has summoned me. Apparently he's found something he wants to show me."

"Ooh! Can I come?" Frances jumped to her feet.

"Be my guest. Although, are you sure? It might not be pretty."

"I'm fine. Come on, let's go."

They found Felix in his brightly lit, stark white examination room, dressed in blue scrubs with a white plastic apron over the top. They knocked on the window.

He spun around and pulled down his mask. His face lit up as he rushed towards them and ushered them inside excitedly.

"So, what is it?" Adam was eager to get this over with for Frances' sake.

"All in good time, my boy. Come this way." Felix peered over the wire-framed glasses that were perched on the end of his nose.

They followed him to a table draped in a blue sheet in the centre of the room.

"As I understand it, this man has been on the missing list for approximately one week, and in that time he's brutally murdered seven people. Is that correct?"

"Sounds about right," Adam said, not in the mood for Felix's theatrics.

Felix folded the sheet down, unveiling the upper body of Miles Muldoon.

Frances gasped.

Adam glanced at her, concerned.

She patted his arm and nodded she was okay.

"Now, what first alerted me that something didn't add up was the clothing which is spotlessly clean apart from his own blood spill. Having just killed two people, you'd expect him to be covered in his victims' blood too."

"Maybe he got changed afterwards," Adam said. "Sally was upstairs most of the evening, so if he was there for a while, she wouldn't have known."

Felix tipped his head in agreement. "Yes. But, if this guy is so worried about cleanliness that he has to change clothing between murders, why the hell didn't he go the whole hog and take a shower?"

"Maybe he did," Frances said."

Felix opened his eyes wide dramatically. "Let's take a closer look, shall we?" He folded the sheet down around Muldoon's waist. "As you can tell by the state of his hands and fingernails, this man hasn't seen a shower in a while. Not even a washcloth in my opinion. He's filthy."

"Well, he *has* been on the run for a week, probably sleeping rough." Adam was impatient to know where this was going.

"I've taken swabs from his nails and hair, but there isn't a single trace of blood, apart from his own, anywhere on his person and yet he's clearly not washed."

"So what are you trying to say, Felix? You think he didn't do it?"

"I'm saying nothing of the sort. You have evidence to support the case. I only want to point out the inconsistencies."

"Is it possible he wore overalls and a hat?" Frances asked.

"Anything's possible, my dear. But did you find any such items at the crime scene?"

"I'm not sure. I wasn't there." She glanced at Adam for the answer.

"I didn't, but I'll check the SOCO report when I get back to the office."

"Another thing that strikes me as odd is his feet." Felix walked to the end of the table and lifted the sheet back to uncover Muldoon's disgusting feet.

Adam had a bit of a phobia about feet. He didn't mind Amanda's feet, or the kids' feet. He was even partial to his own. But dirty, stinky, hairy feet gave him the heebie-jeebies. He dutifully glanced at the feet before him.

"Look how dirty they are." Felix lifted one leg up as if he were examining a flower. "Although he was wearing clean socks and shoes, his feet appear as though he's been barefoot for a while, and lab tests show they are covered in urine and excrement as well as a couple of spots of his own blood."

"Under his socks?" Adam's interest was suddenly piqued.

Felix nodded when he saw the penny drop. "His undies are equally filthy."

Frances heaved and covered her mouth with her hands. Once she was sufficiently recovered, Felix continued.

"His briefs and between his buttocks are caked in human waste as though he'd not wiped for a while. The build-up is disgusting."

"If you even think about getting his arse out now, I'll deck you," Frances said, causing Adam to stifle a laugh.

Felix, eyebrows raised in surprise, shook his head and continued. "His last meal was beans on toast." His eyes fixed on Adam's.

"And?"

"Oh, the guy is living rough, can't find a tissue to wipe his backside, yet he can take the time to cook some toast. Struck me as odd, that's all."

"Felix. Thanks for this enlightening chat, but the way I see it is that Muldoon broke in to the Kemp household, killed the nurse and Mr Kemp, found some clean clothes, shoes and socks and put them on, before lying in wait for Sally to arrive."

"Okay. You're the detective. I just wanted you to see it for yourself. Sometimes a report just doesn't cut it."

"And I'll take into account all of the points you raised. But I really need to be off. Coming Frances?"

Frances couldn't get out of the place fast enough.

Yet something niggled at Adam. He tried to shut down his inner voice. The case was cut and dried, a few more loose ends to tie up, then he was going to visit his wife and newborn son. End of.

As they walked towards the exit, he suddenly stopped. "I won't be a sec, Frances."

He rushed back to the examination room and tapped on the door again.

Felix opened it.

"Could I take a quick look at the shoes he was wearing?" Adam said.

Felix pointed to a plastic bag and went about his business.

Adam pulled one of the shoes out of the bag.

The tread looked similar to that found in the soil outside Charlie Kemp's window. "Is it alright if I take these with me?"

Felix shrugged. "You'll need to sign for them."

Chapter 42

In the car, Adam called Sally's phone again. It went straight to voicemail.

"I might just fly by her place if you don't mind?"

"Not at all," Frances said.

At the apartment, they knocked and rang the bell several times, but Sally didn't appear to be home.

Adam shrugged and turned to walk away, but he heard a bolt sliding open behind the door.

The door opened a few inches before the chain caught with a bang. Sally peeped through the tiny opening.

"Oh, hi. Hang on." She closed the door while unfastening the chain then invited them in.

Sally looked terrible. Her normally beautiful mane of hair was wild and messy. She wore a fleecy, purple robe fastened tight at the waist.

They followed her through to the lounge which had been completely cleaned up since their last visit.

"Somebody's been busy," Adam said, glancing around. "Did you hire a cleaning company?"

"No. I actually enjoy cleaning." She sat down and motioned for them to do the same. "What can I do for you, detectives?" Her voice sounded flat and hoarse.

"We're just checking you're alright. I called the hospital and they told me you'd discharged yourself."

She shrugged one shoulder. "I'll live. No point taking up a bed when I'm not even sick."

"Do you have a friend or family member you might stay with for a few days?" Frances asked.

"My only remaining family members live on The Isle of Wight."

"Did you tell them what's happened?"

Sally shook her head. "I've been putting it off, but I'll call them soon."

"I can make that call for you?"

Sally's eyes flashed, as though considering it, then she shook her head again. "No. I need to do it myself. Thanks though."

"Don't mention it. Anything else I can do for you? Any friends I can call?" Frances pushed. "I think you need someone with you."

Sally's eyes filled and spilled over in an instant. "No friends. Miles said we only needed each other." She began to sob.

Adam jumped to his feet. "I'll fetch you a glass of water," he said, and rushed to the kitchen.

He opened several cupboard doors before finding a glass, and, after running the tap for a few seconds, filled it and headed back to the lounge.

"There you go. Do you need anything else?"

"No, thanks. I'll be fine now. Will I be charged for killing Miles?"

"It is likely there'll be some charges. But considering the evidence against him, and the cold-blooded murder of his victims, this is clearly an act of self-defence. English law permits a person to kill another so long as they are defending themselves and use no more than reasonable force."

"But I will need to go to court?"

"Probably." He smiled sadly. "There will be a trial. A judge will appoint a jury to decide if you used any unreasonable amount of force, but I honestly don't expect them to rule against you. You're the victim and, if anything, you should be rewarded for your bravery."

Sally shook her head and wiped her eyes on a tissue. "You can't call it bravery. I was petrified, but it was either him or me."

Frances rubbed Sally's arm. "Well, we're grateful for what you did. And your dad would be so proud of you."

Sally nodded as more tears ran down her face.

"Just one more question, and then we'll leave you in peace," Adam said.

She blinked in agreement, and made a trumpeting sound as she blew her nose.

"Did you recognise any of the clothes Miles wore last night?"

Her eyebrows furrowed as though tapping into her memory bank. Then she shook her head. "To be honest, I can't recall *what* he was wearing. He could have been naked for all I noticed."

"Thanks, Sally. We'll be in touch in the next few days."

*

Back at the station, Adam requested the SOCO report, but Rachel, his contact, told him it wasn't ready yet. "Can you do me a favour and check if any bloody clothes or overalls were found at the scene?"

"Hang on a sec."

He could hear a muffled conversation going on in the background, but he couldn't tell what they were saying.

"You there, Adam?" Rachel said.

"Uh-huh."

"No. They didn't find anything like that. Sorry."

"No problem. Thanks for checking."

Slamming the phone on the desk, he pinched the point in-between his eyes. Fucking Felix had put a bug in his head, and it was driving him mad.

"Something wrong, boss?" Frances said, handing him a cup of coffee.

"Thanks, Frances. You go home. You've been here ages."

"I'm alright for another hour or so. What's going on?"

"Although it kills me to admit it, I think something's off about the whole thing."

Frances groaned. "Is this because of what Felix said? Because your explanation makes the most sense."

"Maybe. Oh, I don't know. I've hardly had any sleep in days, so maybe I'm not thinking straight."

"Why don't *you* go home and get some rest. I'll stay with Cal. And shouldn't you be with your wife, anyway?"

Cal knocked on the open door. "Something odd, boss. Muldoon had nothing in any of his pockets. He didn't have a bag or keys, not even a penny piece to his name."

Adam closed his eyes and rubbed at his temples. "Let me guess. There were no random cars parked in the vicinity either?

"Nothing," Cal said apologetically.

"He must've had an accomplice. In fact, I don't know why we didn't think of this before."

"Go and spend time with your son, Adam," Frances said. "Come back to it with a clear head and fresh eyes in the morning."

"Yeah, you're right. I'm getting nowhere fast. I may as well be sleeping." Standing up, he shoved the laptop into his briefcase.

"Are you sure you don't mind if I shoot off? I'm neither use nor ornament in this state," he said, joining them in the main office.

"Don't forget these. And tell Amanda congrats from us." Frances handed him the balloons and tucked the teddy under his arm.

"Thanks. I will."

"And I would love to see a photo of baby Stanley tomorrow, if possible."

"I'm hopeless. Aren't I?" He smiled. "Oh, by the way, his name's Andrew."

***

I stand at the door as the detectives walk away. They are totally taken in by everything. Given the energy or the inclination, I would laugh. But a severe depression has descended on me along with the realisation I have committed my final murder.

Outside appearances show I'm in mourning. My dear father was brutally murdered, so, of course, I'm bound to be depressed. But in truth, I'm pleased the controlling old bastard has gone—he'd lingered much too long in my opinion.

I'm aware of the real reason for my depression. Like an alcoholic, or drug addict, the high I'd experienced watching someone take their last breath had awoken a need in me. But I can't kill again seeing as Miles is no longer around to pin it on. The police are stupid, but they aren't that stupid.

As an only child, my father's estate makes me a very wealthy woman. And then there is Miles' life insurance. I hadn't thought to cancel it when he left. I could sell the apartment and move away. Start all over again. Yet, nothing appeals to me. Nothing else in the world can give me the rush I crave.

***

Adam called into the florist on his way to the hospital and picked up the biggest pre-made arrangement he could find. Formal visiting hours were restricted, but partners were allowed in any time between 7.00am and 9.00pm.

He glanced at his watch, just after 3.00pm—much later than he expected to be. Amanda would be wondering where he'd got to.

He headed to her ward first to drop off the cuddly toy, balloons and flowers. He looked like a walking advert for the local florist.

Sandra stood waiting for the lift as he stepped out of it.

"Oh, hi, Adam. Congratulations. Your son is simply delicious."

"He is, isn't he? How's Amanda? I tried getting here earlier, but I've had another shocker of a day."

"She's fine. Apart from being a little weepy earlier today, but that's understandable. As a new mum, being kept from her baby is hard to cope with. But she's fine. I'm going to pick up the kids from school and bring them back for ten minutes to see the baby. Is that okay?"

"Of course it's okay. See you when you get back." He pressed the button to call the lift for her again.

Amanda was standing at the window looking out over Pinevale when he arrived at her room. "Oh, you're here. I've been worried."

"Sorry, Mand. I couldn't get away." He kissed her forehead. Then he handed her the cuddly toy and untangled the ribbon from his hand. "Here you go. The teddy and balloons are from Holly."

She took them from him and smiled. "I wonder if we'll be allowed to put the teddy in his incubator." She tied the balloons to the end of the bed and sat the teddy beside them.

"No harm in asking." He handed her the flowers. "And these are from me to say thank you. You've made me the happiest man alive."

"Aw, they're lovely, Adam. Thanks."

"And they don't need a vase, there's a container inside the stand."

She made a space on the bedside table for them. "How's work? Is everyone relieved the case is closed?"

"Yeah."

"What's wrong? I know that face, Adam. Something's wrong."

"No." He shook his head and pulled her into his arms. "Nothing's wrong, but things are not as cut and dried as I first thought. Anyway, I don't want to talk about work. Do you want to take me to visit our son?"

"Of course. He's missed you, you know?"

"Has he now? And he told you that, did he?"

"He certainly did. Every time the door opened today, his little head bobbed up to see if it was you." She nodded, enthusiastically. "It's true."

"We better head over there sharpish, then. I wouldn't want to upset his nibs now, would I?"

Chapter 43

Sandra and the kids came back soon after. The nurses allowed them in to see baby Andrew one at a time. Considering their ages, Adam was proud of how well Emma and Jacob behaved.

After a few minutes, Adam kissed them all goodbye and left. He was almost dead on his feet.

Arriving home, he groaned as he remembered he hadn't told Amanda of the social workers' visit. He considered calling her, but thought better of it. There was no point upsetting her now.

The flashing of the house phone caught his eye and, following the prompts, he received a message from a Detective Inspector Merchants from Wolverhampton police, who wanted to arrange an interview with him and Amanda as soon as possible.

Although expected, the call made him feel uneasy. He hated the thought of a jobs-worth copper trawling through their private lives, trying to dig up as much dirt up as possible.

Once he'd downed a cheese sandwich and cup of tea, he showered and changed into a T-shirt and sweat pants and opted to get his head down on the sofa.

After staring at the ceiling for what seemed like hours, he switched on the TV and watched a couple of American sit-coms, back-to-back. After an hour of this, he began pacing the room. The discrepancies in the case needed further investigation before sleep would be remotely possible. And although it suited him right now to walk away, he wasn't that kind of detective.

Changing into his trusty black jeans, he grabbed a jacket, his briefcase, and keys and headed back to the station.

*

Ensconced in his office, he pulled out the file and slowly picked his way through it. He made notes on his desk pad as he went.

A week ago tonight, Muldoon argued with Lana, threatened Sally and murdered Michael. The fact they found his DNA all over the apartment couldn't be used as Muldoon lived there for the three years prior.

Evidence against him:

Fingerprints on the crowbar used to gain access to the apartment, and also on the murder weapon, belonged to Muldoon.

DNA from the faeces left on the wall also belonged to Muldoon.

Motive:

He'd threatened Sally earlier for causing trouble between him and Lana. He'd always thought Michael lusted after Sally.

Alternative motive:

Michael could have caught Muldoon trashing Sally's apartment.

On Wednesday/early hours of Thursday morning, Lana and Dean were murdered in their beds. A different murder weapon used from the previous night showed this was pre-meditated.

Evidence:

DNA from the faeces matched that found at Sally's apartment.

A hair belonging to Muldoon was found beside Lana on the bed.

Motive:

Lana had ended her relationship with him after listening to Sally's stories.

Dean assaulted Muldoon when he returned home to find him roughing up his daughter.

Natasha and Angela were murdered late Thursday evening. The killer seemed to be escalating at this point. He attacked both women while they were still awake, and Angela had been undressed, her underwear cut open.

Evidence:

Once again, they found a couple of Muldoon's hairs and his faeces at the scene.

Motive:

Natasha gave a live interview to the local news slating Muldoon and Sally.

Another thing that bothered him about this murder scene was that the path leading up to the house was caked in mud from the recent storm, yet they didn't find any footprints belonging to the killer.

Adam put his pen down and rubbed his chin. It didn't make sense that the killer would so blatantly leave his DNA all over the place, yet cover up his footprints. Plus they hadn't found any more fingerprints at any of the crime scenes which indicated he wore gloves. Why?

He slammed his palms down onto his desk in sheer frustration. Why the hell hadn't he noticed this before?

He returned to the files.

Friday night Muldoon left a message for Adam to find on his car windscreen. Clearly, he wanted to let them know he'd found out where he lived.

On Sunday, Muldoon let himself into Adam's house, somehow knowing the alarm wasn't set and where to find the key. He cleaned the house from top to bottom and left a pile of crap in the toilet—more than a few days' worth, that's for sure. He found and took Amanda's box of clippings.

On Monday morning, an envelope had been left for him in reception questioning Mary's true parentage. Sally received the same type of envelope with several photos inside showing her at her father's bedside the night before. Another taunt, as the house was being watched by the PPU. Then DCI Williamson found another envelope on his desk containing the same information as Adam had.

Later that night, Muldoon lets himself in to Charlie Kemp's house and kills the dying man and his nurse. Afterwards, he disposes of his clothing and changes into a clean outfit before lying in wait for Sally to emerge from the bath.

This had struck Adam as odd when Sally first told him, but he just shrugged it off. But, why did *Muldoon* wait? If his intention was to kill her, why not just march straight into the bathroom and catch her unawares?

Another thing that bothered Adam was the fact *Muldoon* was filthy, as though he'd been living on the streets barefoot for a week. But, it was even worse than dirt from the street. Felix said his feet were covered in human waste and in-between his buttocks caked in excrement, as though he hadn't wiped himself in a while. Adam thought back to Muldoon's car and hotel room. Both were incredibly neat and tidy. It didn't make sense that he'd allow himself to get so dirty.

A thought suddenly struck him. If Muldoon had cleaned Adam's house from top to bottom just the day before, why were his hands and nails thick with dirt and God only knows what else?

He headed into the main office directly to the whiteboard.

Focusing on the images of his house, another thing occurred to him. Scrutinising the image of their bed, it was clear the intruder lay with his head on the pillow. The lowest black mark from their shoes would have been made from that position. The highest mark was clearly made when they sat on the pillow, their back to the wall.

He looked at Muldoon's profile again and nodded. Just as he thought, Muldoon was 6'2". Right now he couldn't be certain, he would need to wait until he went home to measure, but he didn't think the person who made the marks on the bed could possibly be anywhere near 6'2".

Adam was angry with himself for doing what he prided himself on never doing, namely taking the evidence at face value and allowing himself to be blindsided. Now that he was looking at the evidence with fresh eyes, it became clear to him that *if* Muldoon was indeed guilty, he would have had to have an accomplice.

Several things slotted into place in his head making the puzzle complete.

He jumped to his feet as the realisation struck him with the speed and voracity of a freight train. He slammed the heel of his palm to his forehead. How fucking stupid had he been?

The team would take some convincing. And he was aware how crazy it sounded, but he knew without doubt, Sally Kemp was their killer.

Chapter 44

The more he thought about it, the more it became blindingly obvious. But what evidence did he have? He couldn't just march into Sally's home and pray for a confession. She was much wilier than that.

He would even have a job convincing the team, who'd all been thrilled at the current result.

He headed home at midnight, showered, and set the alarm, so he could return to the station by 7.00am.

He was sitting at the communal desk when Calvin breezed in.

"Oh, hi, boss. If I'd known you were here I'd have brought *you* one." He held up a takeaway coffee cup.

"I'm all coffeed out, thanks, Cal."

Eyeing him suspiciously, Cal approached the desk, peering over Adam's shoulder.

Adam pulled down the laptop lid and grinned. "Nosy, aren't we?"

Cal sniggered and trotted back to his desk.

"Can you ask the team to come in for a briefing, Cal?"

"Has something else happened, boss?" He turned to his computer, scanning through his messages.

"Nothing you'll find on there. I'll reveal all once the others arrive."

"Frances too?"

Adam considered this for a moment. Frances would kill him if he left her out after all the effort she put into finding Muldoon.

"Give her the choice, Cal. But only if she feels up to it."

He took his notes and laptop back into his office and checked his emails. The SOCO report had come through and he quickly added a few details to his list.

He called Sandra and caught up with the kids, promising to try his best to pick them up from school and take them to visit the hospital again. He knew they could be a handful, but Sandra sounded happy enough. He hoped to be able to step up and spend much more time with them all as soon as he finished with Sally.

Soon enough, Cal tapped on the door and popped his head in. "They're all here, boss."

Back in the main office, he found his team seated, waiting expectantly.

"Congrats on becoming a daddy." Julie got to her feet and hugged him.

"Yeah. Nice one, boss," Les chipped in.

"Cheers, guys." He winked at Frances who was perched on the edge of Cal's desk.

She smiled.

"Okay. I know you're all wondering why I've called you together. But something else has come to light and I need to run it past you."

"Intriguing," Frances said. They all muttered their agreement.

"What would you say if I told you we missed something vital? And that Muldoon isn't our killer?"

"What do you mean?" Les barked, not amused in the slightest.

"Is this a joke?" Ginger Dave got to his feet.

The others grumbled something but Adam didn't catch what.

He waited for them to settle down again.

"Let's go back to the first murder. What did we learn?"

"Sally's apartment had been trashed and her neighbour knifed to death," Cal volunteered.

"They are the facts, but what did we learn? Frances? What did you learn?"

"About Sally?"

He shrugged. "If you like."

"She'd recently split with her boyfriend, her boss. He left her for another woman. Also a colleague."

Adam nodded.

"What else."

Frances chewed her lip. "We found out Muldoon was abusive and a womaniser."

"Did anything strike you as odd at that moment?" Adam pressed.

"I guess I wondered why she would be so upset with him being such a douche-bag and all."

Adam nodded. "What else did we learn?"

Frances' forehead furrowed. "That Sally was Charlie Kemp's daughter?"

"Okay. So Sally Kemp, daughter of the ex-Chief Constable, is the target. She happened to be away from home at the time which probably saved her life. She's our main priority. Right?"

They all nodded in agreement.

"Michael Curtis, a gentle ex-naval officer, had been either coaxed out of his apartment, or else he heard the commotion and approached the culprit. Either way, he wound up dead. Our first victim."

The team listened intently.

"Lana Davis, the *other* woman, told us she finished with Muldoon because of something Sally confided in her. She said he lost the plot, and when Dean, her father, arrived home they had an altercation resulting in Muldoon being punched by the older man. Nobody saw him after that."

"We know all this, boss. Tell us something juicy," Ginger Dave said.

The rest sniggered.

"All in good time, Dave. Who examined Muldoon's office and laptop?"

"I did, boss." Ginger Dave said.

"And what did you find?"

"Absolutely nothing." Dave shook his head.

"What did his workmates say about him?"

"That he was a nice guy. Hardworking, respectful, but he kept himself to himself outside work hours," Julie offered shyly.

Les nodded. "They all said the same. He was focused and really just lived for his job."

"Didn't that strike you as odd? That a man so devoted to his career would face losing everything over a fling?"

"Stranger things happen, boss." Ginger Dave shrugged.

"I agree. It struck *me* as odd, I must admit," Adam continued. "We interviewed Lana, and that night she and her father were murdered in their sleep. The excrement left at the scene matched Muldoon's DNA. Muldoon was on the missing list, having left without his phone, wallet or car. How can that be?"

He glanced at them all, one at a time. They all shrugged, shaking their heads.

"Imagine there had been no murders. What if a missing person report was the first time we heard of Muldoon? His personal belongings are found at the hotel. His car found in the car park. Vanished off the face of the earth. What would've been our first reaction?"

"Abduction, boss," Julie said.

Adam raised his eyebrows and nodded. "We'd have assumed foul play. A man doesn't just go missing. But because we already have his name in relation to a homicide, we automatically assume he's absconded because he's guilty."

"But the evidence," Frances said. "We found Muldoon's fingerprints on the murder weapon used to kill Michael Curtis, and also on the crowbar used to access Sally's apartment. Not forgetting the bloodstained clothing in his car."

"If you had a man locked up, trying to frame him for something, how easy would it be to get hold of his fingerprints? His hair? His crap for that matter?"

A collective gasp went around the room.

"Natasha Barker, another of Muldoon's exes, spoke to the local news team. She gave Muldoon and Sally a proper slating. That same night Natasha and her friend were attacked and killed. Same DNA, same murder weapon, no fingerprints, no footprints, even though the path leading to the house was a quagmire. Why would someone go to the trouble of hiding these things when he's leaving his calling card anyway?"

"Because it wasn't Muldoon, boss," Cal said.

"Do you all agree that we missed some crucial clues? We all seemed to be suffering from tunnel vision. Beautiful Sally Kemp, daughter of the ex-chief, told us Muldoon did it, and we accepted that as gospel."

They all looked sheepish as they nodded.

"I'm as much to blame. But now, we need to put this right. Agreed?"

"Agreed, boss."

"Several other instances occurred. On Friday night, I saw someone tampering with Amanda's new car. By the time I got outside, they were gone, but as you know I found a message for me on the windscreen. Then, on Sunday, someone entered my house and did the opposite of ransacking it. To be honest, after a hectic morning with the kids, it already looked as though it had been ransacked."

They all laughed.

"Whoever entered, tidied the house from top to bottom." He pointed at the photos showing his kitchen cupboards and the dishcloth over the tap. "They blocked the toilet up with a mound of turd. Then they climbed on my bed, leaving hair on the pillow and marks on the duvet where their shoes finished." He passed the photo around. "Now, I'm six-four and Muldoon six-two. Last night, I measured the marks in relation to the pillow, and there's no way Muldoon did this. This person couldn't have been more than five-seven."

"That's quite short for a bloke," Ginger Dave said.

"Hold that thought, Dave."

"On Monday morning, I received this." He handed the envelope around, giving them a few minutes to get the gist of the contents. "I didn't say anything to you as I just thought it was a wind-up, not for one minute thinking it could be associated to the case. But later on, Sally showed us a similar envelope. It contained photographs of her at her father's bedside, taken the night before, while the PPU were outside."

"Cheeky bastard," Les said.

"That same day, the DCI received an exact copy of that lot." He pointed to the envelope. "He obviously had to report it, and now Amanda and I are under investigation."

"They don't think you kidnapped her though, do they, boss?"

"Of course not. But that won't stop them digging up as much dirt as they can."

"True," Cal said. "I'm sorry, boss. You don't need this right now."

"Monday night, someone broke into the Kemp household and cut the throats of Charlie and his nurse, Dana Morgan. Charlie was already close to death and thankfully wouldn't have felt a thing, but Dana didn't move from her chair when the killer stabbed her in the throat. She bled out fast and furiously, the blood coating most of the room."

He paused as they muttered amongst themselves for a few seconds.

"Sally said she made herself some beans on toast, and after a nap she had a long soak in the bath. Afterwards, she dressed in a silky, satiny number, styled her hair and applied a full face of make-up. She then went downstairs to say goodnight to her dad."

"Goodnight?" Julie said, surprised. "Why did she get dressed and made up just to say goodnight?"

Adam was pleased she'd picked up on that discrepancy. "Yes, I also thought that a bit odd when she told me. Anyway, she got downstairs and Muldoon confronted her in the hallway. After a scuffle, she vomited on the carpet, taking the opportunity to run when he backed off in disgust. He lunged for her, slipping on her vomit and crashed to the floor dropping the knife. Sally raced to grab the knife and stabbed him in the chest. End of Muldoon."

"But I thought the killer wasn't Muldoon?" Julie said.

Adam held one finger up before continuing. "Felix called me to his examination room. Not a drop of blood was found on Muldoon, apart from his own, yet the evidence showed he hadn't washed in a week. His feet were filthy, underneath his shoes and clean socks." He opened a box and took out a bag containing a pair of running shoes and handed them to Cal. "He wore freshly laundered clothes, but he was caked in dirt, mainly faeces. Felix said in-between his buttocks looked as though he hadn't wiped in a while."

Frances gagged again.

"Look at the laces, Cal. What do you see?"

"The knots are the wrong way round, as though someone else tied them from the front." Cal smiled, pleased with himself.

"And Felix found Muldoon's own blood on his foot, underneath his socks and shoes, indicating someone put them on after Muldoon was stabbed."

"In fact, under his clothes, he resembled a person who'd been shut up in a room for a week. And get this, his stomach contents revealed beans on toast."

Ginger Dave shook his head. "You mean to say—"

Adam held up his hand. "Hold on, before you say anything, let's examine the evidence."

Chapter 45

Adam straddled a chair before continuing.

"Okay, now think. Who is the only other person who had a grudge or anything to gain from each of the killings? Aside from Michael Curtis, whose death was most likely collateral damage?"

He glanced around at the blank faces. Ginger Dave looked bored.

Adam took a deep breath before continuing. "Lana Davies betrayed Sally in the worst way possible—she stole her boyfriend. Getting rid of Dean was a smart move, and something Miles would have done if he was indeed the killer."

"Still don't get you, boss," Cal said, looking at the rest of the team.

"You will. Think of the news interview. Natasha Barker blamed everything on Sally calling her some terrible names. Angela Smith just happened to find herself caught up in it all."

"Now hang on a minute." Ginger Dave said, suddenly interested.

Adam raised his hand again. "Charlie Kemp was all but dead anyway and possibly becoming a nuisance. Or maybe he and Dana Morgan witnessed something." He dropped his notepad to the desk.

"There are a lot of maybes in your theory, boss," Les said.

"I know. But bear with me. When Frances and I visited Sally's apartment yesterday, she proceeded to tell me how much she enjoys cleaning. I offered to fetch a glass of water for her and, after searching several cupboards for a glass, I noticed each cupboard was in perfect order, just like this." He pointed once again at the photo. "And her dishcloth was folded perfectly and hung on the tap exactly like someone had done at my house." He glanced around at them all again. They all stared at him, open-mouthed. "Sally is five-seven, an incredibly good actress, but she is also our killer. Of that I'm in no doubt."

"What about the photos taken from outside the house showing Sally at her father's bedside?" Frances said.

"Most phones and cameras have built-in timers. A great way of cementing her place as a victim and a target," Adam said.

"But...I still don't understand. The house was being watched. How did she get past the PPU?" Julie asked.

"That was one of the sticking points I had last night, but this morning I read the reports, and they mentioned the comings and goings of two nurses, one driving a green Volkswagen Passat, the other a blue Honda. There was always at least one nurse with Mr Kemp at all times. But sometimes they both stayed." He let the information sink in for a few seconds. "So, I got to thinking, after a long shift, why didn't they leave as soon as the next nurse arrived? One night the second nurse arrived, the first one left, only to return again two hours later."

"So what does all that mean? I'm still lost," Frances said.

"I called the nursing agency and they informed me that Dana Morgan was the only nurse on their books working for Mr Kemp. His daughter was his second carer."

Frances drew a sudden breath. "But why did the PPU think Sally was the nurse?"

"She more than likely wore a disguise, and used a different car. I checked the number plate details off the PPU report and the supposed nurse's green Volkswagen Passat was registered to Charlie Kemp."

"Fuck me, boss! You're amazing," Les said.

Ginger Dave threw his hands in the air. "Nah. I still don't buy it. No way would little Sally do that. Not to her own dad." He began pacing, angrily.

"Dave, the little girl you remember grew up. And she's clever. She *almost* got away with it. But believe me, she did this."

Dave scowled at Adam and turned away.

"So what do you want us to do, boss? It seems you've got enough to go on already," Cal said.

"As far as my superiors are concerned, we've had a result—Muldoon is out of the picture and everything is cut and dried. No loose ends. Just the way they like it. Now I have to go back to them with this little lot and convince them we've made a mistake. The problem is Sally makes a convincing victim. If we don't have enough evidence, she'll walk."

"So we need to do some digging?" Julie said.

"Exactly. We need to find out every little detail of Sally Kemp's past. She's clever, but we're one step ahead because she isn't aware we're on to her. We need to find out where the hell she kept Muldoon locked up. It would need to be somewhere isolated. Otherwise, somebody surely would've heard his cries for help or, at the very least, witnessed some strange comings and goings."

They clambered to their feet, eager to begin.

"Frances, I don't intend for you to stay. Get off home. I'll keep you updated."

"Not on your life, boss. I want to stitch the bitch up as much as you do."

"Please yourself. I'll begin compiling the evidence. Cal, could you arrange a meeting with the DCI for this afternoon? Hopefully we'll have more to show him by then. If not, I'll just wing it."

"Will do, boss."

"Julie. Will you check Monday morning's CCTV footage from the front desk? Let's see who dropped the envelope off."

Julie nodded and rushed to her desk.

Ginger Dave turned and strode from the room.

"Where's he going?" Frances asked.

Adam shook his head. "I've no idea." He left them all hard at it and went into his office. DCI Williamson wouldn't have time to spare to listen to the whole scenario. He would break it all into bite-sized chunks, and hope he had enough to convince his boss they needed a search warrant, if not a warrant for Sally's arrest.

Cal appeared in his doorway. "Appointment booked for three-thirty, boss. The DCI only has ten minutes to spare, though."

Adam shook his head in annoyance. "How the hell will I condense this little lot down to ten minutes and get him to take me seriously?"

"I can help you, boss."

Adam scrubbed his hands over his face and groaned. "Nah, you're alright, Cal. I can do it."

The reports spoke for themselves. Yet trawling through them would take more than the allotted ten minutes, so he compiled a bullet list with a reference link to the relevant report.

He knew the DCI wouldn't want the shit storm without concrete evidence, yet looking at the list it was all circumstantial.

He could hear the DCI's comments without even showing him. Nothing he hadn't said to himself several times already. But call it a gut feeling—he knew. He just fucking knew.

After a few hours reading and re-reading the file, he got to his feet and stretched. Without more evidence, an arrest was out of the question. Unless Sally made a full and frank confession based on what he already had. But there was little or no chance of that.

"How's everyone doing?" he asked hopefully, as he walked into the main office. He nodded at Ginger Dave who had returned and was sitting back at his desk.

Everyone shook their heads apologetically.

"Nothing yet," Frances said. "She's got no prior convictions. In fact she's squeaky clean."

"I'm trying to find any derelict buildings close by, but I'm not having much luck," Les said.

"Maybe she used her apartment?" Cal piped up.

Adam shook his head. "It was a crime scene for a few days and he definitely wasn't there then."

"Oops, I forgot." Cal winced.

"No, it's okay. The place must be somewhere as close and as convenient as the apartment. But where?"

Cal shrugged.

"Maybe check with the council. See if either Sally or Charlie Kemp own any other properties in the area."

"Will do, boss."

"I need to stretch my legs and get some fresh air. What do you all want from the bakery? My shout," Adam said.

Ginger Dave suddenly perked up and rubbed his rotund stomach. "Steak pie and a custard slice for me, boss."

"Julie?"

"Hmm, the same as Dave, please."

"Les?"

"Nothing for me, thanks. I brought a packed lunch."

"You sure? How about a cake?"

"I have some rich tea biscuits, I'm fine."

Adam shrugged. "Suit yourself. What can I get you, Frances?"

"Oh, surprise me. I'll make a pot of tea."

"Cal?"

"A chicken salad roll, please?"

"Okay, shan't be long."

Adam strolled along the street to the bakery in the next block, calling Amanda as he walked.

"Hi, Daddy. We were just talking about you," she said.

"Who's *we*?"

"Me and baby Andrew. I was saying you'll come to see us as soon as you can."

"Sorry, Mand. Are you in the baby unit?"

"No. He's in my room. With me."

Instantaneous tears pricked his eyes and he had to blink them away. "You're kidding? He's out of the incubator? Is he alright?"

A woman overtook him on the pavement giving him a strange look.

"Sorry," he mimed at her.

"He's been doing great. They took him off the machines last night and brought him to me first thing. I was going to call but wanted to surprise you instead."

"That's fantastic news, Mand. I can't tell you how relieved I am."

"I know. He's a little bit jaundiced, but the nurse said that's to be expected and should come right in a few days. At the moment, he looks as though he's been to Spain on his jollies."

"What do you mean?" Adam asked, suddenly concerned again.

"His skin has a yellowy tinge to it, and reminds me of a sun tan."

"Are you sure it's normal? I had a mate who had jaundice once, and he had liver cancer."

Amanda chuckled. "He's fine. Stop panicking. Most newborns get it, and it should go once he's drunk enough fluid."

"So is he feeding normally now?"

"I fed him for the first time this morning. The nurses gave him a bottle in the night, too. And he's also had his first pooey nappy."

"That's my boy. Tell him Daddy's proud of him."

"I will do, love. How's it going at work?"

"I've got heaps going on. I'll fill you in later. I don't know what time I'll make it though. I told the kids I'd try to pick them up from school and bring them to see you, but I'll have to cancel that now."

"Okay, love. Don't worry. Just whenever you can is fine. I'll call Sandra and tell her you can't make it."

"Thanks, Mand. Love you."

He hung up as he reached the bakery and stood in line. The woman in front of him turned and smiled at him and he recognised her as the one who passed him in the street. He smiled back.

"Sorry, I wasn't being nosy back there, but I couldn't help overhear—do you have a new baby?"

Slightly taken aback, Adam nodded. "Yeah, that's right. A little boy, he's three days old."

"Congratulations. You must be very proud."

"Thank you. Yes, I am." He smiled, a little uncomfortable as other people in the queue turned to look at him.

All of a sudden, it occurred to him how Sally knew where to find the key to his house. She must have overheard him when he left the pub that night. It all made perfect sense now.

He collected the food and raced back to the station.

Chapter 46

The CCTV footage showed a local scally, Austin Fitzpatrick, dropping the envelope off. Julie and Les had gone to search the streets for him, knowing where he often hung out.

No other evidence had come to light by the time Adam left for London. He told the team he would call, with a yay or a nay, as soon as he got out of his meeting.

His phone rang when he was almost in the city. He hit the centre console to accept the call.

"Stanley," he said.

"Hello, detective. It's DI Merchants here. I left a message on your home phone yesterday."

"Ah, yes. Sorry, for not getting back to you but I'm in the middle of a homicide investigation."

"I appreciate that, but I also have a job to do. Can I arrange to visit you and Mrs Stanley tomorrow morning?"

"That might be a problem. My wife gave birth to our son three days ago. He was six weeks early and they're still in hospital."

"I could visit the hospital, if that's possible. The sooner we do this, the sooner we can put it all to bed."

The detective's words assured Adam he wasn't out to cause trouble and so he decided to accommodate him.

"What time?"

"The journey will take around two and a half hours from Wolverhampton, so shall we say, ten-thirty?"

"Okay. Amanda's in room three of the maternity annex at Pinevale Hospital."

"Great, see you then."

He needed to tell Amanda but would wait to tell her in person. She'd not mentioned the *Mary* issue since being admitted to hospital, and he guessed she was just burying her head in the sand.

He parked up and trudged across the car park to Police Headquarters.

DCI Williamson came out of the gents, zipping up his trousers. "Ah, Stanley. Bang on time, as usual." He held out his hand.

Adam shook it, before discreetly wiping his fingers inside his jacket pocket.

Once they were sitting across the desk from each other, Adam pulled out the file.

"Wonderful result, by the way, Stanley. The Chief-Super is impressed."

"That's the reason I'm here, sir. I don't think Muldoon was our killer after all."

His boss groaned and buried his head in his hands. "Then what was the whole manhunt about? You were certain when I met with you last week."

"I know, sir. But once we got him, more evidence came to light and I think Muldoon was framed."

"Who by?" he said, impatiently.

"That's the thing, sir." He took a deep breath. "I'm pretty positive our killer is Sally Kemp."

DCI Williamson snorted. "Old Charlie's daughter? You're 'aving a laugh, aren't you?"

"Hear me out, will you. The thing is, after the first murder, Sally pointed the finger at Muldoon. She's a credible witness and, when we couldn't locate him, we thought she was right. Muldoon's DNA was found at each murder scene. But no fingerprints or footprints, just faeces and hair."

"We've convicted bigger and better than him for less, Stanley. DNA is DNA when all's said and done."

"Not if Muldoon had been abducted and his DNA planted at the scene."

"And you think that's what happened? You think young Sally is capable of that?"

"Sally isn't the young girl you remember, sir. She's grown into a dangerous and wily young woman. I agree, on first impressions, she comes across as the innocent victim, but you've got to look beyond all that."

"So what evidence is there?" He glanced at his watch.

Adam passed the folder to him. "A lot of it is circumstantial, I admit. But I'm working on that." He watched as his boss read the bullet points on the top page.

The DCI paused, his pen pointing half-way down the page. "So Felix reported he thought Muldoon had been held against his will?"

"Yes, sir. Everything's in there."

He continued reading. "Okay, I think there may be a case, but you need something more concrete."

Adam released his breath in a whoosh.

The DCI continued. "But only Felix's report will have any credibility in court. The rest, as you said, is circumstantial. The fact Muldoon's blood was found underneath his socks is also a bonus, but a good lawyer would easily argue that it could have been cross contamination."

Adam nodded. "I know, sir."

"Where are you up to with Sally? Has she been charged with Muldoon's death yet?"

"Not yet. I was going to arrange to get her in for questioning tomorrow. I've warned her what to expect, so she won't think anything of it."

"And are forensics finished with the crime scene?"

"I'm not sure, but I wanted to search Sally's apartment as well as Charlie Kemp's house anyway. So I'll need a warrant—if that's okay, boss?"

DCI Williamson got to his feet. "Leave it with me. I have another meeting to get to, and then I'll go through all the evidence. Can I call you in an hour or so?"

Adam felt dejected as he left the building. He'd been certain at one point that the DCI was on board, but when he backed off at the last minute, Adam wanted to kick something.

He called the station and Cal answered almost immediately.

"How'd it go, boss?"

"Pretty good. He accepted it was a possibility, which I didn't think he was going to at first. He too remembers Charlie Kemp's gorgeous little girl. He wants to go through the file before he agrees to the warrant."

"Oh, well. He took it better than you expected, I guess."

"Yeah, definitely. I'm going to arrange for Sally to come in for an interview tomorrow. She's expecting it, but thinks it's just a formality for us to charge her with Muldoon's death."

"Good idea."

"The DCI also reminded me that forensics might not have released Charlie Kemp's house yet. If that's the case, we can search it without a warrant."

"I'll get onto them now."

"Cheers, Cal. I'll call you back once I hear from the DCI. Hopefully then, we can organise a warrant for both properties."

The motorway on-ramp was more or less at a standstill. It took over half-an-hour to travel a few hundred metres. He took the first available exit and headed straight to the hospital via the back roads.

His phone rang, and the caller display flashed DCI Williamson. Clearing his throat, he hit the console.

"Stanley," he said.

"Looking at this lot, I agree we need to take it further. You have my backing to do what you must, but I'm sure you don't need me to tell you to proceed with caution. From the looks of things, she's not behind the door and will do you over like a kipper, given half a chance."

Adam punched the air. "Great. And yes, I will do."

"Keep me updated every step of the way. I won't inform the Chief Super yet. I'll wait until there's more to go on."

"Okay, and thanks again, sir."

Adam rang Cal back right away. "Can you make an application for a warrant for both addresses? The DCI's on board."

"That's a relief."

"Yes. I'm going to call Sally now and arrange for her to come in tomorrow afternoon, around one. Could you sort out two search teams? I don't want her spooked before then. The crafty bitch thinks she's got away with this, and that's the way I want it to stay."

"Consider it done. Shall I let the rest of the team know?"

"If you don't mind, thanks. I'm on my way to the hospital to hold my baby for the first time. He's finally out of the special care unit and in with Amanda."

"That's great news, boss. Tell Amanda I said hi."

"Will do. I'll see you tomorrow."

As he pulled into the hospital car park, he called Sally. It rang a number of times, and he resigned himself to leaving a message when she finally answered. "Hello." She sounded wary.

"Sally? It's DI Stanley. How are you today?"

"I'm good. Still a little down, but I guess that's normal, considering."

"I'm sure it is. Listen, I'm sure it's the last thing you feel like doing, but can you come into the station tomorrow to finalise the case?"

"Are you going to charge me?"

"I warned you a charge would be necessary. A jury will need to decide your fate, I'm sorry. We've just got to present the facts."

"Okay. What time shall I come in?"

"Can you meet me there at one? You might want to bring your solicitor."

"What for?"

"Bearing in mind you're likely to be charged with murder or at the least manslaughter, your solicitor will want to be present."

"I'll be there." She hung up without another word.

"You have a good night too, Miss Kemp," he said to nobody, shaking his head.

Chapter 47

Amanda's room was full to bursting. Mary sat on the armchair beside the bed cuddling the baby who was dressed in a lime green and white outfit. Amanda and Sandra were on the bed, and Emma and Jacob lay on the floor on either side of the room wheeling a car to each other.

"Hello, you lot."

"Adam!" Emma jumped to her feet and ran to him.

He lifted her up onto his hip and kissed her head.

Jacob, a little slower than his sister, did the same.

Adam picked him up too and hugged him tight. "Well, that was a nice welcome." He walked around the bed and carefully bent to kiss his wife on the lips.

Amanda laughed and reached up to meet him. "Put them down, or you'll do yourself an injury."

He pretended his back had broken and made as if to drop the kids onto the floor to the sound of raucous laughter. After a few minutes, the children went back to playing with the toy car.

"Hi, Sandra. Sorry about today." He hugged his mother-in-law.

"It's not a problem, Adam. You know I like to feel needed."

"You'll always be needed, especially now there's another little terror to add to the mix." He approached Mary. "And how are you, squirt?"

"I'm okay. Do you want to hold him?"

"You're alright. I can wait." He crouched beside her and gazed at his son who'd already changed so much in just a few hours. "What do you think of him?"

Mary smiled. "He's so cute. I could cuddle him forever."

"Maybe we'll remind you of that when he's screaming in the middle of the night."

She giggled, shaking her head. "No. You can cuddle him at night."

Adam shook his head in mock disgust.

"Right, time to go." Sandra got to her feet and grabbed the pile of coats off the end of the bed. "We can pick up fish and chips on the way home if you like?"

"Yes!" they all said together.

Amanda got off the bed. "Are you going to give him a kiss goodbye, love?"

Mary nodded and gently kissed the baby's cheek before Amanda took the tiny tot from her.

The two youngest couldn't wait to get out of the place once food was mentioned, but Sandra called them back to say goodbye to their mother and the baby.

Moments later, they'd gone.

"Phew! Thank goodness for that. I'd forgotten how noisy they can be." Amanda's eyes twinkled. "Sit down." She nodded towards the chair.

He did as he was told, and she promptly placed his son in his arms.

"Oh heck. I've never held such a tiny baby before." He felt self-conscious and clumsy, all of a sudden.

"Don't worry. You'll be throwing him around in no time." She smiled, stroking the baby's cheek.

The baby opened his mouth and turned his face towards her finger.

They both laughed.

"He's hungry again." She shook her head, amazed. "I only fed him an hour ago."

"He's making up for lost time." Adam, suddenly emotional, couldn't describe the immense love that came over him when he gazed into his son's face. "How's he been?"

"Absolutely perfect. The nurses are astounded by how well he's doing. They think he's been here before."

"And there's nothing else to worry about? You know, with him being so early?"

She shook her head. "No. They said the medication they gave him when he was first born would have helped to strengthen his lungs, which was the main reason he had to go into the unit in the first place. But other than being slightly jaundiced, he's fine."

"That's amazing."

She nodded. "They also said if he'd gone full term, he would've been huge."

"But he's dinky!"

"He is to us, but I met another mum yesterday whose baby was due around the same time and I couldn't believe how tiny her little girl was—less than two pounds."

"Wow! He's double that," Adam said.

"I know. We're so lucky."

The baby began to stir and squeak.

Adam gasped, amazed. "Is that his cry?"

"Yes. He's quiet, but I'm sure he won't stay that way for long."

"Do you want to take him? I haven't a clue what to do."

Amanda plucked the baby out of Adam's arms, and he felt able to breathe again.

"That was so scary," he said.

"He's a little baby! How can he possibly be scary?"

"I've dealt with mass murderers that are less scary. He's too little for me. I feel as though I might hurt him without meaning to."

She climbed back onto the bed and placed the baby on her lap while she unfastened the top two buttons of her nightie.

"Shall I leave?"

"No." She laughed, shaking her head. "I've never seen you so out of your comfort zone."

"I'm sorry. It's all new to me. Can I do anything to help?"

"You can pour me a glass of water, if you don't mind."

Within a minute or two, baby was feeding away happily and Adam was back in his seat.

"Is it okay to talk to you while you're doing that?" he asked, nodding at her boob.

She giggled again. "It's fine. Imagine I had a bottle in his mouth. Would you talk to me then?"

"Of course."

"This is no different. What do you want to talk about?"

"Mary."

Amanda's face dropped. "What about her?"

The other morning, I had a visit from two social workers. They wanted to talk to you but I told them you'd just had the baby. Anyway, we had a little chat, and I told them we think it's a load of old rubbish, but even if it wasn't Mary is in her rightful place with us."

Amanda nodded as she stared at the baby.

"They said they were happy to leave her with us while they conducted their investigation. I also told them I was concerned what this could do to Mary if it got out, and they agreed not to say anything for now."

"Well, we both know what they'll find, don't we?"

"Yes, but I wanted to buy some time while you were in here. We've not even had a chance to talk to Mary ourselves."

"I know. And, of course, you're right."

"There's more."

Her head jerked up, and she frowned at him. "What now?"

"A Detective Merchants is meeting us here at ten-thirty tomorrow. He's coming from Wolverhampton, which must have been the district Mary was snatched from."

"He's coming here?" She jumped and the baby began to whimper when her nipple popped out of his mouth.

Adam waited while she reattached him. "He knows the situation and said he won't stay long, but we need to get it over with. We can't ignore it forever."

"I'm aware of that. I'd put it to the back of my mind, to be honest."

Adam stayed at the hospital until well past visiting time, briefly shooting off to grab some burgers for them both.

Afterwards, he went straight home to bed. He set the alarm, and once again, arrived at the station in the morning before the others.

The first thing he checked was that the warrants were in place. They were. Cal had organised for two search teams to be ready to move in as soon as they got the go-ahead.

As always, Cal arrived first and the others trickled in behind him, including Frances.

Her face appeared gaunt and her eyes reddened from crying. Her normally slim figure bordered on skinny, the jeans and T-shirt she wore hung off her.

"I'm sure you're supposed to be on leave," Adam said.

"And miss this? Most excitement I've had in ages. Where are we up to with everything?"

"All on track. Sally's due here at one. I told her to bring a solicitor, but I don't know if she will. Cal's arranged for two search teams to be ready once we give them the nod. I'm happy for any of you to join them in the search if you like?"

"I think I might," Ginger Dave said. "I'm still not convinced Sally is responsible, and if there's anything to find I'd like to see it with my own eyes."

"Fair enough. Choose which team you want to be with and sort it out."

"Will do, boss."

"Are you going to sit in on the interview with me?" he asked Frances.

"I was hoping to, yeah."

"Good, she trusts you and may let her guard down. We need to spend a bit of time going through each of the points, so we're on the same page."

"Sounds good. How's Amanda and the baby doing?"

"Oh, sorry. I meant to tell you. Baby Andrew is out of the special care unit. They're both doing really well."

"That's fantastic news!" Frances said. The rest of the team chimed in with their congratulations.

"Maybe we'll have a double celebration later?" Les raised his eyebrows comically. "Wetting the baby's head and wrapping the case up once and for all."

"Here's hoping, Les." Adam winked at him.

He pulled Frances to one side. "I have an appointment with a detective from Wolverhampton at ten-thirty. Can we catch up once I get back?"

"Of course we can, boss. Good luck."

Chapter 48

Amanda's hair was still wet from the shower when Adam arrived a few minutes after ten. "Oh, good. Did you bring me a change of clothes?"

"I certainly did." He handed her a cloth supermarket bag and kissed her head.

"Cheers, I won't be a sec." She scooted back into the adjoining bathroom.

Adam stepped over to the bassinet and gently moved the pale-green sheet away from the baby's face, so he could take a good look at him. He still couldn't get over the all-consuming love he felt for the tiny bundle who didn't even know his daddy existed yet.

When Amanda returned, wearing a pair of navy-blue leggings and a baggy white blouse, she looked more like her usual self—minus the bump, of course.

"That's better." She fussed about, tidying the bedside cabinet, shoving things in the drawer and cupboard, stacking magazines into a tidy pile. "I'm nervous. Are you?"

"A little." He smiled reassuringly. "But he did sound like a nice guy on the phone."

"I hope so. I didn't sleep a wink last night."

They heard a gentle tap at the door.

He glanced at Amanda and raised his eyebrows. "You ready?"

She took a deep breath and nodded.

Adam opened the door to a tall, wiry man with thinning, flyaway blond hair. He wore a grey suit, white shirt, and a blue and mauve paisley tie. He had a file wedged under his right arm. "Hi. You must be Detective Merchants?" Adam held out his hand.

"Yeah, but we can do away with the formalities. Call me Johnny." He shook Adam's hand warmly.

"Come on in then, Johnny. I'm Adam and this is my wife, Amanda."

In two strides, the detective stood beside Amanda shaking her hand enthusiastically. "Congratulations on the new arrival." He nodded at the baby. "I'm guessing a boy?"

"Thank you, yes. His name's Andrew."

"All the *A's*," he said.

"Yeah, I never thought about that." She gave a fake tinkling laugh.

Adam pulled up a plastic chair and offered the armchair to Johnny. Once seated, the detective opened the file.

"I appreciate you seeing me, considering the timing of all this." His forehead crinkled.

Adam nodded and glanced at Amanda.

She looked as though she may burst into tears any minute.

"I just need you to tell me what you know about Mary's early years and her parents, etcetera."

"Very little, I'm afraid," Amanda said. "My brother, Andrew, went missing when he was fifteen years old, and I actually thought he was dead. We were abused as children you see, and after Andrew left, I discovered I was pregnant. I was fourteen." Amanda began to shake, and a solitary tear rolled down her cheek.

Adam jumped to his feet and sat beside her on the bed. "I can send you the case notes if you like, Johnny. I'd prefer it if Amanda doesn't go into too much detail about that part of her life."

"Of course, I understand. When did you first meet up with your brother again?"

She pulled a tissue from the box and dabbed at her eyes. "A couple of years ago. He was living in the country with his wife and Mary. His wife was suffering from acute MS and died soon after. That's when I discovered Andrew was responsible for several murders including that of our father. Before he absconded for a second time, he asked me to look after his daughter for him."

"Did he tell you anything about the child?"

"He told me she was born in France. His ex, Mary's natural mother, didn't want to be tied down and left the baby with Andrew. He brought Mary back to England when she was around five, I think."

"Do you have a copy of Mary's birth certificate?"

Amanda nodded. "Yes. It's in French. I got all her legal documents from their house after she came to live with me."

"Would it be okay if I examine them? I'll return them of course."

Amanda looked at Adam.

Adam nodded. "I can pick them up for you later. I'll send them internally, if you like?"

"I'd appreciate it."

"What do you make of all this, Johnny?" Amanda asked. "Up to now, that is?"

The detective seemed uncomfortable as he glanced between each of them. "Well, I'm not sure if you were told, Amanda, but the child you gave up for adoption was indeed the child who was kidnapped a few years later. So the information we were given was correct in that respect."

"So, this means if Mary isn't her, my little girl is still missing?"

"I'm afraid so."

"I'm not sure what's worse now, to be honest. Finding out Mary *is* my daughter, or finding out she's not."

"What would happen if she is?" Adam said. "Surely there's a family who've been searching and pining for her all these years. Would she have to go back to them?"

"Both adoptive parents passed away a few years back. And, to be honest, I've never had a situation like this one, so I haven't a clue what will happen." He got to his feet just as the baby began to squeak and snuffle. "Thanks for your honesty, I appreciate how delicate the subject is, and I can assure you I'll do my utmost to wrap this up as soon as possible."

Amanda shook his hand before reaching into the cot for the baby.

Adam walked him to the lift. "I'll send you those case notes later. I've got a huge investigation going on at the moment, and I imagine I'll be tied up for the rest of the day, but I promise to have Mary's birth certificate, and anything else I can find, in the mail by tomorrow."

The lift door opened and several people got out, two of them carrying flowers.

Johnny sidestepped them before getting in the lift. "I appreciate it. Thanks, Adam."

Adam raced back to Amanda. The time was ticking, and he still had a lot to do. He found her sitting on the bed, the baby attached to her breast.

"Who knew what a good little actress you were?" he said, kissing her head.

"Do you think he bought it?"

"Hell, yeah. But it was mostly true anyway. How can they prove Andrew told you anything else?"

"They can't. And I'm exhausted now."

"Get your head down once his nibs has had his fill. Promise me, Mand. Turn your phone off and get some sleep. You won't get the chance once you're back home."

"I will. I promise."

"Good. Right, I've got to dash. I'll be back later. Has anybody told you when you can come home?"

"Maybe tomorrow. I'll need you to buy a car seat though. That's one of the things I hadn't got around to shopping for."

"I don't know anything about car seats, but I'll ask one of the sales staff. Is there anything else?"

"We need a pushchair, but we can go shopping together once I'm home. I think we're fine for everything else."

"Alright. Give me a kiss." He kissed her lips and then the top of baby's head before rushing off.

*

He got back to the station with only an hour to spare. Ginger Dave was heading down the stairs as he arrived.

"How's it going, Dave? Did you sort it out with the search team?"

"Going over there now."

Dave couldn't even raise a smile which was unlike him. "Are you alright, mate. You don't seem yourself."

"No offence, but I can't wait to watch you eat your words. That poor girl's just lost her only living parent, and now she's got you persecuting her."

Adam was completely taken aback. "Hardly persecuting her, Dave. If there's even a remote chance Sally could be our killer, then even you must agree we're obliged to follow it through, regardless of who her father was."

Dave shook his head and shoved past him.

Adam turned and watched the older man leave. He'd never had a cross word with Ginger Dave in all the time they'd worked together.

The rest of the team were standing in a huddle as he walked in. They sprang apart, seeming relieved it was him.

"Something happened?" he asked.

"Ginger Dave just blew up at us all," Frances said. "We were talking about having a whip-round for the new baby, and he started ranting about déjà vu, and how he remembered having a whip-round for Charlie Kemp's little girl—the one we're all trying to *frame!*"

"He said that? He thinks we're trying to frame her?"

They all nodded.

"He's too close to it. I should have realised and put him to work on another case. He'll calm down," he said, trying to reassure them. "Now come on, we've not got much time left. Frances, are you ready to go through that list with me?"

"Yes, of course."

They had little over half an hour before Sally would be there. "Cal, are the teams on stand-by?"

"Not yet. They'll call when they are."

Adam nodded. "Okay. Tell them I want to know immediately if they find anything."

"I already have, boss."

He followed Frances into his office and closed the door. "I wish I could be in three places at once," he said.

"You could be, you know. If you tell her something's come up and make her wait, you could be part of both searches."

"I know. But I really don't want to put the wind up her. We've got very little proof as it is. We need to shock a confession out of her, if we can."

"How did you get on with the detective?"

"He was a nice bloke, really. He just has a job to do. And he doesn't seem to be out to screw me over like some would."

"Good. That's a relief."

He pulled up the list on his laptop and sent it to the printer.

Frances reached behind herself and grabbed the two sheets of paper.

"Okay. Most of the points are straight forward. Just read through them, and if you need any further information let me know."

Cal tapped on the door and brought in two cups of coffee.

Adam took the cups from him. "You're a life saver, Cal. I haven't had anything all day."

"If you get stuck in the interview room, you might not get the chance to have anything until later." He produced a packet of biscuits from under his arm.

"I could kiss you," Adam said, as he opened the chocolate digestives and crammed one into his mouth.

"Better watch out or people will begin to talk." Calvin exaggeratedly minced out of the office.

Adam laughed. "Want one?" He offered the packet to Frances as she glanced up from the file.

"No, thanks. And all of this looks pretty much straight forward."

"I'll take it in with us anyway. Get your coffee down you. She'll be here any minute."

Chapter 49

I leave the house on time, dressed to kill in a skin-tight scarlet pantsuit and over the knee black boots. The outfit is finished off with a classy, black jacket that boasts a fluffy collar.

I climb into my two-door Audi and head off in the direction of the police station. A little further up the road, I turn and double back. I spot the van on the other side of the street, just up from my apartment. I can imagine the commotion inside right now as they prepare to get to work.

I park up and watch them for a few moments, but I'm soon bored. I decide to leave them to it.

On the other side of town, I get out of the car and lock it. Glancing around me, I slowly walk through the gate and up the path. The front door is open a few inches and I push it, tapping my highly polished, red fingernails on the glass. "Knock, knock." I call.

A woman, who looks to be in her late fifties with fashionably short, grey hair, appears at the top of the stairs. "Oh, hello. Hang on a minute."

This throws me. Who the hell is this woman?

The woman rushes down the stairs towards me. "Sorry about that. How can I help you?"

I give her my warmest smile. "I'm looking for Amanda. Is she home?"

"Oh, no, she's not. Are you a friend of hers?"

My brain went into overdrive as I tried to remember as many details as possible from the secret box. "Yes. Although I've not seen her in ages. Not since she split with Michael."

"Gosh, that was a while ago. Come on in."

I follow her inside, closing the door behind me.

She walks through to the kitchen. "Fancy a cuppa?"

"I'd love one, actually," *I say, holding my hand out towards her.* "I'm Sally, by the way."

The woman folds a tea towel and throws it onto the counter. "Sorry, I'm Sandra, Amanda's foster mum."

"Oh, Amanda told me a lot about you. It's nice to finally be able to put a face to the name." *Flattery always works, and, when the woman smiles I know I'm in.*

"That's nice. How do you and Amanda know each other?"

"I used to go out with Kevin, a friend of Michael's, and Amanda and I were often thrown together. We got on well. But Kevin and I split up before they did and I moved away. She sent me a message on Facebook, telling me all about Michael, of course." *I didn't know what the hell happened to Michael, but something clearly did, or else they'd still be together.*

"Of course. Tea? Coffee?"

"Black coffee, please." I perch on a stool beside the breakfast bar.

Sandra fills the kettle and grabs a couple of cups from the shelf. "Sugar?"

I shake my head. "No, thanks. So, where is she? Amanda?"

"She's in hospital. Nothing nasty, she's had another baby. A little boy."

"That's lovely. Congratulations! She must have three now?"

"Yes. Unless you count Mary, she's Amanda's niece who lives here too."

"So she's got four kids. Wow! Busy lady."

"Do you have a family, Sally?" Sandra scoops instant coffee into the cups and pours boiling water on top.

"Not yet. A career girl, me. But, I must admit, my biological clock's ticking away."

"Don't leave it too long, love. I speak from experience." She hands me a steaming cup.

"Is that what you did?"

Sandra nods, sadly it seems. "I was in my thirties when we began trying, which isn't late in this day and age. We expected it to happen right away. All my sisters were popping them out for fun. But it wasn't meant to be."

"So you decided to foster instead?"

Sandra's eyes lit up. "I did, and I loved every minute of it. Amanda stayed with us the longest, and I class her as my own. We're close."

"She thinks the world of you."

"It's so nice of you to say that. I've been looking after the children while she's been in the hospital, but she's due home tomorrow, the reason I'm here, actually. I thought I'd give the house a once over. You know what men are like when they're left to their own devices."

"I do indeed. He's a detective I believe? Amanda's new fella."

"Yes, that's right. He's lovely."

"I was hoping to meet him and the children. I'm only home for a few days, and then I'm shooting off to the States for a year or two." I eye the knife holder on the kitchen side. The police took my hunting knife away.

"Sounds fabulous, if not a little scary. I tell you what. Why don't you surprise Amanda at the hospital? She was going stir-crazy yesterday."

"I'd love that. Are you sure she won't mind?" I finish my coffee and hand her the cup.

"I'm positive she'll love it. Tell her I'll pop in after school, will you?" Sandra jots Amanda's ward number on a pad.

"Of course, I will. And thanks, Sandra, Amanda's a very lucky girl."

I walk to my car with a spring in my step.

Chapter 50

"Where the hell is she?" Adam said, pacing up and down the front office.

"She left her apartment at a quarter to one." Cal glanced at the wall-clock. "They thought she headed this way."

"That was almost an hour ago."

"Yes, and the search teams are getting tetchy. What can I tell them?"

"Tell them to go for it. What choice do we have?"

"Okay, boss." Cal walked around his desk.

Frances came back from the toilet. "Heard anything?"

"Not a peep. I might give her a call." He pulled his phone out as it rang. *Home* flashed on the display.

At first he considered ignoring the call, but then he remembered there shouldn't be anybody at his house. "Hello?"

"Hi, love. It's me," Sandra said. "I'm sorry to disturb you at work, but I'm at your house and a friend of Amanda's just called around."

"That's nice." He rolled his eyebrows at Frances and mouthed *Sandra*.

"She left a few minutes ago. I think she plans to visit Amanda in hospital. But the thing is, she said something that worried me."

"What's that then, Sandra?" He scratched his head, agitated.

"She said Amanda told her all about Michael on Facebook."

Suddenly on full alert, he turned to face Frances. "Amanda doesn't have a Facebook account."

"That's what I thought, love. But you know what I'm like with those things. I thought I must have been mistaken. Anyway once she left, I checked Amanda's address book and she doesn't even know anybody called Sally."

Adam couldn't breathe. Frances appeared in front of him, her mouth opening and closing, but he couldn't hear a word.

Then Cal grabbed him by the shoulders and began shaking him. He dropped the phone and he vaguely remembered Frances picking it up and talking into it.

When time caught up, the sound came back to Adam in a whoosh.

Frances said, "Oh, my God. Sally's gone to the hospital."

"Get a squad team to the hospital, Cal." Adam sped from the room. "And call hospital security immediately!"

He sensed Frances behind him on the stairs.

"If she's done anything to them, I'll kill her with my bare hands," he roared, as they dashed across the car park to his Mondeo.

Frances tried to call Amanda's phone but it went to voicemail.

"She's having a sleep." Adam slammed his hands on the wheel. He drove to the hospital like a raving lunatic. Several people honked their horns and made rude hand gestures, but he didn't care, his only thought was for the safety of Amanda and their new baby.

He parked across the entrance of the hospital and he could hear several sirens approaching.

"You take the stairs, Frances." He bashed the lift button several times. "Amanda's on the fourth floor. Room three."

She nodded and disappeared through the door.

Four uniformed constables ran into the foyer.

Adam turned to them and quickly flashed his ID. "We're looking for Sally Kemp, an attractive redhead in her late twenties, early thirties. She's wanted for a number of homicides. I've got reason to believe she's here. My wife and newborn son are her targets."

The lift door opened and he left the officer in charge barking orders to the others.

The maternity annex was deathly quiet. The swing doors stood wide open and the main desk eerily vacant, but as he approached he noticed three nurses gossiping in the back room. He rapped the palm of his hand on the desk and continued towards Amanda's room.

He tried to calm his breathing, fearing Sally would hear him coming a mile off.

Taking wide strides, he made it to Amanda's door horrified to find the curtains closed and the room in darkness. He paused, mentally preparing himself for anything and trying to call on his training to stay in control. He slammed the door open and barged in.

Amanda squealed and jumped up in bed, disorientated. "Adam! What the hell?"

He ran to the window almost tearing the curtains down in his haste to get some light into the room.

Amanda noticed the empty crib at the same time he did and began screaming hysterically.

He had no time to waste.

A hefty nurse appeared in the doorway, alerted by Amanda's screams.

"Someone's taken the baby," he barked. "Stay with her."

One of the officers came out of the lift as Adam ran from the annex.

"She's taken the baby."

The officer got on his radio, informing the others.

An alarm sounded from the stairs.

Adam ran to the stairwell and paused, working out that the wailing alarm came from above. He launched himself up three steps at a time.

"Frances?" he yelled.

"Up here, Adam. She's got the baby."

He thought his head might explode. But he knew the importance of staying in control. He reached the eighth floor, the voices were coming from higher still. From the roof.

He cleared the final steps and burst through the doors at the top.

He quickly assessed the situation. The large, open rooftop had a helipad at the far edge, with a bright yellow air ambulance parked in the centre of it.

He saw Sally beyond the helicopter. The wind whipped her long red hair ferociously. She clutched the baby in her arms.

Frances was also on the pad, slowly approaching Sally, her arms held out, clearly trying to calm the woman down.

A hospital security guard on the ground in front of him approached the helipad with caution.

Adam had seen this scenario played out hundreds of times on the TV. Every time he'd scream at the screen how far-fetched it was. Yet here they were—a mad woman holding his newborn son close to the edge of a hospital roof.

His shoes felt filled with lead. It took all his effort to move forward an inch.

Instead of climbing the steps, the security guard moved off to the side.

Adam didn't pay him much attention. He was too focused on Frances and Sally who were moving out of his vision on the other side of the helicopter.

He climbed the steps and approached, little by little.

Their voices carried on the wind. "I gave him everything," Sally shouted. "And he left me for that bitch."

Adam reached the helicopter and still couldn't hear Frances' response, but could make out her calming tones and body language.

As though out of nowhere, Ginger Dave sprinted past Adam, yelling, "I'm sorry, boss. This is all my fault."

"Dave! Stop!"

Hearing this, Frances turned to see what the commotion was behind her. She held her arms out, trying to slow Dave down. He dodged past her.

"Don't come any closer, Dave." Sally said. She spoke calmly.

He stopped running, but continued walking forward at a fast pace. "I trusted you. Put my job on the line for you. Why would you do this, Sally?"

"Dave! Stop! She's got the baby," Frances yelled.

He slowed down as though he'd only just spotted the baby.

Sally, still backing up, was about two feet from the roof edge.

Adam reached Frances, and together they approached, slowly. Out of the corner of his eye, Adam noticed the top of the security guard's head as he crawled around the lip of the helipad, behind Sally.

Adam held his breath.

"Why would you want to hurt your dad? He loved you so much," Dave continued.

Sally's lip curled. "If only you knew how much, Dave. After Mum died, he wanted special cuddles—you know what I mean?"

"Liar! Your father was an honourable man. I won't have you sullying his good name with your despicable lies."

The security guard was only an arm's reach away from Sally, and she still hadn't noticed him.

"He was no better than the disgusting letches he locked up," she spat.

As though in slow motion, everything happened at once.

Sally turned and noticed the guard.

Dave roared and shot forward.

The guard reached for the baby.

Adam ran towards them in sheer panic.

He reached them as the mass of bodies toppled off the edge of the building.

Chapter 51

Frozen to the spot, Adam couldn't believe his eyes. A scream from the street below confirmed what he imagined had just happened. But he couldn't look. He couldn't do anything.

He stared, mouth agape, as Frances peering over the edge.

Her hand pressed firmly to her mouth stifling her cry. Suddenly she dropped to her knees. "Adam! Come quick."

He moved to her side on automatic pilot. Hearing a strange squeaking to the side of him, he turned to see the security guard crouching on the lower ledge holding the baby.

Adam almost collapsed on the spot. He didn't realise, he wasn't breathing—positive the baby and the guard had gone over the side with Sally and Dave.

He grabbed the bundle and slid to the floor, unable to control his emotions one second longer. Hot salty tears ran down his cheeks and dripped off his chin onto the sleeping face of his beautiful little boy.

Within moments, the roof was crawling with uniformed men.

Frances helped him to his feet. They walked down to the eighth floor in silence, both horrified by what they'd just witnessed. They got the lift down to the fourth floor. Frances hung back, indicating she had a call to make.

A female officer barred the doorway of Amanda's room, but she stepped aside with a smile as he approached.

Amanda cried and ran to him, snatching her baby from his arms. "Oh-my-God! Oh-my-God!" she squealed repeatedly. Then, finally satisfied her baby seemed oblivious to his ordeal, she turned back to Adam. "Are *you* alright? You look terrible. Come and sit down."

Hearing his mummy's voice, baby Andrew began squeaking and snuffling at his tiny fist.

Stunned, Adam sat beside her on the bed while she prepared to feed the hungry baby.

"What the fuck just happened? Who took him and why?"

He couldn't seem to string a sentence together and was relieved when Frances appeared and explained everything.

Horrified, Amanda held the baby tight to her breast. "And Ginger Dave? Is he...?"

"He's dead. They both are." Frances looked at Adam as she spoke.

Adam nodded. Considering the height from which they'd fallen, he hadn't expected any other outcome.

"Thank the Lord that security guard acted on his instincts the way he did. I've no doubt things would have been much different if he hadn't," Frances said.

"Where is he?" Amanda sobbed. "I need to thank him from the bottom of my heart."

Frances placed her hand on Amanda's. "I imagine he's quite busy right now, but I'll ask him to check in on you later."

Adam got to his feet and bent to kiss Amanda's forehead. "Try to rest? I'll come back as soon as I can."

"I'll never sleep again. I only wanted a nap inbetween feeds, and that crazy bitch sneaks in and takes my baby. I didn't hear a thing."

He shook his head. "She's not coming back, Mand. I promise you'll be fine now."

"Why don't you stay?" Frances placed a hand on his shoulder. "I'll do what I can until you're feeling up to it."

"I need to deal with this mess now. I'm okay."

Adam and Frances travelled to the station in silence, both absorbed with their own thoughts. Cal jumped up when they entered, clearly distraught by the news.

Adam nodded at him, trying desperately to swallow the lump that had returned to his throat. "Where's Les and Julie?"

"They've gone to Charlie Kemp's house. Ginger Dave called here after he and the search team found an old music room in the basement. He realised you were right."

"Did you tell him Sally was at the hospital?"

"I did. I'm so sorry." Cal plonked down on his chair.

Adam sighed. "Hey, it's not your fault. You didn't know what he'd do."

"Yeah, but…"

"Sally's the only person to blame in all this." Frances walked around Cal's desk and gave him a hug.

"Has anybody called the DCI?" Adam still felt in shock.

"He's on his way in to inform Dave's wife with you."

Adam's stomach dropped. He'd not even thought about that. Ginger Dave and Pixie had been married for over thirty years.

"What happened? Why did Sally go to the hospital?" Cal asked.

Adam shrugged. "I'm not sure of that myself, Cal."

"Ginger Dave told her of our plan," Frances said. "She knew we'd find the room in the cellar once her dad's house was searched, and so she figured she had nothing to lose."

"Dave informed her? Did she tell you all this while you were up on the helipad?" Adam spun around to look at Frances.

"Yes. She went to your house for Amanda and found Sandra instead. She considered doing away with Sandra but thought the baby would make the biggest impact."

"Fucking crazy bitch," Cal said, shaking his head. "Are Amanda and the baby okay?"

Adam nodded. "They're fine, thanks, Cal."

The door swished open, and DCI Williamson walked in dressed to the nines. "Stanley. I don't know why I ever doubt that instinct of yours. It hasn't let you down yet."

"Hi, sir. It didn't turn out to be the clean cut arrest I'd imagined," he said, flatly.

"Shall we go into your office? You can bring me up to speed."

Adam raised his eyebrows at Frances and Cal, and followed the DCI into his office.

*

Once Adam filled the DCI in on the day's events, they paid a visit to Ginger Dave's widow.

Pixie, named because of her petite stature and elfin face, had already guessed why they were there by the time she opened the door. Just having the DCI in attendance spoke volumes. She gripped the silver Saint Christopher that hung around her neck and staggered backwards, shaking her head.

Thankfully, the DCI took the lead. Adam was too shell-shocked to cope with much more that day.

Afterwards, back at the station, he completed the relevant paperwork, and it was close on 8.00pm before he was able to leave for home.

He collected the paper package that Frances had left for him on her desk, and dialled Sandra's number as he headed to the car.

"Sandra, it's me. Is Mary with you?"

"Yes. Why, is something wrong?"

"No. But we need to have an important chat with her. Can you tell her I'm on my way? I'm taking her to the hospital."

"We've just got back from there. Are you sure Amanda's up to this? She looked totally washed out when we left."

"We've left it too long as it is. Best we do this now."

"Well, if you're sure. I'll go and tell her to get ready."

He pulled up outside his mother-in-law's house. Mary appeared at the window.

He waved and she closed the curtain and ran out the door a few seconds later.

She opened the car door and an icy blast preceded her.

"Hurry up, get in. It's bloody freezing out there."

"Am I in trouble?" Mary asked, wide-eyed.

"No! Of course you're not. We just want to have a word with you without the others making a racket."

"What about?"

"All will be revealed, young lady."

"Did you know a lady tried to kidnap our baby today?"

"I did. Who told you?"

"I heard Amanda telling Nana."

Adam laughed. "Not much gets by you, does it, Miss Mary?"

Mary seemed pleased with herself. "I'm not a baby anymore. I can work things out for myself."

"I don't doubt that for a minute. Now, fasten your coat up. We're here."

They got out of the car and ran hand in hand to the main doors. "Woo! I think it might even snow!" he said as they waited for the lift.

He regretted not calling ahead and telling Amanda he planned to bring Mary, but he figured she'd only stress if he warned her.

Visiting time was over and they had to be buzzed in by the nurse. "We're only planning to be here for a short while," he said, when she scowled at them.

Amanda was sitting up in bed watching the TV. "Oh, I thought you weren't going to make it." Her smile faltered as she noticed Mary behind him.

"I told you I'd be back. I brought Mary so we can have that little chat."

Chapter 52

Amanda's heart thundered in her chest. She was confused that Adam would arrange to speak to Mary like this without even warning her. She braced herself.

Adam took her hand and began to stroke her fingers. Looking into her eyes, he gave her a reassuring nod. "It's better this way."

Noticing Mary's worried expression, Amanda took a deep breath, smiled, and held her hand out. "Come here and sit with me, sweetheart."

Mary climbed up on the bed beside Amanda. Her huge blue eyes appeared too big for her face as she looked at them both expectantly.

Adam cleared his throat. "Mary, you remember the other day when you found Amanda's box of memories?"

She nodded, gulping on nothing, and she gripped Amanda's hand tight.

"Well, you asked if you were the baby she gave up for adoption all those years ago."

She nodded again.

Amanda rubbed the girl's arm as she began to tremble.

"This scenario hadn't occurred to us at the time, but your question made us wonder. Didn't it, Mand?"

"Yes," Amanda whispered. She turned back for him to continue.

"So we did a bit of investigating, and although your birth certificate says you were born in France, we're not actually sure if that's true."

"So, what does that mean?" Mary seemed much older than her thirteen years all of a sudden.

"There's a chance you could be Amanda's child."

Mary gasped as tears sprang to her eyes.

Amanda reached out and pulled her into her arms. "I know it's a shock, but we needed to tell you, sweetheart."

"There is one way to find out the truth," Adam continued.

Mary turned to face him again. "How?"

He pulled out the paper bag from his pocket. "We could do a DNA test."

"Would I need to have an injection?"

"No, nothing like that." He pulled open a plastic container and removed a large cotton bud. "I'll just need to run this around the inside of your mouth for a second. Is that alright?"

Mary pushed herself back into a sitting position. "Okay." She opened her mouth while he took the sample.

He wrote Mary's name on the plastic container after placing the sample inside. "Now, we need the same from you, Amanda."

Afterwards, he returned to his seat. "Any questions?"

"Will you send me away again?"

"No!" Amanda cried and pulled the child towards her again. "I'll never send you away, Mary. I love you as one of my own, whether you are or not."

Ever the practical one, Adam had to warn them both it might not be up to them. "There will need to be an investigation by the police and social workers. If you aren't Andrew's daughter, then you were kidnapped from your adoptive family. You do understand that, don't you, Mary?"

"Will they want to take me back there?" Mary buried her head in Amanda's shoulder as though not wanting to hear the answer.

Tears streamed down Amanda's face. It broke her heart to see Mary so upset, but Adam was right—it was better this way than her finding out from someone else.

"Not if we have anything to do with it. But the social workers and maybe even the police will probably want to talk to you," he said.

"How long will the tests take?" Amanda asked.

"I'll push them through and try to get a result by tomorrow."

"That soon," she gasped.

"We'll find out tomorrow if I'm your daughter?" Mary turned to look at her.

"Sounds like it. How will you feel?"

"Will I have to call you Mummy?"

Amanda shrugged. "Only if you want to."

"Can I go home now?" Mary got to her feet and walked to the door without a backward glance.

Adam also stood up. He bent to kiss Amanda. "Maybe you should call Sandra, fill her in before I drop Mary off," he whispered.

Amanda nodded. Feeling abandoned and dejected, she watched them leave. Mary had a lot to process, but she wished she'd said more, told her how she felt.

Tomorrow couldn't come soon enough. At least the truth would be out, and she wouldn't have to lie anymore.

***

"Penny for them?" Adam said as they approached Sandra's street.

"If I *am* the baby, Amanda won't want me. She gave me away once before."

He indicated and pulled the car over to the side of the road before responding. He swivelled around in his seat. "You need to understand something. Amanda was only fourteen—just one year older than you are now."

Mary scrutinized her hands as though trying to read and process information written between her fingers.

"She didn't have a loving family like you've got. She was treated badly, often worse than you'd treat a dog."

Mary gasped and tears began to spill from her eyes.

He didn't know how graphic he should be, but he wanted it to hit home how terrible Amanda's situation had been.

"When the baby was born, Amanda didn't even lay her eyes on it, and she was in a trance-like state for weeks afterwards. The doctors said it was trauma."

"She didn't wake up?"

He shook his head. "Not for weeks. It took a lot of years for her to recover from her ordeal. Sandra and her husband helped a lot, but, if I'm honest, she's still scarred to this day."

Two deep grooves appeared between Mary's eyebrows.

"So she wasn't in her right mind at the time the baby was born. You've seen what a good mum she is to Emma and Jacob. Do you really think she'd have turned her back on a defenceless little baby if she'd had the choice?"

Mary shook her head, sadly.

"If you are that child, I know Amanda will be overjoyed. There's always been a part of her missing, and it would make her complete."

She began to sob.

As best he could, he leaned over the handbrake and hugged her until her tears stopped.

"Come on. Let's take you back to Sandra's."

*

Adam sent the samples to the lab first thing the next morning. He stressed to Jemima the importance of getting the results back before close of business.

He contacted Detective Merchants, as well as Cordelia Brampton from the social services, informing them of the DNA test. He knew that would be the next step anyway, and no doubt they would still want to perform their own in case of tampering.

He also arranged for Cordelia to interview Amanda and Mary at the house at 4.00pm Monday afternoon. At least Amanda had the weekend to prepare.

Sandra called to tell him Mary didn't feel too well and wanted to take the day off school. He knew she probably hadn't slept a wink and agreed she should stay home for the day.

Mid-morning, he called Amanda.

"So what's happening?" he asked.

"I'm waiting for the doctor to come around, and if all's well, we can go home."

"Brilliant. Mary's home today, so I might go and pick her up, if you don't mind."

"Of course I don't mind."

"Good. Call me as soon as the doctor's been."

He hung up and called Sandra's house.

"Hello?" Mary said, in a worried little voice.

"Hi, love. It's only me."

When she gasped, he realised she thought he'd got the news.

"I've not heard anything yet. I just wondered how sick you really are?"

"Erm."

"Don't worry. I'm not going to make you go to school. But I wondered if you fancied coming with me to buy a car seat for the baby. I'm rubbish at that sort of thing."

"Okay."

"Great. I'll be over soon."

He'd hoped to have everything tied up by now so he could enjoy his son coming home for the first time.

When he and Mary arrived at the hospital, Amanda was dressed, all her belongings piled on the bed, ready to go.

She beamed at the red car seat they'd bought.

"It even has a carry handle so you don't have to wake him up if he's sleeping," Mary said.

"Brilliant. And who chose the colour?"

"I did. He wanted to get a boring grey one." Mary laughed.

"Then I'm glad one of you has a bit of taste. This one will match my new car."

"See." Mary turned to Adam smiling.

"I told you I was no good at that sort of thing. So shoot me." He held his hands up.

They fastened the baby into the seat, piled everything in the car and headed off for home.

He didn't hang around long. Sandra was already at the house waiting for them, and he knew he was leaving Amanda and baby Andrew in safe hands.

Before heading back to the station, he did a detour to Frances' house.

Val answered the door. "Oh, come in, lovey. Holly's in her room. I'll give her a knock."

He wandered through to the kitchen while Val ran upstairs.

Moments later, Frances appeared. "Is everything alright?"

"Yes. I just wanted to let you know what's happening."

She indicated he take a seat, and she sat beside him on the stool.

"Amanda's home. She'd love to see you when you feel up to it."

"Oh, great news. And baby's okay after yesterday?"

"He didn't bat an eyelid, thank God."

"Did you talk to Mary?"

He nodded. "Last night. She was shocked when we told her but seems back to her normal self today."

"That's good. I was wondering how she'd take it."

"We're just waiting on Jemima to get back to us with the lab results."

Val was fussing around, filling the kettle and preparing tea.

"Not for me, thanks, Val. I've got to get back."

"That's a shame. But I know you're a busy man."

He turned back to Frances. "The reason nobody heard Muldoon's cries in the basement was because he'd been kept in a soundproof music studio. The last owner had it built."

"Ah, makes sense now."

"Scary to think she almost got away with it, isn't it?"

"I'll say. That must be why she turned her focus to you—well, to your baby."

"Holly told me what happened, Adam." Val placed a cup in front of Holly. "You must have been beside yourself."

"It's not something I'd like to go through again, believe me."

"No. You cherish that little boy, lovey. None of us know what tragedies are around the corner."

Adam placed a hand on her arm. "How're you coping?"

"Oh, me? I'm fine. We'll be better once we get Tuesday out of the way, won't we, Holl?"

Frances nodded. "It feels like we're in limbo. That's why I've been wanting to come into work. Poor Val's had nothing to distract her though, have you?"

"So what do you intend to do after the funeral? Will you go back to the Isle of Wight?" he asked.

"No. There's nothing there for me now."

"I've told her to stay on here. We built the extension for her, this is her home now," Frances said.

"What a fantastic idea," he said.

"I don't want to be a nuisance."

Frances drew air between her teeth noisily. "You're not a bloody nuisance. What will I do without you here? And besides, it's what Steve would want."

"Well, I'll stay for now. I don't have anywhere else to go anyway."

"Exactly." Frances patted the older woman's hand.

His phone buzzed. The message on the screen told him he'd received an email from Jemima.

"DNA results," he said as he opened it, knowing what he would find, yet needing to see the proof.

Frances' breath hitched.

His eyes flew over the scientific jargon to the area of interest. "Positive."

"Shit! That was fast, even for Jemima."

He got to his feet. "I'd best go home and break the news."

"Good luck."

Epilogue

Adam opened the car door for Mary and ran around the other side to help Amanda get the baby out. He looked at the sun, high in the sky, and smiled. "It's going to be another beautiful day."

"Can we go for ice-cream when we leave here?" Mary asked.

"I don't see why not."

Amanda linked her arm through Mary's, and Adam carried the car seat towards the quaint old building.

Cordelia Brampton met them at the entrance to the court. "Oh, you're early too. I was going to stand in the sun for a few minutes. It's freezing inside."

"Good idea," Adam said, backing up and falling into step beside her, until they were standing in the sun. "These old buildings are always cold and draughty."

"How are you feeling, Mary?" Cordelia smiled, kindly.

"A bit nervous."

"There's nothing to be nervous about. We're here to finalise everything, that's all."

Mary nodded, still looking petrified.

"Do you intend to go in?"

Mary nodded again. "If I'm allowed."

"Yes, of course you're allowed. But you don't have to. We've already submitted a report which states your wishes."

"Do you foresee any hiccups with this case, Ms Brampton?" Amanda asked.

"It is, as you know, a highly complex case, but the facts remain, Mary is in the best place she could be. You have myself and the child's lawyer fighting your corner, and you already have a residence order in place. The fact no other parties are fighting against you is also a plus."

"Oh, good. We intend to adopt Mary too. Make her legally ours," Amanda shrugged at Mary, who was still holding her hand.

Cordelia's eyes lit up. "How lovely. How do you feel about that, Mary?"

Mary smiled up at Adam shyly then turned to face the social worker. "I'd like that."

"Good. Well, the court isn't likely to rule against any of your wishes. They'll take into account Mary's emotional and educational needs. Also, the likely effect any change of circumstances would have on her. In other words, she's happy, nurtured, and well cared for where she is. They wouldn't dream of taking her away from that."

"That's a relief, isn't it Mary?" Amanda said.

Mary smiled, a genuinely happy smile this time, and nodded, sliding her other hand into Adam's.

THE END

I hope you enjoyed reading *Prima Facie*. If so, would you please consider posting a short review? Genuine feedback is the best *thank you* an author can receive.

ABOUT THE AUTHOR

Netta Newbound, originally from Manchester, England, now lives in New Zealand with her husband, Paul and their boxer dog Alfie. She has three grown-up children and three delicious grandchildren.

For more information or just to touch base with Netta you will find her at:
www.nettanewbound.com
Facebook
Twitter

For more books by Netta go to

Amazon

Amazon UK

Printed in Poland
by Amazon Fulfillment
Poland Sp. z o.o., Wrocław